TIME
TO
RUN

◆

Marliss Melton

WARNER

FOREVER

NEW YORK   BOSTON

Copyright © 2005 by Marliss Melton
All rights reserved. No part of this book may be reproduced in any form or by any electronic or mechanical means, including information storage and retrieval systems, without permission in writing from the publisher, except by a reviewer who may quote brief passages in a review.

Warner Forever and logo are registered trademarks of Time Warner Book Group Inc.

Book design by Stratford Publishing Services.

Warner Books

Time Warner Book Group
1271 Avenue of the Americas
New York, NY 10020
Visit our Web site at www.twbookmark.com

Printed in the United States of America

First Paperback Printing: February 2006

10 9 8 7 6 5 4 3 2 1

IN THE DARK

"Fantastic . . . keeps you riveted . . . will keep you guessing . . . Well done!" —OnceUponARomance.net

"A strong thriller . . . Action-packed . . . will keep the audience on the edge of their seats." —Blether.com

"Hooked me from the first page . . . filled with romance, suspense, and characters who will pull you in and never let you go." —Lisa Jackson, *New York Times* bestselling author of *The Night Before*

FORGET ME NOT

"Refreshing . . . fine writing, likable characters, and realistic emotions." —*Publishers Weekly*

"An intriguing romantic suspense . . . Readers will take great delight." —*Midwest Book Review*

"The gifted Melton does an excellent job building emotion, danger, and tension in her transfixing novel." —*Romantic Times BOOKclub Magazine*

"Entertaining . . . moving and passionate . . . with plenty of action and suspense . . . *Forget Me Not* is a winner; don't miss it." —RomRevToday.com

more . . .

"A wonderful book, touching at all the right heartstrings. I highly recommend it!"   —Heather Graham, author of
Dead on the Dance Floor

"Amazing . . . fantastic . . . a riveting plot, engaging characters, and unforgettable love story . . . not to be missed."
—NewandUsedBooks.com

"A thrilling romance."   —TheBestReviews.com

"Riveting . . . you'll definitely want to pick this one up."
—RomanceJunkies.com

"Wonderful, thrilling . . . loved it!"
—RomanceReviewsMag.com

Also by Marliss Melton

Forget Me Not
In the Dark

This one's for you, Sunshine. Thank you for the inspiration.

✦

For my Broken Arrow cousins, the nicest bunch of people you could ever hope to know.

Acknowledgments

A lot of super people had a hand in creating this book, but my editor gets first mention for her skill in taking a rock of a manuscript and finding the diamond in it. Thanks so much, Devi, for your faith in me.

Special thanks to three very loyal readers who offered their time and talent in proofreading this manuscript: Kerry Sehloff, Cathy Goldman, and Lisa Panzarella. I'm so very grateful to you.

Thanks, also, to Louis Dooley and John Polak of the Virginia State Police Fifth Division Bomb Squad, for sharing your expertise with me, not to mention a thoroughly enjoyable luncheon, and to my dear friend Laura for hosting it.

And thank you to my Broken Arrow cousins, Tom and Lynn Lewis and Jennifer Anthis, for all your help in making my setting as realistic as possible.

Big thanks goes to all my children and stepchildren: Bryan, Tricia, Conrad, Chauncey, and Grace, for putting up with me being chained to my computer the entire summer while shrieking, "Be quiet! I have a deadline!"

Lastly, thank you, Alan, my sweetheart, for just being you.

Prologue

Sara was diligent in putting away the frozen groceries first, the way her husband expected. Food requiring refrigeration came next, each item neatly placed into its proper receptacle within the stainless-steel refrigerator. The packages and boxes were already stowed in their respective cupboards, but cans still littered the granite countertop. Hearing Garret emerge from his study, Sara hurried to put them away.

Any minute, Garret was going to poke his head through the door to inquire what her plans were for supper and, unfortunately for her, she hadn't given a thought yet as to what they were going to eat.

Working quickly, she slid the cans one by one onto the cabinet shelf, alphabetizing as she went. Baked beans went before chicken broth, which went before green beans; then mushrooms, ravioli, stewed tomatoes, and three-bean salad.

On second thought, maybe the broth ought to be classified with soups, or would that annoy him?

Transferring the chicken broth to the soup shelf, she

stepped back to double-check the order: broccoli, celery, chicken broth, chili, gazpacho, lentil, then tomato.

Wherever there were two cans of the same kind, one went behind the other, and the can in front had to have an earlier expiration date.

With a huff of annoyance, she shut the cabinet door. She didn't have time to check the expiration dates, which were all years from now, anyway. If she didn't think of a meal to cook tonight, Garret would find something else to take away from her.

She opened the stainless-steel freezer and frowned at the contents. What was wrong with her that she couldn't remember to take the meat out in the morning? Garret was bound to lecture her. *Forethought, Sara, is all that this requires. Or are you too simple to plan ahead just a few hours?*

Simple? No. She had a master's degree from the University of Virginia, which she'd earned before she met him, of course. If he knew how truly clever she was, how masterfully she kept her secrets from him, he'd lock her up in the attic.

She snatched up a package of frozen hamburger meat and tossed it into the microwave.

The throbbing of a bass drum had Sara glancing up with consternation. What was Kendal doing playing his music that loudly? Surely he knew that his father worked at home on Wednesdays.

She drew an agitated breath. If he didn't turn the volume down, they were both bound to face some kind of reprimand.

Abandoning the kitchen, Sara hurried through the marble foyer toward the stairs to warn him. She slowed when she saw that the door to Garret's study was open. That's right, she'd heard him leave his study just moments before. She realized that he was already upstairs having words with Kendal. *Oh dear.*

The sudden silence told her that Garret had ripped the stereo plug from the wall. She could hear his voice now, harsh punctuations of sound that she couldn't make out words to. With a foot on the bottom step, she listened. Garret didn't like it when she interfered.

An awful silence ensued.

"No!"

Kendal's wail galvanized her. Sara took the broad, curving steps three at a time, her heart jumping up her throat as she envisioned what Garret could have done to elicit such a cry of protest. He'd never laid a hand on Kendal as far as she knew.

She arrived at the second floor in the same instant that Garret stalked from Kendal's bedroom, Mr. Whiskers dangling from one hand. "Throw this away," he commanded, thrusting the French Lop rabbit at her as he stormed past. "That ought to teach *your* son not to disturb me when I'm working."

Sara caught the limp creature in her arms. She could tell right away that it was dead.

She looked down at it, stunned. There was nothing visibly wrong with it—no open gashes, no blood anywhere, but it was definitely dead.

The sound of Kendal panting had her hurrying forward. "Sweetheart?"

She found him on the edge of his bed, arms clasped to his midsection, staring wide-eyed at the empty rabbit cage.

"Honey?" She eased onto the bed beside him, dead

rabbit cradled in her arms. "What happened?" She'd never seen him like this, gasping as if he'd been punched in the stomach. "What did your father do?" she asked, shaking his arm when she got no answer.

"Strangled," he whispered, through bloodless lips.

"What?" Horror squeezed Sara's heart. Garret wouldn't have strangled Kendal's rabbit to death—or would he?

The boy continued to pant as if desperate for air. She jumped up to find something he could breathe into. There was a lunch bag, filled with school supplies. She emptied it and brought it to him. "Breathe into this, honey. You need to calm down."

Calm down? The suggestion was ludicrous! How could anyone be calm in this nerve-wracking environment?

Kneeling on the plush carpet, she watched the bag inflate and deflate. Kendal's panting subsided, but his face still reflected shock. How many times had she looked into the mirror and seen herself looking like that?

Volcanic, maternal rage boiled within her. It was one thing to let Garret intimidate her; it was another thing to let him victimize her son. How dare he threaten her baby, her reason for enduring this marriage in the first place?

No more. This was where she drew the line, where she pulled together her fragmented plans for freedom and made them a reality. "Listen to me," she whispered, placing the dead rabbit on the floor to grasp his knees. "We are going to leave him, Kendal. We don't have to live like this."

He looked at her. At last, she had his full attention.

"I have a plan," she admitted, speaking so quietly that even if Garret had planted a listening device in Kendal's room he couldn't overhear. "I can't tell you what it is, but it's going to work. We are going to leave," she said again, "and we're never coming back," she added fiercely.

The scales of shock fell from Kendal's eyes, giving way to hope. "He'll find us," he whispered fearfully.

"No, he won't. I've kept a secret from him. Something that he doesn't know."

The boy's gaze fell to the lifeless bundle at their feet. "I'm afraid," he admitted.

"I know, sweetheart." *I am, too.* "That's why I can't tell you any more. You'll just have to trust me."

He gave a tentative nod, which Sara took as a token of his agreement and, hopefully, his cooperation when the time came.

She needed more than that, though.

She needed a miracle to help them get away.

Chapter One

Chief Petty Officer Chase McCaffrey stalked into the Trial Services Building on Oceana Naval Base in a piss-poor mood. He hadn't put a dent in the paperwork piled on top of his desk at the Spec Ops and, already, he was having to pack his bags and leave—not on an assignment this time, but to claim the land his stepfather had left to him, land he never wanted to go home to.

The young, African-American security guard on duty greeted him warmly. "How you doin', Chief? I ain't seen you here in months!"

"Twelve to be exact," Chase told him, slapping the envelope he'd brought onto the X-ray belt. He withdrew his pistol, a SIG Sauer P226, out of the holster on his battle dress uniform belt and surrendered it to the guard, along with his cell phone, neither of which was permitted in the building.

"Where you been?" Petty Officer Marcelino Hewitt asked. "Oh, wait, I guess you can't tell me that. It's classified."

"Somewhere hot," said Chase succinctly. Which had to

be obvious, given his savage tan and sun-bleached eye-brows. He stepped through the metal detector, feeling vulnerable. But this wasn't Malaysia. In this building, he was safe from everything but long lines and red tape, neither of which he had time for today.

"What's wrong, Chief? You don't look so chipper today," Hewitt needled, reverting to their habit of harassing each other.

"I am never chipper," Chase articulated, with a scowl that was half-genuine, half-pretend.

"Jolly, then," Hewitt amended, with a straight face.

"Fuck you," Chase said, without heat. "You're the one who's jolly." His gaze fell to the petty officer's ample midsection. "I thought I told you to lose weight. You've put on at least ten pounds."

The man chuckled. "You said to lay off the donuts. You didn't say nothin' about no honey buns, though," he retorted gleefully.

Chase snatched his folder off the X-ray belt as it reappeared. "No pastries, period, Hewitt," he suggested. "And lay off the soda," he added, pointing out the can of Coke in the guard's work area.

"Aw, Chief!" Hewitt protested with exaggerated grief.

But Chase was already halfway down the hallway. All he needed was for Commander Spenser, a JAG lawyer, to sign off on the document Chase carried, stating that he agreed to represent a petty officer third class in Chase's platoon who'd cracked a few skulls at the waterfront.

With a mutter of annoyance that his job at home port amounted to babysitting, Chase stalked into the lounge area outside the counselor's chambers. To his relief, only one other person, a woman, sat waiting. But then he noticed that the lawyers' offices were empty. Through the milky glass windows in the door across the hall, he could see that they'd come together in a meeting.

"Fuck me," Chase growled, throwing himself down into a hard, plastic lounge chair. Out of the corner of his eye, he saw the woman's head come up sharply. "Sorry," he apologized glancing her way.

Their gazes locked in mutual surprise as they recognized each other.

She was Sara Garret, wife of the infamous prosecuting JAG from Lieutenant Renault's court-martial last year.

She'd intrigued him then. Her gray-green eyes had the same effect on him now as they moved over him, taking in his sun-streaked goatee, his jungle-camouflage BDUs, and his black, lace-up boots.

"Do you know how long they're going to be in there?" he asked, unsettled by her scrutiny.

"Um, I don't know," she admitted, biting her lower lip. "Maybe half an hour longer?"

He couldn't look away from her, just like at last year's court-martial. He'd tried to speak with her at the trial's end, only she'd darted into the restroom, frustrating his attempt. He could assuage his curiosity now. "Have we met before?" he asked, certain that they had. "Before the court-martial, I mean."

Her face took on a certain radiance. "Well, yes, actually. You were in San Diego about four years ago?"

How'd she know that?

"You jump-started my car in the library parking lot," she explained. "I'd left the lights on, and the battery was dead."

He didn't remember.

"Then a couple years later, I rammed my shopping cart into yours, right here at the local commissary."

Now that he kind of remembered. Her cart had upset the six-pack of canned soda he'd slung over the side of his. Two of the cans had plummeted to the floor, spraying carbonated soda all over his pant legs. The woman had been so shaken that he'd had to call for the mop to do the cleanup himself. "That was you?" he asked.

"Yes." Flushing with chagrin, she focused on the notebook in her lap, which was what she'd been doing when he walked in.

He let himself consider her. From her mousy brown hair to the shapeless beige dress she wore, she wasn't much to look at. She was nervous and tense, and she'd perfected the art of blending in, a skill detectable by one who hid for a living, a sniper like him. He'd wondered last year what she was hiding from. He was still wondering.

"My name's Chase," he volunteered. "Chase McCaffrey. Some folks call me Westy."

"Sara," she said, with a shy nod. She kept a firm grip on her pencil. No hand-shaking allowed.

"Whatcha workin' on?" he asked, wanting to put her at ease, to solve the riddle that she presented.

"Lesson plans," she admitted, scrunching up her shoulders as if doing that would help her disappear.

She reminded him of a wild animal, wary of humans. He'd tamed a number of wild animals when he was younger. All it took was time, gentleness, and patience. "You're a teacher?" he inquired. Aside from the bun confining her hair, she didn't look like a teacher.

"English tutor," she corrected him. She glanced at her watch, and a crease appeared between her slender eyebrows.

"Something wrong?" It wasn't in his nature to be nosy, but he could feel the tension building in her. Not because of him, he hoped.

"Oh, no. I'm . . . supposed to tutor at the Refugee Center in an hour, but . . ." She glanced toward the closed door where the lawyers convened, and frustration dimmed the clarity of her eyes.

"You don't drive," he guessed.

A flicker of anger came and went. "Not lately," she said, looking down at the notebook.

He wasn't making much headway. Some wild animals took months to tame.

"Could you use a ride?" he heard himself ask. Like he had time to drive her places with all the paperwork waiting for him.

That got her attention. "Excuse me?" she squeaked.

"I was offering you a ride," he explained, figuring he'd overstepped his bounds.

"To the Refugee Center," she clarified.

"Of course." Jesus, did she think he was picking her up? He wasn't that hard up to be chasing a JAG's wife, let alone one who dressed like a nun.

"No, thank you," she murmured, with a pretty blush.

He watched her scratch a word onto the list that she was making. The longer he looked at her, the more tightly she gripped her pencil.

"Ma'am?" he said, startling her head up. "Could you do me a favor?" he asked. He couldn't sit here any longer, feeling the tension in her. "Could you give this envelope to Commander Spenser when he comes out of the meeting?"

"Sure," she said, managing a wobbly smile.

"Thanks. Tell him, he can mail the document back to the return address after he signs it."

"Okay."

Coming out of his chair to extend her the envelope, Chase felt like he was jumping into one of the green-gray pools at the base of a Malaysian waterfall. Her eyes were exquisite. "Take care," he said, unsettled by their unexpected pull on him.

"You, too," she said, radiant again.

He stalked toward the exit, trying to get his mind on all the things he had to do before taking leave. But as he paused by the security checkpoint to collect his SIG and cell phone, he asked Petty Officer Hewitt, "So what's the deal with Captain Garret's wife?"

"Miss Sara?" Hewitt countered with a pitying shake of his head. "She sits in there all day sometimes, waitin' for him to leave work."

"Why?" Chase asked.

Hewitt shrugged. "Captain Garret don't let her out of his sight. Sweet lady, too. It's a shame he treats her so bad."

Chase turned away. He wished he hadn't learned that. "See less of you later, Hewitt."

"Not a chance, Chief." Hewitt chuckled.

As he pushed out of the building into the balmy September afternoon, Chase felt for the woman trapped inside. She must long to be freed to the wild outdoors. He shook his head, picturing her husband, a man whose arrogant demeanor betrayed an overinflated ego.

Men who dominated women belonged to the same category as the terrorists that Chase annihilated. Too bad he'd never get orders to take that fucker out.

Twenty-four hours later, Chase filled his duffel bag with what he'd need for three weeks' leave. He stood halfway between his dresser and his bed, emptying the drawers he'd just filled a few days ago.

Jesse, his black Labrador retriever, lay with his head on his paws, ears flattened, looking devastated.

Chase couldn't take it anymore. "You want to come with me, boy?" he relented. For the last twelve months, the dog had stayed with a friend. It wasn't fair to Jesse to leave him again.

Jesse's head popped up.

"Want to go to Oklahoma? It's a long drive."

The dog's mouth parted in what had to be a smile.

"Hell, you might like it so much you won't want to come back," Chase mused, picturing the woods and the stream where he grew up, paradise for a hunting dog. Jesse wagged his tail as if he could see the pictures in Chase's head.

Pictures that went from good to bad in the blink of an eye. He envisioned his mother on the front porch holding the squalling baby. *"Linc, stop it!"*

Linc had Chase by the scruff of his shirt. Ignoring his wife's pleading, he flung Chase as hard as he could into the door of the two-toned, 1976 Chevy Silverado. The impact was stunning. Chase felt the bone in his nose crack. Hot blood gushed out, running over his lips.

With a mutter of annoyance, he flicked the memory off. He couldn't believe Ol' Linc had gone and left him the ranch. It was probably mortgaged to the eaves, and this was his last bid, even from the grave, to torture his stepson.

If his real father hadn't originally bought it, Chase would let a Realtor sell it. He couldn't care less about the place.

But it was McCaffrey land, not Sawyer land. His daddy had bought it for his mama before he was born. "So, suck it up," he muttered to himself.

He was stuffing his socks in the bag when his cell phone rang. "Yes, sir," he said, having recognized the executive officer's extension.

"I know you're trying to leave, Chief, but did you ever get the lawyer to sign off on the paperwork for Dewey?" asked Lieutenant Renault, who was known to his friends as Jaguar.

He was referring to the document that Chase had left with Sara Garret. "It should be in the mail today or tomorrow, sir. I'll double-check that."

"Just give me a call back if there's going to be a problem."

"Roger, sir."

"Listen, drive safely, and take your time. Vinny's got your paperwork covered. Luther's got the range. If you need more time, just let me know."

"Will do. Thank you, sir."

"No problem, Chief."

Chase ended the call, then looked up a number in his dial-up menu. Commander Spenser's phone bumped him over to voice mail. If he left a message on a Friday afternoon, the lawyer might never get around to calling him back.

With a long-suffering sigh, he descended the stairs to his kitchen, where he pawed through the phone book. Hopefully Sara Garret's number was listed, and hopefully she'd be home to take his call.

Her name wasn't listed, but her husband's was, identifiable by his rank, *Captain* Garret. Chase dialed *67 to conceal his number from caller ID. As the phone rang, he pictured her exquisite eyes and his pulse quickened inexplicably.

The jangling of the telephone startled Sara from counting her money on the bathroom floor. Stuffing the bills back into the tampon box, she shoved it under the sink before hurrying to the adjoining bedroom to snatch the phone off the cherrywood secretary. "Hello?"

"Mrs. Garret?" asked a male voice. The familiar drawl made the air back up in her lungs.

"Yes."

"This is Chief McCaffrey. I left an envelope with you yesterday at the Trial Services Building?"

"Yes," she said, rendered almost mute by the fact that he was calling her. Her thoughts ran wildly before her.

Chief McCaffrey. Four years ago, he'd approached her stranded car in the parking lot, offering to help. He'd been so considerate, so competent, so handsome in a rough-and-ready way, that she'd been in a daze when they parted company. Garret had berated her for her tardiness the instant she arrived home.

Running into him again at the base commissary, here in Virginia Beach, had struck her as a marvelous coincidence. And he'd been just as cordial and considerate as

the last time, even though she was fully to blame for toppling his soda cans. She'd left the store amazed that such
a man existed, only to have Garret seize her checkbook
because she'd splurged on strawberry shortcake.

Now Chase McCaffrey was on the phone, calling her!

"Sorry to bother you, ma'am, but I need to know if you
were able to give Commander Spenser that envelope."

"Oh, yes," she said, disappointed that the call wasn't
personal, of course not. "I handed it to him right away,
along with your message."

"Thanks," he said. "I'm headed to Oklahoma this afternoon. Just wanted to tie up all my loose ends."

Oklahoma? Had he just said *Oklahoma*? The word
jolted her like an electric shock. Sara sputtered, searching
for an appropriate way of asking whether he could give
her and Kendal a ride.

"Why . . . why are you going to Oklahoma?" she stammered, her head spinning so fast that she could hardly
think.

"Family member died," he said shortly. "Left me some
land."

Sara licked her dry lips, desperate to put her question
to him. But within the confines of a casual phone call, it
was inappropriate. Besides, she could hear Kendal's bus
coming up the road now, hydraulic brakes screeching as it
slowed beside the bus stop. "Please, can . . . can I see you
before you go?" she added before she lost her courage.
"There's something that I have to ask you."

He kept notably quiet, no doubt thinking she had lost
her mind.

"There's a park in my neighborhood," she persisted,

sacrificing her dignity for Kendal's sake. "I'm taking my son there today at four. Could you meet me there?"

"Well, I'm pretty busy packin' and all," he answered, but he actually sounded like he was thinking about it.

"Just give me ten minutes." She wanted to melt into the Berber carpet for being reduced to begging favors from a stranger, but the opportunity was too golden to pass up: a ride out West without having to use public transportation.

"The park on Sherwood Drive?" he asked her.

"Yes," she confirmed, her hope flaring, "just past the pool."

"See you there," he said, ending the call.

Sara stared at the phone in her grip, dazed by the possibility that the miracle she'd been praying for had just dropped in her lap. Who better to help her and Kendal slip away than a Navy SEAL? He'd been so helpful in the past; surely he'd consider helping just one more time.

Her gaze shifted out the window to where ten-year-old Kendal was getting off the bus, his shoulders bowed beneath the weight of his backpack. He'd dressed all in black today, still mourning his rabbit.

His teacher had called yesterday evening, the day after Mr. Whiskers's death, alarmed by the change in Kendal's demeanor.

Sara was also alarmed. But she wasn't going to waste time wondering where the downward spiral would end. She was taking every conceivable measure to get her and Kendal out of this nightmare before another incident took place.

Chapter Two

Chase nosed his older model sports car between a BMW sedan and a Range Rover. The park in Sara's neighborhood looked like Disneyland, with an elaborate plastic playground, pool, and clubhouse, all surrounded by million-dollar mansions.

What the hell am I doing here? Chase wondered.

But there was Sara Garret, standing on the edge of the play area, with one hand fisted at her hip, the other raised to shield her eyes from the setting sun. And even with fifty yards between them, he could feel her pull on him, her silent cry for help. He had to know what she wanted from him.

The park was packed with privileged children and their white-collar, upwardly mobile parents enjoying the cooler weather on this second day of fall. It was a whole different cosmos from the world of conspiracy and terror that Chase lived in.

As well it should be, he figured.

The challenge would be not drawing notice to himself. Given the silver hoops in his ears, his goatee and ponytail, that wouldn't be easy. He pulled the bill of his baseball cap down to shield his eyes and got out.

Sauntering toward a bench that was hidden in the shade, he sat down and waited for Sara to see him. He took brief inventory of the children scrambling over the equipment and tried to guess which boy was hers.

He could tell the exact moment that Sara spotted him. Like a jackrabbit spying a predator, she froze, eyes fixed, shoulders tensing. But unlike a rabbit, she didn't dart away. She put one foot in front of the other until she was standing by his bench. Keeping her eyes forward she sat down stiffly.

Chase took wry note of her clothing. Today she wore a dark brown jumper over a white button-up blouse. Was it possible for any woman to have such poor fashion taste?

"Nice evenin'," he noted, breaking the ice for her.

"Yes, it is," she agreed, wetting her lips with a dart of her tongue.

"That your boy?" he asked, following her gaze to where a dark-haired boy, maybe ten years old, sat on a swing, scuffling his toes into the mulch.

Chase had seen the resemblance immediately in the downcast eyes and the curve of the boy's chin. He hid his face behind the bangs growing over his eyes. "What's his name?"

"Kendal. He's the reason that I have to leave," she added quietly.

Leave? Chase swung a startled glance at her, and their gazes collided. He experienced the same cinching sensation in his gut, the same compelling attraction. Her gray-green eyes were incredibly beautiful.

At the same time, the pallor in her face assured him that she was serious. So why was she telling him?

"We need a ride out West," she added, urgently. "I have money. I can pay you if you like. Please . . . take us with you when you leave for Oklahoma."

All he could do was look at her. "Mrs. Garret—" he began.

"Sara," she corrected him, with a flash of those magnificent eyes.

Obviously, she couldn't stand the sound of her husband's last name. "Sara," he began again, "I can't help you with this."

"I've thought it out," she interrupted, reaching inside the voluminous pocket on the front of her jumper. "Kendal's Boy Scout troop is hiking at Seashore State Park tomorrow." She pulled out a folded flyer. "The place is completely remote. We could slip away from the rest of the Scouts and meet you in the overflow parking lot." She thrust the flyer at him.

Chase unfolded it, took note of the pertinent information—place and time—and handed it back.

"I can't help you," he repeated.

He knew exactly when his message got through. She blinked and turned her face.

He felt like he'd slapped her. *Jesus.*

He glanced at her son, who'd buried his Converse tennis shoes completely under the mulch.

Shit. Why would she want to leave her privileged lifestyle unless Captain Garret abused both of them?

"There's gotta be an advocacy group that can help you," he insisted quietly. He willed himself to stand up and walk away.

She still wouldn't look at him. Her face was a mask, with tear-bright eyes made of jade. She'd probably exhausted all her options. She didn't strike him as the type to act impulsively, to solicit the help from a perfect stranger.

"Good luck," he told her, not knowing what else to say. He put his hands on his knees and pushed to his feet.

He wished she'd look up at him or at least acknowledge his refusal, but she didn't.

He felt subtly reprimanded, like he had no right to let her down.

With a scowl, he walked away, determined not to feel guilty. He got into his car and slammed the door shut. What the hell did she expect of him? It would ruin his career if he was caught stealing away a JAG officer's wife and kid. His career was all he had.

Sorry, but he couldn't do it, regardless of Sara's strange pull on him. He'd never let a woman get under his skin before. He wasn't about to start now.

Sara dragged her heels. Hiking along the edge of a marsh was pointless when Chief McCaffrey had made it clear he wasn't going to be here. If it weren't for Kendal, who'd loved nature since he was a baby, she would just as soon have stayed home. And unless Kendal managed to muster some enthusiasm himself, this tramp through the woods amounted to wasted time.

Three cars had been parked in the overflow parking lot, and none of them were Chase's. She'd seen what he drove yesterday—an older blue sports car that was probably halfway to Oklahoma already.

She couldn't blame him for not wanting to get involved. Who would, when Garret had made a reputation for securing some of the harshest sentences in naval history?

And yet . . . she'd expected better from Chase. After all, he'd taken care of her twice in the past, why not this time?

In a moment of foolish optimism, she'd even stuffed her backpack with everything they needed, just in case he did show up: toothbrushes saved from a dentist visit, eight hundred and three dollars, plus a change of clothing for both her and Kendal.

She regretted that impulse. What if Garret, ever suspicious, delved into the contents of her bag? He'd guess her intent to flee in an instant. He'd never let them out of his sight again.

She shivered, clinging to her secret, desperate to relieve the tension building inside of her. She'd sworn to herself that she and Kendal would never suffer another one of Garret's consequences. But unless she found a way to flee, and flee soon, it was inevitable.

Down a tree-shaded foot trail, she plodded. Wasn't there any way to Texas that couldn't be traced? Public transportation was not an option, not in this post-9/11 era, when even bus stations were equipped with video monitors.

If only Chief Chase McCaffrey could have plucked them from Garret's world and taken them to another! It had seemed like providence that he'd blown into her life when she most needed him. Nothing so promising would ever come her way again.

With a blind eye for the flora and fauna Sara trailed seven boys and their Scout leader down a steep ravine. Up the other side they climbed, on steps created by underlying roots. At the crest of the hill, she and Kendal paused, while the others rushed pell-mell toward the swathe of marshland below, eager to spot wildlife but more likely to frighten it away.

The sulfuric tang of mudflats commingled with the fresh-scented breeze. Weighted with depression, they followed the others more sedately.

When they arrived at the bridge that spanned a snaking creek, the others were far ahead. In the quiet lull, Sara discerned the cry of an osprey and looked up.

What would she give to be free like that bird? Free of Garret's unrelenting expectations.

But the sun beat down, and the backpack bit into her shoulders, reminding her that she was earthbound.

Kendal stopped in his tracks, and Sara stumbled into him. "Honey, what—"

"Look, Mom."

His request had her peering down the glinting stream. To her astonishment, there was Chief McCaffrey paddling toward them in a camouflaged canoe.

"He was at the park last night," Kendal said, proving he was more observant than he'd let on.

Chase's hot blue gaze captured Sara's startled one. He'd come after all. God in heaven, he'd actually come for them! Disbelief, relief, then urgency stormed her sensibilities.

"Mom, what's going on?"

They were still alone on the bridge, the others far ahead. With a swish of his paddle, the SEAL maneuvered the canoe alongside them. "Jump in," he said.

"Mom?"

She rushed to explain. "Remember when I told you that I had a plan, Kendal? That we were leaving?"

He darted a stunned look at Chase.

"This is it," she confirmed. "We're leaving now. Get in the boat, sweetheart. Hurry!"

Sara threw a leg over the rail.

But Kendal didn't move. He looked back and forth between her and the stranger. "Who is he?" he wanted to know.

"He's a Navy SEAL," she answered. "He can protect us. Kendal, please get in the boat."

The scowl on Chief McCaffrey's face could have dissuaded even the most fearless individual. "We can't miss this chance, sweetheart!" Sara pleaded, her heart pounding. "Hurry, before the others come back."

Her urgency finally galvanized him. Kendal scrambled over the railing, stepping down into the boat before she'd thrown a second leg over.

"Sit on the bottom," Chase instructed him.

Sara took that cue to position herself on the front seat.

No sooner were they in the boat than Chase launched them into the current. Stabbing his paddle into the stream, he swept them around the bend, taking them quickly out of view of the bridge. The tide was low, and the marsh provided concealment.

A cooling breeze dried the sweat on Sara's upper lip. She glanced back at Kendal, who gripped both sides of the boat, his eyes wide and disbelieving. Behind him, their unlikely rescuer, wearing a baseball cap and cutoff T-shirt, kept a steady stroke on the paddle.

She wanted to thank him, only the frown wedged between his eyebrows kept her mute.

Her heart pattered with hope and fear. She glanced down at the ring pinched between her fourth finger and the canoe's edge. If she didn't think she might need to pawn it one day, she'd take it off right now.

They kept close to the mudflats, moving with such stealth that she could hear fiddler crabs scuttling between the reeds. A blue heron froze on one leg as they glided by.

Sara was just beginning to breathe more easily when they came across a pier and a lone fisherman. He lifted his gaze from a crab pot to greet them.

Chase pulled the bill of his baseball cap down as he nodded back. Plunging his paddle deeper, he whisked them out of the stranger's sight.

It seemed an interminable amount of time before the canoe eased toward a forested shore. The SEAL drove the prow onto land and wedged the paddle into the mud to keep it there. "Hop out," he invited.

Sara clambered out. She held the canoe to keep it from wobbling as Kendal, then Chase followed suit. The bark of a dog drew her gaze to a black Lab sitting in a familiar sports car, parked beneath the trees.

Chase pulled the canoe ashore and flipped it over. "Stand back." With that brief warning, he delivered a swift kick to the underside, leaving a gaping hole. In a brisk, forceful move, he shoved the boat back into the cove, where it started to sink.

"Let's go," he said, heading toward the car. He opened the passenger door and flipped the seat forward. "You'll have to sit with the dog," he said to Kendal. "Back, Jesse."

Kendal dove into the cramped rear seat. "Hey, boy."

As Sara dropped into the front seat, Chase rounded the car to take the wheel. "Buckle up."

With competence and speed that had her holding her breath, he backed them down the rutted track. They came to a clearing, where he reversed direction. And then they took off again.

The dirt track turned into a gravel one before spitting them out into the overflow parking lot. "I used to fish back there," he explained in response to her wondering look.

That was why he knew about the cove, why he'd chosen it as a remote spot to get her into his car without witnesses. She shrank down in her seat, reluctant to be seen by the handful of visitors getting in and out of their vehicles.

Leaving the park, they merged smoothly into the traffic on Shore Drive. Sara sat up straighter and wiped her palms on her shorts.

"Hope you've got everything you need in there," Chase commented, darting a look at her backpack.

"Yes," she said, relieved that she'd planned for the unlikely.

He switched gears. "So, what made you think I'd even show up?" he demanded. The question betrayed an element of self-directed anger.

"I don't know. I just couldn't accept the alternative, I guess."

That answer earned her a conjecturing look.

She glanced back at Kendal. "Oh, honey, you didn't put your seat belt on."

"The dog's sitting on it."

"Jesse, scoot," Chase commanded, and the dog immediately made room.

Mother and son shared a look. The SEAL sure had his dog well trained. Kendal fastened his seat belt with a *click*.

It was then that the full impact of their departure hit

Sara. Mr. Hale, the Boy Scout leader, was probably frantic right now, wondering what had happened to them. The authorities would soon be notified, then Garret. There was no going back now.

"We're not going to stop anywhere, are we?" she asked on a note that betrayed her fear.

"No," he said. Accelerating, he swept them up an exit ramp onto the highway that would lead them north and west, toward the Blue Ridge Mountains and beyond. In just three hours, or so, they'd be in the western half of Virginia, far from the search that would be taking place for them at Seashore State Park. She would breathe a whole lot easier then.

"Do you think that fisherman is going to be a problem?" she asked beneath her breath.

To her deepening concern, Chase didn't answer right away. "He wasn't there when I approached the rendezvous point. If he had been, I would have turned around."

In which case, she never would have known that he'd intended to rescue her, after all.

"Thank you," she murmured, thinking those two words fell woefully short. "I promise you won't . . . regret it," she added, forcing those words through a tight throat.

She was certain that he'd heard her, but he didn't answer. It was probably too late, and he probably already did.

Chapter Three

For the next four hours, very little was said. The radio kept up a steady barrage of music and advertising. The highway unraveled before them like an endless, asphalt ribbon.

Chasing the sun westward, they arrived, at last, at the foothills of the Blue Ridge Mountains, where the cooler clime had already turned the trees to crimson and gold. The setting sun lit the peaks of the mountains in a blaze of color.

"Gotta love the mountains," Chase finally said, breaking the silence.

"Yes," Sara agreed, exhaling a sigh of relief that he was speaking again. With every passing hour, the fear that Garret would catch them diminished, but Chase's brooding presence had kept her from relaxing.

"We'll stop on the other side of Roanoke, near Bristol," he indicated, turning down the radio.

Sara nodded her agreement. She'd been hoping for a potty break. "How long will that take?"

"'Bout two more hours."

She glanced at Kendal, who squirmed in the backseat.

Riding on roadways that weren't absolutely flat, he had a tendency to get carsick. "How do you feel, honey?"

"Okay," he said, but to her discerning eye that wasn't the case.

"I brought your medicine," she said rummaging in the backpack. "Oh, but I don't have anything for you to swallow it with." She started to put the medicine back.

"What's that?" Chase asked.

"Dramamine. Sometimes he gets carsick."

Garret had scoffed at Kendal's condition. Surely a Navy SEAL would also view it as a weakness. But in the next instant, Chase was easing into the breakdown lane. "There's water in the back," he explained. He stopped the car, jumping out to fetch them each a bottle.

The considerate gesture was deeply reassuring. Kendal swallowed his pill, and they were off, climbing up into the mountains. But Chase had lapsed back into silence.

"How many days does it take to get to Oklahoma?" Sara inquired. Could she endure that many hours with a brooding driver?

"Three days more or less," he said shortly.

"Why are we going there?" Kendal asked in a sleepy voice. The Dramamine was having its usual effect on him.

"I'll explain later, honey." The less Chase knew, the safer it was for all of them. She looked out the window to avoid his quick glance.

Three days! She'd been so focused on getting away that she'd spared little thought as to what it would be like in the hours and days following their departure. The idea of being cooped up that long brought little relief to her nail-biting anxiety.

By the time they pulled into a roadside motel, it was

dark, and her stomach was rumbling. Chase unlatched his seat belt.

"They'll want a credit card imprint," he said, as she tried to hand him some money. "I'm only gettin' one room."

With that, he was gone, notching Sara's tension to the snapping point. She hadn't considered that they would have to share a room.

Jesse whined, as eager to get out as she and Kendal were.

Minutes later, Chase reappeared. Guiding them along the shadows, he escorted them to their room, shut the door, and drew the curtains before flicking on the lights. Kendal stumbled sleepily toward the bathroom.

"I'll be right back," Chase said. "I'm gonna walk the dog and take a look around."

As he slipped out again, Sara locked and latched the door. She turned and eyed the double beds. Was this forced intimacy just a means for him to take advantage of her? Surely not. He'd given her no reason to think he'd helped her for any reason other than human decency.

Besides, she knew what she looked like. She'd dressed this way intentionally for years. And for good reason.

Kendal came out of the bathroom, looking lost.

"Feeling better, sweetheart?" she asked. She crossed the room to catch his face between her hands. He was almost as tall as she was.

"Where are we going?" he demanded ignoring the question. "Not with him, I hope."

"No," she reassured him. "Chief McCaffrey is going to take us as far as Oklahoma," she explained. "From there we'll get a ride to Texas."

"Why? What's in Texas?"

The time had come to share her burning secret. "My real mother is in Texas. I was adopted, Kendal. Your father doesn't know that."

Kendal's jaw dropped. His gaze flicked over her like he'd never really seen her before. "Cool," he finally said. A glimmer of hope lit his eyes.

"That's why this is going to work," she insisted. "We're going to start all over again, with new names and everything."

"But what about all my stuff?" he asked with belated regret. "My PlayStation and my computer?"

"I'll buy you new stuff," Sara promised. "After we get settled and I get a job. It isn't going to be easy, honey," she admitted. "But it will be better. We'll make our own decisions. We'll do whatever we want without constantly having to worry whether we'll upset your father."

He gave her a searching look. "You would've stayed, wouldn't you, if Dad hadn't killed Mr. Whiskers?"

"I couldn't stand to watch him hurt you," she admitted.

"But he hurt you all the time."

He'd noticed, then, despite her efforts to protect him. Hiding her stricken look, she kissed his cheek and moved past him, into the bathroom.

When she reemerged, Kendal was watching TV. Chase knocked on the door, and she went to let him in.

"Spotted a Super Kmart across the street," he announced, letting Jesse off the leash. "I'm gonna run over there and get us what we need."

Sara snatched up her backpack, pulling out two twenty-dollar bills. "Take this," she said, holding out the money. "I need some scissors and some hair color." She wanted something in a blond shade. "Maybe we should come with you?"

He took the money, sliding it into his pocket. "Not yet. Stay away from the windows, and keep the door locked," he instructed. "Oh, and Kendal?"

Kendal lifted wary eyes at him.

"You mind feedin' the dog for me? His food and bowl are in that plastic bag right there. Don't forget to give him water."

" 'Kay," the boy said, slipping off the bed.

With a wink at Sara, Chase was gone, shutting the door behind him.

Reassured by the wink, Sara drew the latch a second time. "I know he sounds rough, honey," she said, as much for herself as for him, "but he helped us four years ago, back in California, when our car wouldn't start at the library. Remember that?"

Kendal had been six years old, then. "No," he said, dropping nuggets into Jesse's metal bowl.

Sara plopped down on the edge of a bed and watched him carry the water bowl to the bathroom. It was obvious that Kendal didn't trust the stranger helping them. She couldn't blame him. Chase had been silently forbidding since his appearance at the park, not exactly the laid-back, considerate gentleman he seemed to be before.

Trust me, no one's going to hurt you again, Kendal, she swore to herself, watching as he offered the dog water and petted his broad head.

An hour later, she had to wonder if she'd let him down already. In addition to the sandwiches that they'd wolfed down, Chase had bought a deluxe hair-cutting kit that included an electric shaver.

"We need to cut the boy's hair," he'd said to Sara.

She'd been so eager to start coloring her own hair that she'd agreed to his offer to do so. The bathroom door was left ajar, reassuring her further as she stood before the desk, using the mirror in the room to put dye in her hair.

Entering the bathroom fifteen minutes later, she found Kendal's hair buzzed down to a smart, military cut.

"All set," Chase said, whisking the boy's neck and ears with a brush. Kendal winced at the dusting. Chase pulled the poncho off.

With the look of a wounded animal, Kendal pushed past his mother and went to flop down near the TV and sulk.

"It'll grow out," Chase called after him. He sent Sara an apologetic grimace. "Sorry 'bout that. I should've used a different size head," he muttered.

"That's okay." The apology appeased her. Not once in eleven years had Garret ever apologized.

Skirting around Chase, Sara dropped to her knees beside the tub and stuck her head under the faucet.

Warm water sluiced by her ears. Yellow-brown dye rushed down the drain. She was conscious of Chase coming to stand behind her.

"You're missing some," he observed, and suddenly his hands were cradling her head, angling it under the stream to ensure that all the excess dye got washed out.

A gasp wedged itself into Sara's lungs.

He was touching her, and she could feel the strength in his gentle fingers all the way down to her toes.

"All set," he said, turning the water off.

Sara fumbled with the conditioning tube, squirting the white stuff into her palm and rubbing it briskly into her hair.

Before Chase could help her again, she rinsed it out, not bothering to wait the requisite two minutes.

He plopped a towel over her head. She came shakily to her feet, wondering when he intended to step out.

"How do you want your hair cut?" he asked her.

"Oh." From beneath the towel she added, "I think I'll cut it myself." Although, on second thought, Kendal's haircut had looked professional.

"Suit yourself," Chase replied. "Concealment's what I do for a living. I know how to make you look different," he added.

Sara wavered. Pulling the towel off her head, she looked at him.

"Trust me," he said, his blue eyes compelling.

She wanted to. She was longing to put her whole faith in him. If he could just act like the laid-back cowboy who'd rescued her in San Diego instead of this serious, uncommunicative commando.

"All right," she agreed, taking her chances. She positioned herself before the mirror.

"Color looks good on you," he said, lifting the comb and drawing the snarls out of her shoulder-length hair.

She thought so, too, but watching him groom her was distracting. He was perhaps just six feet tall, several inches shorter than Garret, but his shoulders were twice as broad, making her seem petite by comparison.

"I was blond as a child," she admitted. At one time, she'd been told that she resembled Meg Ryan, but that was way back before she'd started planning her escape.

Chase put the comb down and picked up the scissors. He began by hacking four inches off her hair.

Sara gaped.

"Just need a place to start," he explained, with a hint of humor in his eyes.

His fingers slid into her hair, just above her scalp. He tugged and snipped. Three more inches fell away. He repeated the movement, and this time it felt like a caress, which he repeated, over and over again.

Sara relaxed by degrees. In place of her tension came a heightened awareness of him as a male, touching her in a way that Garret had never touched her. It wasn't meant to be sexual, but it made her acutely aware of her femininity.

"You gonna change your name?" he inquired. He seemed to know exactly what he was doing, moving without hesitation, from front to back, snipping off tendrils that drifted toward the floor to layer over Kendal's darker hair.

It wouldn't hurt to tell him, would it? "Serenity," she admitted. She'd chosen the name when she'd first considered leaving, right after Kendal's birth.

The look that he bounced off the mirror went straight through her. "Serenity what?"

"I'd rather not say," she hedged.

He was silent a second. "Good," he decided. "It's smart to be cautious."

In lieu of asking more questions, he started twisting strands of her hair and snipping the ends. The shortness of the cut had Sara holding her breath, though she dared not complain. The idea was to change her look completely, and he was definitely doing that.

"Face me now," he instructed.

She did so, her pulse fluttering as she stood within six inches of him, gaze riveted to his muscle-corded neck and the pulse that thudded steadily at the base of it. Drawing a secret breath, she decided that he smelled like fresh-cut wood.

"Close your eyes," he said, going to work on her bangs. *Snip, snip, snip.*

She heard the scissors slide onto the sink. Chase ruffled her hair. "You're done," he said.

Sara turned toward the mirror. "Oh, my," she exclaimed, discovering that she looked more like Meg Ryan than ever. She touched the soft, spiky strands by her ears. "How'd you learn to cut hair so well?"

"No barbers in the places I go," he answered matter-of-factly. "While I clean up in here, why don't you check out the clothes I bought for you?"

She'd seen the bags that he'd brought back from the Super Kmart. This was her getaway, and yet he seemed to be masterminding it.

Kendal stared at her as she stepped from the bathroom. "You look like that movie star," he commented.

"Meg Ryan?"

"I don't know her name." He went back to watching TV.

Moving past him, Sara spilled the plastic sacks open on the second bed. *Oh, no.* For a shocked minute she stared at the clothes and accessories that Chase had bought her: shorts from the juniors department; baby-doll T-shirts in every pastel hue imaginable; two pair of sling sandals, pink and green with sequined flowers on them, and a bag-ful of makeup.

She couldn't dress like this! She would look like . . . like a completely different woman, a teenager, practically.

She glanced up as Chase stepped into view, carrying their hair in a sack. He paused by the bed, taking in her reaction with a challenging lift to his eyebrows.

"This had to have cost more than forty dollars," she said, trying to find some way around having to wear what he'd bought.

"End-of-summer sale," he countered, eyes narrowing. "Sixty percent off."

She just looked at him. "So, no refunds then."

"Nope."

With a nod, she started putting the clothes away. "Kendal's going to need clothes, too."

"You can shop for him tomorrow," Chase said.

Sara drew a deep breath. "You know," she said, giving rare voice to her opinion, "I wouldn't have bought these kinds of clothes for myself," she dared to tell him.

A tiny smile touched the edges of his mouth. "I know. And trust me, ma'am, I don't get my kicks out of tellin' you what to wear. But this is what I do for a living. You wear these clothes, and no one's going to recognize you."

His argument was infuriatingly reasonable. With a sigh of surrender, Sara put the clothes in the bags for the night.

Chase went outside to toss their hair in the Dumpster. When he came back in, he grabbed sweatpants from his duffel bag and disappeared into the shower.

Sara went to sit with Kendal. Everything was happening so quickly, yet, at the same time slowly enough to fray her nerves. What if, in the next twenty-four hours, Garret guessed how she'd engineered her flight?

Impossible. He didn't even know that she knew Chief McCaffrey. How could he guess he'd helped her get away?

The bathroom door yawned open, and Chase materialized on a puff of steam, wearing nothing but a pair of gray sweatpants.

She and Kendal both stared. Sara had never seen a man

more powerfully put together. His was the body of a warrior, with muscles that came from daily, rigorous training, and scars suggesting deadly hand-to-hand combat, not to mention a fearsome black tattoo on his left triceps. The rest was golden skin and tawny fur, a combination that left her dry-mouthed.

He crossed in front of them, heading toward his duffel bag, and his footfalls were undetectable.

He leaned over his bag, and when he straightened again, he was holding a gun in his hand.

Sara gasped, reaching for her son.

"Relax," Chase told her, keeping it pointed at the floor. He carried it over to his bed, pulled the quilt down, and stuffed it under the pillow. "It's my security blanket."

"Is it . . . loaded?"

He sent her an incredulous look.

"Stupid question," she acknowledged.

He sprawled with masculine grace upon his stomach, and her gaze slid helplessly to his tattoo. Four skeletons rose from a common gravesite. *Good heavens.*

He was a far cry from the clean-cut, starched-shirt officer she'd married. She'd once credited Garret with traits that he didn't posses: fairness and self-control.

What if her evaluation of Chase was equally flawed?

Officer Stan Laughlin of the Virginia Beach Police Department Crime Unit cast a trained eye around the study in Captain Bartholomew Garret's upscale mansion.

The study, with its burgundy walls and heavy mahogany furniture, was a true male retreat. The wall behind the desk displayed Garret's credentials: diplomas, plaques, and certifications. The man was obviously successful. Too bad success couldn't shield a man from crime, which leached upward through the layers of society like an overflowing septic tank.

It was 10:00 P.M. on Saturday evening, and Stan had a judgment to make based on scant evidence. One eyewitness had placed the wife and son of Captain Garret in a canoe that day, in the company of a stranger. Because stranger abductions were the most dangerous to children, it was in Kendal Garret's best interest for Stan to issue an Amber Alert, a cooperative agreement between law enforcement and broadcasters, sponsored by the US Department of Justice.

But, in this situation, the mother had disappeared, as well, making it equally feasible that Mrs. Garret had abducted her own son. Feasible, but not likely, given Captain Garret's fervent assertion that he and his wife were happily married; that Sara was not at all the type to do something so irresponsible.

Following intensive questioning, first at the park, then at the police station, Stan had followed Captain Garret home to get more recent photos than those he carried in his wallet. It was taking the man an inordinate amount of time.

Stan got up and paced. The carpet under his feet kept his footfalls silent. He circled the room, making note of the impersonal wall art.

He read through the diplomas declaring Captain Garret an honor's graduate from Harvard University and the Marshall-Wythe School of Law at the College of William and Mary. The man was definitely an overachiever, and given the dust-free surfaces in his study, not to mention the starch in his golf shirt, he was also a perfectionist.

All of which led Stan to wonder if Sara Garret didn't secretly long for a more carefree existence than that of a housewife living the all-American dream.

"Sorry that I took so long," Captain Garret said, startling Stan from his contemplations. "I'm not sure what Sara did with the rest of the photo albums. This is the best I can offer."

Stan cast a jaundiced eye at the two photos. "When was this picture taken?" he asked, studying the one of the boy first.

"I believe he was eight, then."

"And he's ten now? Don't you have any school pictures hanging on the walls?"

Captain Garret looked muddled. "No, I . . . perhaps Sara took them to work with her."

She volunteered as an English tutor at the Norfolk Refugee Center. Stan made a note to check there Monday morning. He glanced at the second photograph, the one of Mrs. Garret. It was blurry. Not only that, but it captured a woman with indistinct features, medium brown hair, and baggy clothing. "And this is the only picture you could find of your wife," Stan marveled.

"She's the self-effacing sort," Garret explained. "She doesn't like to have her photo taken."

Stan could see that. She didn't look like the type to abduct her son, either. "These will have to do," he decided, sliding them into his breast pocket. "I'll need to run if I'm going to get these into the Sunday paper."

"Then you're issuing an Amber Alert," Garret guessed with a look of relief.

"Yes," Stan decided. "We can't rule out the stranger at this point."

"Thank you," Garret replied, with a hitch in his voice.

Normally Stan was moved to pat the shoulder of a distraught parent, but something about this father—his extreme height, perhaps—kept him from being that demonstrative. "By dawn, the search for your wife and son will go regional, and from there, national," he comforted.

"Do you think you'll find them?"

Stan didn't want to raise the man's hopes too high. "It really depends on the identity and motivation of their abductor. You have no idea who the bearded stranger might be?" It was the tenth time he'd asked that night.

"No," Garret said, tiredly. "I have no idea."

"Well, then." Stan offered him a grimace and a nod. "We'll be in touch in the morning. Let us know if you hear anything on this end."

Garret escorted him through the marble foyer and out to his car. When Stan pulled away, speeding to deliver the photos to the press, a glimpse in the rearview mirror showed Garret still standing on the curb, looking forlorn.

Chapter Four

Chase awoke as the first hint of sunlight framed the motel curtains. He swung his feet to the floor, beset by the instinct to keep moving. But the two dark lumps in the bed next to his were sleeping peacefully—at last. He'd heard Sara toss and turn late into the night. He didn't have the heart to wake her.

He dressed in shorts and a T-shirt, put on his running shoes, and brushed his teeth. Jesse wagged his tail as Chase scooped up his leash. *Go for a run, boy?*

It could be Chase's imagination that had him thinking that Garret was dogging his heels. The best way to find out would be to pick up a morning newspaper. He'd do that and squeeze in a run at the same time.

Grabbing money and the room key, Chase let himself out into the cool mountain air. The hills were bathed in dawn's first rays. They brightened by degrees as the sun climbed higher.

"Hup," Chase said to Jesse, and they took off across the parking lot, setting a strong, steady pace that helped relieve some of Chase's tension.

He'd never put his career on the line for anyone before. It had to be his dislike of Captain Garret that made him do it. The man's arrogance at last year's court-martial had made Chase envision a humiliating defeat for the prosecution—not that vengeance had ever been a motivating factor for him.

The sky warmed to the color of butter as Chase cut across a grassy knoll, urging Jesse to cross a quiet intersection. Arriving at the Super K, he fed the newspaper machine seventy-five cents and whipped out a paper. Shaking it open, his gaze fell to the article emblazoned across the lower portion of the front page, and his heartbeat faltered.

AMBER ALERT ISSUED FOR KENDAL GARRET. Below that were three pictures: One of Kendal, one of Sara, and a composite sketch of their kidnapper. *Oh, fuck.*

Chase angled the paper so that the sun illumined it fully. "Jesse, sit," he ordered, as the dog snuffled out a piece of trash.

He read the article once quickly, then again more carefully. The sweat he hadn't managed to break on his run poured from him belatedly, coursing down his back in rivulets.

Son of a bitch! A statewide search was under way for Kendal Garret and his mother Sara, both of whom were believed to have been kidnapped at Seashore State Park yesterday afternoon by a bearded stranger.

With a scowl, Chase assessed the composite sketch of himself. The one witness to the abduction, the fisherman on the pier, had remembered Chase as having a full beard, like the one he'd grown for his mission to Malaysia. With the bill of his cap pulled so low, his features, thankfully, hadn't been clear.

Even Kendal's picture wasn't the best representation of him. It'd been taken a while ago, and his hair had been even longer than it was yesterday before Chase cut it.

As for Sara, her photo captured a woman with drab, shoulder-length hair, unremarkable features, and baggy clothing.

There was hope, yet.

So what if a statewide search was under way for them? Chase had been in tighter situations and come out on top. He didn't need to panic, necessarily. What he did need to do was to get the hell out of Virginia.

"Come on, Jess," he called, leaving the paper for someone else to pick up. He wasn't about to send Sara into panic mode by telling her what kind of publicity her disappearing act was generating.

With Jesse at his heels, he sprinted back to the motel. Pausing at the door, he took five seconds to slow his breathing, opened the door, and let the sunlight pour in. "Time to get up," he said brusquely.

Both of them jumped like squirrels on a high-voltage wire.

"Sorry," he apologized, taking in Sara's wild-eyed disorientation. "But we need to go."

She threw back the covers, offering instructions to her son as she gathered up her new clothes and scurried into the bathroom.

Chase and Kendal waited, wolfing down the donuts he'd bought last night.

"Save some for my mom," Kendal demanded, with knee-knocking bravado.

It was the first sentence he'd spoken directly to Chase. "She can have the rest," Chase assured him. Each one was the other's defender, he realized. It'd been the same with him and his mama.

Half an hour later, the dog was in the car, the car was running, but they were still waiting. "We have to *go*," Chase growled, knocking on the bathroom door.

"Okay, I'm done." And there she was, brushing past him in her new clothes. "I'm sorry," she said, snatching up her backpack. She was out the door without even looking at him.

Chase followed with his eyes glued to her legs. *Holy . . . fuck.* She had legs. Gorgeous, soft-looking legs that went all the way from her trim ankles up to the hem of the shorts that barely covered her cute-as-hell ass.

"Mom, you look like a girl," Kendal said, in accents of disgust.

Woman, Chase corrected mentally. She was all woman from the rear. He hurried to overtake her, dying of curiosity to see how she looked from the front. The first thing he saw was cleavage. The pale yellow T-shirt not only revealed ample breasts but, thanks to the hip-hugging shorts, it exposed her belly button and subtly curving hips, as well. No wonder she'd taken so long to come out of the bathroom. She'd have to work up her courage, first.

He opened the car door, which gave him time to assess her transformation. The spunky haircut, makeup, and clothing made her look ten years younger. The only thing missing was a belly button ring.

She glanced at him uncomfortably as she took her seat. Her eyes had been merely extraordinary before. Accentuated by eyeliner, shadow, and mascara, they were a punch in the gut.

Feeling dazed, Chase rounded the vehicle to slip in behind the wheel. *Focus,* he commanded himself, pulling them out of the parking lot. He needed to find Route 11 West, which would put them on a less-traveled roadway crossing into Tennessee.

But even as he merged into traffic, hunting for road signs, his gaze strayed toward Sara's thighs, her waist, breasts, face. She was so unexpectedly appealing that he had to lecture himself not to get any more involved in her life than he already was.

"Aren't we going to the Super K?" she asked him, as they roared right past it.

"Not this morning," he retorted curtly. *Hell, no, not with Kendal's picture on the front page of the newspaper.* "We'll stop in Tennessee somewhere," he added on a gentler note.

His curt tone rendered her silent. She stared out the window at the hills, quilted in autumn colors. "Look at the stream, Kendal," she said, and Kendal put his chin on the back of her seat to admire the stream that ran alongside the roadway.

Chase considered explaining his haste. How would Sara react to knowing that her escape was in the public eye, and he'd been cast into the role of kidnapper?

Glancing her way, he was struck by how long and graceful her neck was. She sat with her palms on her thighs, trying in vain to cover them. She looked so vulnerable eyeing the horizon for peace of mind that he bit the words back.

She didn't need to know. Why scare her more than she was already scared?

Ten minutes down Route 11, Chase cursed his luck.

It can't be, he told himself, scanning the area for a quick exit. But there wasn't one, and it was.

He swallowed a lurid curse, knowing that the worst thing he could do was to alarm Sara or her son.

Too late, she'd already seen the blue lights flashing up ahead. "It's a roadblock," she croaked, bracing herself as if they were going to crash straight through it.

"Breathe," he replied, using the voice he used on junior SEALs when coaxing them out of the plane on their first nighttime HALO jump. "The worst thing you can do is to show fear. Kendal, I want you to pretend you're sleeping. Turn your face away from me," he instructed. "Sara," he added, putting a hand on her knee because that was what he did with his men. "I want you to smile," he said, giving her a reassuring squeeze.

"Smile," she repeated, darting an unsettled look at his hand.

He wished he could keep it on her leg a little longer. Instead, he had to reach into his glove compartment for his registration, slowing at the same time behind the line of cars in front of him.

"They're looking for us, aren't they?" Sara inquired. She was pale and trembling, not at all the smiling companion he needed her to be.

He flipped down the visor in front of her. "Look in the mirror," he commanded. "What do you see? Is that Sara Garret?"

She stared at her reflection, swallowed heavily, and shook her head. *No.*

"It's how you wear the concealment that counts," he added, easing them forward.

Sara drew a deep breath. To his surprise, she propped a

sandaled foot up on the dashboard, leaned her head back against the headrest, and sent him a relaxed smile.

He caught himself staring. "Good," he muttered. He dragged his eyes forward again to assess the looks on the state troopers' faces as they bent to address the vehicles ahead of them. "Let me do the talking," he added, fishing his wallet from his back pocket.

Finally, it was their turn. Chase reached back and nudged his dog. "Jesse, speak." He lowered his window and the Lab started barking.

"Good mornin'," said the middle-aged trooper, who took a quick step back as Jesse shoved his snout through the opening between the front seat and the backseat and let loose with a series of strident barks.

"Howdy," said Chase. "Hush, Jesse," he ordered, only Jesse didn't know that command.

Keeping his distance from the dog, the trooper glanced at Chase's license and registration. He then handed Chase a flyer. "We're looking for this boy and his mother. They disappeared yesterday from the Virginia Beach area," he explained, speaking over the dog's loud barks.

"I heard about that," Chase answered, frowning at the pictures on the flyer—same as the ones in the newspaper.

The trooper tried to peer at Chase's passengers. He caught sight of Sara, who sent him a friendly smile. "Where are you headed?" the trooper asked.

Jesse, who blocked the man's view of Kendal, barked again.

"Knoxville," Chase replied loudly. "My sister-in-law's place."

The trooper nodded. "Ya'll have yourselves a nice drive," he said, and he waved them on.

As Chase eased them out of the bottleneck, Sara snatched the leaflet off his lap. He heard her stifled cry. "Oh, my God," she breathed, staring aghast at the photos of her and Kendal. "They think we were kidnapped," she realized out loud. "They've issued an Amber Alert!" She raised her horrified eyes at him. "Oh, Chase," she breathed with bottomless regret. "I had no idea it would come to this, I swear," she added, her concern, apparently, all for him. "You can drop us off at the next bus station if you don't want to take us. I totally understand—"

"I'm not droppin' you off," he told her, holding her gaze for a reassuring moment.

As she considered him through tear-bright eyes, her slender eyebrows came slowly together. "Why aren't you upset? Or surprised?" she added with belated suspicion.

"I saw it in the papers this morning," he admitted.

He could see her reviewing the morning in light of that confession. "Why didn't you tell me?" she demanded.

He shrugged. "Didn't want you to worry."

"But you were worried," she recalled.

He didn't bother to deny it. He sensed he'd just earned a portion of her faith by trying to protect her.

"Mom, I feel sick again," Kendal interrupted.

"Honey, we just started driving."

"I need my medicine," he insisted.

With a sigh, Sara turned and pawed inside the backpack.

Chase checked the impulse to say something. It wasn't his place to point out that maybe Kendal was just stressed out—not that he blamed him. Besides, a dose of Dramamine wasn't going to hurt. It'd keep him from getting restless till they could afford to stop, on the other side of Tennessee, if Chase had his way.

"Navy SEALs kill people, don't they?"

The question popped out of Kendal, as Chase slid his gun under the pillow on the bed closest to the window of their motel room in Memphis. Sara had just retreated into the shower. There wasn't any chance in hell that she'd save Chase from having to answer.

"SEALs protect the interests of the free world," he replied, sitting down. He put his back against the head-board and focused his gaze on the fishing show that Kendal had found on television. "Sometimes we kill terrorists because they've hurt innocent people and intend to do it again."

Obviously that wasn't enough to satisfy the boy. "Bet you're a hunter, too," he continued several minutes later, "which is why you've got a retriever." He glanced at Jesse, who lay sprawled in front of the door.

"He retrieves ducks," Chase conceded, "but that's pretty much all I hunt. And I never kill more than I can eat."

That earned him a horrified look.

Chase scratched his head and tried again. "My grand-father was a Creek Indian. He taught me to respect life, not destroy it."

The atmosphere in the room shifted. "A real Indian?" Kendal asked, darting him a dubious look.

"Hundred percent Indian."

The interrogation continued. "What was his name?"

"Jeremiah Blackbird. He taught me how to trap beaver

and tame a bobcat," Chase recalled with remembered pleasure.

"You can't tame a bobcat."

"Did once. Back when I was ten. We had a couple o' bobcats on the ranch. I tamed one of their cubs so that it'd come to me when I called it."

"No way," Kendal scoffed, looking at him.

"Way," said Chase, staring him down.

They went back to watching the TV as the angler snared another fish.

"What other animals live on your ranch?" The hostility in Kendal's voice was gone.

"The usual: 'coons, and squirrels; badgers and jack-rabbits; eagles, owls, egrets, and three-toed box turtles. Those're my favorite."

"So you know lots about animals."

"Grew up with 'em. The ranch is fifty acres or so," he added, picturing it in his mind's eye. "Most of that's forest, some pastureland. There's a creek you can wade in when it gets too hot." He experienced a tremor of excitement at the realization that he'd see it all again, soon.

Reflective silence sat between them. "Maybe I could visit," Kendal suggested.

"Maybe," Chase replied. *Maybe not.* He'd be out of his mind to take them any farther than the Muskogee Turnpike, Oklahoma. At that junction, they'd head south to Texas, and he'd head northwest to Broken Arrow.

But then he pictured Sara and her son at the ranch, and the thought occurred to him that Garret would never find them there.

Forget that shit, he sternly commanded himself. He'd gone above and beyond the call of duty where those two were concerned. He wasn't going to get into any more trouble than he was already begging for.

Sara awoke from a paralyzing dream, trembling and covered in goose bumps. It took her a moment to recollect where she was—in a motel room in Memphis, not in her bedroom in Virginia Beach, cringing from Garret's sexual advances.

She turned her head, seeking reassurance in the form of Chase's silhouette, on the bed next to hers. The pale expanse of sheet was all she saw.

With an indrawn breath, she jerked to her elbows, seeking him in the room's dark shadows. Where was he? Not here. Could he have taken off, abandoned them? She wouldn't blame him if he had.

She rolled out of bed, straining to see in the darkness. To her great relief, she spied Jesse, guarding the threshold. No way would Chase have left his dog.

She crossed the room to peek outside. A man loomed on the other side of the glass, startling a gasp from her. She realized it was Chase, standing with his back to the window. She glanced at the nightshirt she'd bought while buying Kendal clothes at a local Walmart this evening. Heck, it covered more of her than the clothes she'd worn all day. Nudging Jesse aside, she squeezed through the door to talk to Chase.

His head turned as she stepped into view. Silvery rain dropped like a curtain on the other side of the balcony, hemming in the walkway. Wearing nothing but his gray sweatpants, Chase seemed to take up an awful lot of space.

"What are you doing?" she asked him.

In the dark, his eyes glinted like pools of water. He shrugged. "Couldn't sleep. You all right?" he asked her.

The drumming of rain created a peaceful atmosphere that drew her out to join him. "Bad dream," she admitted, letting the door close softly behind her.

She had to wonder if she was still dreaming. Against the backdrop of the rain, Chase struck her as reflective, nonthreatening. In the semidarkness, the angles of his face didn't look so fierce. She even considered that his broad torso might be a comfort to lean against—like a pillar of strength or a safe haven.

"A dream about Garret?" he guessed, insightfully.

She hugged herself against the wet breeze and nodded.

Silence fell between them, but it wasn't fraught with tension as before.

"I had a dream, too," he admitted.

She could tell by his tone that it wasn't a good dream. She shivered, overwhelmed by the sense that it was just a matter of time before Garret caught them both.

"We'll go our separate ways tomorrow," she reminded him. They'd discussed a plan before going to bed. In Muskogee, Oklahoma, he'd help her find transportation to Dallas.

"I've been thinkin' 'bout that," he admitted. "Any type of shuttle is going to ask you for identification, and you don't have any."

"We'll take a taxi," she offered, wanting to put his worries at ease.

"Too expensive."

Another reflective silence swept between them. Chase broke it, with a decisiveness that told her he had just made up his mind. "There's something I can do for you," he offered quietly. "I have a friend in Washington who makes documents for me when I go abroad. I can get you any form of identification you need."

"What do mean, like a birth certificate?" she asked, stunned.

"Birth certificate, driver's license, transcripts, anything," he answered, watching her carefully.

The offer made her head spin. "Oh, I can't," she decided. "You've done enough, more than enough—"

"How are you going to get a job without a social security number?" he pressed her. "How's Kendal going to go to school without transcripts?"

She put a hand to her forehead. He made the future sound impossible. "I don't know, I—" She'd been naïve enough to think that she could say that Kendal had been homeschooled. Chances were that someone would eventually question that. "It's not your problem."

He gave a humorless laugh. "You made it my problem when you asked me to help you."

"I'm sorry."

"I'm not asking for an apology. I just want you to trust me."

Trust? She would never fully trust a man again.

"Enough to answer some questions," he amended, "so that I can send my buddy information, and he can put some stuff together for you."

She drew a troubled breath. She didn't want Chase to find himself court-martialed one day, should Garret somehow find her. On the other hand, Garret stood less chance of that if she accepted Chase's offer.

"I'd also like for you to come to Broken Arrow with me," he added unexpectedly. "My stepdad left behind a truck. If I can get it running, you wouldn't have to take a bus or taxi. You'd have your own wheels."

Her very own car to drive? This offer, like the last, was equally hard to refuse. More than that, she'd been dreading the moment of separation, when she and Kendal were thrust into the hostile world, where some stranger might just recognize them. The thought of being detained and questioned and ultimately reunited with Garret terrified her.

Chase's invitation erased those wretched pictures and replaced them with visions of something far less threatening.

But what if he exploits you? whispered the voice of caution.

She immediately quelled it. Chase might have brooded for two days straight, frightened her with his terse efficiency, slept with a gun under his pillow, but he'd acted honorably in every conceivable way. Surely she could trust him to see to their well-being just a few days longer. "Okay," she agreed. "I'm not in a rush."

His lagoonlike gaze held hers captive. "You're gonna have to tell me what your last name's gonna be. Everything."

She queried her judgment one more time. She would have to tell him that she and her birthmother had corresponded via e-mail for months now; that she planned to live with her in Dallas, tutoring immigrants to earn a living. "I'll tell you tomorrow," she promised, too weary tonight to go into detail tonight.

"Fair enough," he said, his gaze lingering. "You gonna be able to sleep now?"

"I think so."

"Me too. Let's get some shut-eye."

His arm brushed her breast as he turned toward the door to put the keycard in the lock.

Sara gasped, surprised that the contact felt pleasurable. She trembled to think of how vulnerable she truly was, how easily Chase could take advantage of her.

"Go ahead," he said, holding the door.

She dove into the dark room, resolved to remain watchful.

Chapter Five

A hush fell over the occupants of the sports car as Chase turned off the asphalt road onto a dirt-and-gravel driveway to his ranch outside of Broken Arrow, Oklahoma.

It was 4:00 P.M., several hours past their anticipated arrival time. But they'd dawdled in Memphis that morning, where Sara had answered Chase's questions—Where in Texas was she headed? Who was waiting for her? What did she want to do for a living?

They'd stopped at a postal store on their way out of the city, and Chase had put all the notes he'd gathered that morning into an envelope and mailed it to his contact in DC. In ten days or so, she could expect her new documents to arrive at her birthmother's home in Dallas.

In the seven hour road trip that followed, Chase must have sensed Sara's misgivings for having revealed so much. He spoke to her—actually opened his mouth—and told her a little of his past and of the ranch where they were headed.

She'd been surprised to hear that he'd left Broken Arrow

the day after high school graduation, driving a beat-up GTO all the way to California, where he joined the Navy and was accepted for training to be a SEAL.

"Didn't you miss your family?" she'd asked him.

"By then, there was only my stepfather," he explained, frowning.

They'd all died? He'd mentioned earlier that his father had fallen off a ladder when he was quite young. His grandfather had come to live at the ranch to help his mother cope. Then Lincoln Sawyer, the foreman who worked the ranch, had asked his mother to marry him.

"You didn't get along with him, did you?" she'd dared to ask.

"Used to work me like a rented mule," he admitted shortly.

That was her first inkling that Chase's happy childhood had gone swiftly down the drain. To hear that everyone but Linc had died, including his mother, whom he'd spoken of so tenderly, cemented her conclusions.

Sara peered down the driveway now, curious to see what kind of place had produced a man like Chase. The trees pressed in on either side—scrub oaks, sassafras, and persimmon. Wildflowers shot color through the overgrown grass edging the road.

She glanced at Chase's profile to assess his state of mind. He'd lapsed into silence, his eyes watchful, his expression grim. Dappled sunlight flickered over the tops of his hands as he adjusted the steering wheel to keep from driving through potholes.

A hundred yards down the driveway, the trees gave way to prairie grass interspersed with towering sunflowers and Indian paintbrush. The driveway curved, and a bungalow, complete with stone chimney, sloping roof, and covered porch came into view. It stood in the clearing, flanked by a red barn and shaded by a mammoth pecan tree.

One of the tree's limbs had been sheared by lightning and lay across the driveway. Chase drove around it, into the tall grass, which tickled the underbelly of his car.

As they pulled up before the house, she could see that weeds choked the steps to the porch. A window on one side had been broken, leaving behind a gaping hole. At least the structure itself was standing and appeared intact.

Chase cut the engine and stared at it grimly.

"It's in worse shape than you thought?" Sara guessed.

"It's pretty run-down," he agreed.

Obviously it was going to be a chore to fix it up in a couple weeks' time.

Kendal gave a sudden gasp. "Look, someone's runnin' into the woods!"

They peered in the direction that he pointed, catching sight of a man dodging through the tall grass, headed for the trees.

Chase jumped out of the car and flipped the seat forward. "Get him, Jess!"

Jesse bolted. Whether he'd seen the man flee was anyone's guess, but he took off in the direction that Chase had indicated, tearing after the trespasser with every indication of knowing what he was doing.

Chase reached under his seat for his gun, causing Sara's pulse to quicken. "Stay put," he instructed, heading for the house.

"Kendal, keep your head down," Sara advised her son.

Welcome to the Wild West, she thought, with an inappropriate urge to giggle, as she and Kendal scrunched down in their seats.

Time slowed to a crawl.

"Was someone s'posed to be here?" Kendal whispered.

"I don't think so," Sarah admitted. It flashed through her mind that Garret had guessed her destination and set a trap for her, but she dismissed the thought as paranoid. The police would have been waiting for them if that were the case.

Chase emerged from the house scowling. He whistled for the dog, a sound that must have carried for miles.

"House is clear," he said, opening her door for her. "It was just a squatter hopin' to lay claim to an empty building. He left a mess behind, though. Come on in. We'll get our stuff later."

They filed out, trailing Chase up the porch steps. Ceramic pots of every shape and size littered the porch. Some previous occupant had liked to garden. Chase's mother? she wondered.

Chase pushed the door open. A musty odor greeted them as they stepped into a dark interior. "Electricity's turned off," he explained. He pulled heavy drapes away from the window, and light flooded in.

Sara's eyes widened. The main room boasted a stone hearth, exposed beams, a large sofa, hardwood floors, and a rust-and-cream-colored rug. "Oh, this is nice," she said, noting the gold-framed mirror and faded prints on the once-white walls.

"Kitchen's over here," Chase said, turning away.

Following him, she noted the dated cabinets and orange Formica countertops, littered with empty wrappers. Chase hadn't exaggerated to say that the squatter had left a mess behind. Dirty dishes filled the sink, and the garbage overflowed, making Kendal pinch his nose.

Muttering under his breath, Chase carried the garbage can through the rear exit.

"Barn's out this way," he called through the screen door. "There's the truck I told you about."

She glimpsed a vintage Chevrolet, parked in the shadows of a two-story barn, and tried to picture herself behind the wheel.

"Bedrooms are on the other side of the house," Chase said, herding them toward a hallway.

The odor of must and stale liquor kept them from venturing inside the first room.

"This was Linc's study." Chase braved the stench to throw back the curtains and wrestle the windows open, one of them with the broken pane that she'd noticed out front.

The sunlight revealed a room crammed with books, magazines, and pamphlets. A gun cabinet took up one entire wall. From what Sara could see through the grimy glass, it housed an arsenal of rifles. "Gracious," she said, drawing Kendal closer.

Chase regarded the cabinet with a frown. He shook the lock that kept the cabinet shut, felt above it for a key, then turned to Linc's desk to sift through the drawers, but he came up empty-handed.

"What's inside the other rooms?" Kendal asked, enjoying the suspense.

"More work," Chase muttered. He visibly braced himself before opening the second door.

Right away, Sara realized that the room had once been his.

A narrow bed took up one wall. Mismatched furniture lined the other three. Even with blinds filtering the sunlight, she caught sight of half a dozen wooden sculptures.

"Look, Kendal," she called, drawn to inspect the carvings more closely. "Did you make these, Chase?" she asked in amazement.

He remained at the doorway with an odd expression on his face. "Whittled," he confirmed.

Sara ran a finger over a replica of a squirrel, realistically carved, right down to the mischievous gleam in the agate-chip eyes. "Who taught you to do this?"

"My grandfather," Chase admitted. "I'm surprised Linc kept all this stuff," he said gruffly.

"How could he have thrown it away?" She and Kendal moved around the room, admiring the other carvings—a bear, an eagle on a tree branch, and a beaver with a hatch-marked tail.

"Can we stay here, Mom?" Kendal pleaded.

Sara glanced at Chase. "We will, honey, until Chase gets the truck running."

"This here's the main bathroom," Chase called from across the hall. "Needs work," he added.

Sara peered past him, taking in the yellow tiles, rusty fixtures, and ceramic bowls.

"This was my mother's room," he added, recapturing her attention as he opened the last door.

Sara stepped into a room with cream-colored curtains, double bed, antique armoire, and family photos in gilded frames. The patchwork quilt drew her deeper. Its pastel roses had faded, but its charm had not.

She turned to smile at Chase, but the door stood empty.

Chase was gone. His mother's death—the details of which weren't known to her—obviously still bothered him.

Sara stepped over to the family portraits to inspect them. The young woman featured in several of the black-and-white photographs had to be Chase's mother. Her complexion was darker, but her nose and eyes were identical to his. Chase bore more resemblance to his father, a strapping man with light-colored curls and a winning smile. Heavens, was that baby in his lap Chase?

Studying the bright-eyed cherub she could see that it was. A wondering smile touched her lips.

"Mom," Kendal cried, wandering in with moccasin boots up to his thighs. "Look at me!"

"You need to ask Chase before you help yourself to his things," Sara cautioned. Hearing his voice out front, she hurried for the front door.

"Jesse, what'd you find, boy?"

The dog panted and danced at his feet, but unless Chase could read his mind, there was no telling what had gone on between the dog and the squatter.

Sara pushed through the door as Chase deposited their possessions on the porch. "I'm going into town," he said, brusquely. "Need to get the power turned on before nightfall. I'll get us some food and cleanin' supplies, too."

"Shouldn't we go with you?" she asked, worried that the squatter might come back.

"Jesse'll keep watch. I just need a minute . . ." He didn't finish his sentence, but she could tell that this homecoming had rattled him.

It put a strangely tender feeling in her chest to discover that he was human. "I'll help you," she heard herself offer.

"You've done so much for me and Kendal. Let me help you clean this house up."

He contemplated her with a frown. "It's gonna be a lot of work," he warned. "You're probably not used to that."

"I don't mind," she reassured him.

He glanced at the cracked pots on the steps. "Okay," he agreed. "I'll be back before it gets dark," he promised. "Stay inside with the dog and keep the door locked."

She withdrew into the house. From behind the screen door, she watched him execute a swift U-turn, bypass the fallen limb, and roar down the driveway, kicking up dust.

Turning to regard the house's dark interior, Sara felt immediately that there were eyes on her—ghosts or people? she wondered, securing the inner door as Chase had advised.

Standing in line at the grocery store, Chase felt like he was fifteen years old again, buying food 'cause his mama was too sick to get out of bed.

He shifted uncomfortably, glancing to his left and right. So far, no one had recognized him. Broken Arrow had grown to almost unrecognizable proportions, but the landmarks were the same, like the old grain elevator, visible for miles. The two-story buildings on Main Street housed the same businesses, including Tim & Louie's barbershop, a family law firm, the same dentist's office. The city's growth was more to the south of the tracks, extending into what was once pastureland.

The breadth of his shoulders and his beard might buy him anonymity, but only for a while.

Lining up goods on the checkout belt, Chase asked himself if he'd bought enough food for three people, along with every scrubbing agent in the cleaning aisle. He figured he'd need all of it to combat years of neglect.

He hadn't brought Sara here to clean for him, though. A gently bred lady like her wasn't supposed to get on her hands and knees and scrub. But Linc's drinking had obviously gotten the better of him. The place was a pigsty. Cleaning it up in the leave time that was left to him would be a chore.

Which was why he'd accepted Sara's offer to help. Besides, who knew if Linc's old truck was even running. Could take him a while yet to fix her up.

"Chase McCaffrey, is that you?" exclaimed a woman pushing an empty cart into the store.

Heads turned. Chase winced. It'd taken less than an hour for him to be recognized. He sent a wry smile at Linda Mae Goodner, his mother's best friend and closest neighbor. Her blond curls had faded to silver; her blue eyes had receded in the soft folds of her face, but her welcoming smile was still as sincere.

Abandoning his groceries, he eased out of the aisle to greet her.

"Oh, Chase!" she cried, going up on tiptoe to kiss his cheek. She was the one soul in Oklahoma with whom he'd kept in touch, sending a yearly letter. "Just look at you, darlin'! How big you've grown!" she exclaimed, holding him at arm's length. "I was hoping you'd come back and claim your property," she added, her eyes sparkling happily.

"Yes, ma'am," he said, feeling fifteen again and unsure.

"How long are you stayin'?" she demanded, as friendly and curious as ever. "I don't suppose the Navy's ready to give you up yet."

"Not yet," he admitted. "I'll stay long enough to fix the place up. Plan on rentin' it out."

Linda Mae grimaced. "Well, at least ol' Linc had the good sense to leave it to you, though I was hopin' you'd come home to stay this time."

Never, Chase thought. "How's Mr. Goodner?"

"Same old cowpoke he always was. Why don't you come over for supper tonight? He'd love to see you."

Chase glanced back at the cash register. "I just bought food for tonight," he hedged. "But I'll be sure and stop by sometime."

"You'd better," she warned, giving his cheek a pat. "It's so good to see you again. Your mother would be so proud. Do visit soon," she added, letting him go. "We've lots of catching up to do."

Feeling curious eyes on him, Chase went back to pay for his purchases. His anonymity was gone. He'd bet the contents of his wallet that by tomorrow morning, everyone he'd ever known would have heard that he was back in Broken Arrow.

Mrs. Goodner was as informative as the local newspaper, which meant that Sara—Serenity—would need to keep a low profile for as long as she stuck around.

"Kendal!" Sara called her son's name louder, only to be answered by silence. "Kendal?" With growing consternation, she abandoned the kitchen, which she'd been tidying, to peek into Chase's old bedroom, but Kendal was gone, and so was the dog.

Don't panic, she told herself, hurrying to the front door. She found it unlocked. Kendal had come this way before her. "Kendal!" she shouted from the front porch. Her voice sounded small in the open space. The sweet smell of prairie grass was a welcome contrast to the stuffy odor of the house.

"I'm here," came the answering call from the vicinity of the pecan tree. "Come and see, Mom!"

The urgency in his voice had her running down the steps and down the driveway. She finally made him out, hunkered in the shade of the tree's heavy boughs.

"What are you doing?" she asked him. At the same time, she saw what had captured his attention. There were three—no, wait—four headstones jutting out of the tall grass. "Oh, my goodness," she exclaimed, drawing up short.

"I figured out one of 'em," said Kendal, parting the grass on the one nearest him. The inscription read, *Jeremiah Blackbird, 1923–1983*. "This is Chase's grandpa," he revealed excitedly. "He was a Creek Indian, and he taught Chase how to tame bobcats."

"Really," said Sara, wondering when Chase had imparted that tall tale.

"But I don't know who this is," said Kendal, stepping toward a headstone that was yellowed with lichen.

Aaron McCaffrey, 1947–1976, Sara read. "I think that's Chase's father," she guessed, noting the common last name. She pictured the golden-haired man in the family portrait.

"And then there's a small one," Kendal added, pointing out a tiny, marble headstone buried in the grass.

Sara bent down to read it. The cherub sitting at the base of the marker and the single name, Blessing, confirmed that this was the burial spot for a child. *Feb–April, 1984.* Heavens, had Chase had a baby sister?

With a sense of premonition, Sara turned toward the last headstone. Parting the grass that grew up around it, she read, *Marileigh Sawyer, 1947–1985*. The last name was different than Chase's, but she knew this was his mother.

"Who is Mary—" Kendal stumbled over the name.

"Marileigh," Sara guessed, pronouncing it *merrily*. "It's got to be Chase's mother."

Kendal looked up at her sharply. "Why did they all die?" he asked, sounding scared.

"I don't know, honey," Sara answered, putting a hand on his narrow shoulders. "Sometimes it just happens." Looking at the four headstones, she was reminded of the tattoo on Chase's left arm. *He carried them with him wherever he went,* she realized, with a chill.

Kendal looked up at her, his eyes luminescent in the shadows. "I don't want you to die," he whispered.

Goose bumps sprouted all over her body. "I'm not going to die, sweetheart," she reassured him. "Not for a long time. Why would you say that?" she added, prompted by something in his expression.

He shook his head, unable to answer, her.

"Are you thinking of Mr. Whiskers?" she guessed.

Kendal swallowed hard. "His eyes bulged out when Daddy strangled him."

"Oh, honey," she murmured. She put a protective arm around him, furious with Garret for branding that terrible memory into Kendal's consciousness. "That's all behind us now," she whispered, rubbing her cheek against his shorn hair. At least she hoped it was. They regarded the headstones at their feet. "Come on. Let's go inside where Chase told us to stay."

Kendal broke away, calling for the dog as he ran for the door.

Petty Officer Marcelino Hewitt looked up to see Captain Garret leaving work for the day. It was his first day back since the disappearance of his wife and son. The man had lasted just three hours.

Hewitt had never liked Captain Garret much, mostly because he'd caught Miss Sara looking sad when she thought no one could see her. But he'd have to be heartless not to feel for the JAG today. The captain's black tie was askew. He stood more stoop-shouldered than ever, a frown on his narrow face. Obviously, he was overwrought by the tragedy.

"Have a good day, sir," Hewitt offered gently, handing the man his cell phone. "And . . . and I'm so sorry to hear about Miss Sara and your son," he added, forcing himself to issue condolences. According to the Sunday paper, they'd mostly likely been kidnapped.

He found himself the focus of Captain Garret's black-as-ink eyes. "You knew her on a first-name basis?" the man inquired quietly.

There was something threatening about the question. Hewitt took a small step back. "She . . . she asked me to call her Miss Sara," he reassured the man swiftly.

"Really? But then, you were both here all day together. You must have become quite friendly."

Hewitt didn't know what to say to that. Clearly the man was out of his mind with grief.

"Was she friendly with anyone else?" he continued. "A man with a beard, perhaps?"

It wasn't grief that Hewitt saw in the man's eyes. It was something far colder than that, something calculated.

"A beard, sir?"

"Do you have trouble hearing, petty officer?" Garret inquired.

"No, sir."

"Have you ever seen her with a bearded man?" the lawyer repeated.

Hewitt felt like he'd taken the witness stand and was being interrogated. He searched his memory. The only bearded man that came into the Trial Services Building was Chief McCaffrey, the Navy SEAL who verbally harassed him while his blue eyes gleamed with wicked humor. "No, sir," he replied, knowing the chief would never have to resort to kidnapping to get himself a woman.

"No? Why the hesitation, Petty Officer . . ." He had to look down at the name tag, "Hewitt?"

Chief McCaffrey not only knew Hewitt's last name, he also knew his first—Marcelino, which he'd teased him about, of course. "No reason, sir."

"I see," the captain answered. His mouth drooped with disappointment. Without another word, he turned and stalked through the exit, straight into a downpour.

Chapter Six

The thumping on the roof abated suddenly, causing Sara to pause as she swept the kitchen floor. She'd elected to work indoors, while Chase tackled the exterior. She was able to select her own tasks, as Chase had placed no expectations on her whatsoever. Exposing the innate charm of the bungalow was its own reward, making every chore a pleasure.

The screen door yawned open, and Chase came in with a scowl on his face, holding his thumb.

He went straight to the sink and stuck it under running water. Sara propped the broom against the counter and stepped closer to assess the damage.

"Hammered it," he said shortly.

His thumbnail was already purple. With a grimace of sympathy, Sara turned toward the freezer and pulled out an ice tray. She whipped a plastic bag from a drawer and filled it, handing it to Chase, who dried his thumb with a paper towel. "Thanks."

They stood there a moment, taking stock of each other. Chase's shirt was damp with sweat. Sara was perspiring lightly herself, in the absence of air-conditioning. Among the long list of items to be fixed was the central air.

Chase looked around, taking in the work that Sara had already accomplished. He opened a cabinet she'd emptied earlier, throwing away items that were broken or unusable. She'd wiped it out and put the dishes back in, stacking them neatly.

"You've been workin' hard," he commented, opening the next cabinet over, where she'd ordered the cans and spices, some of which Linc or the squatter had left behind. In defiance of Garret, she'd lined the cans up smallest to biggest. What a pleasure that had been!

She gave a start of surprise when Chase caught her wrist and scrutinized her reddened palm. His sure but gentle grip left a burning ring on her skin. "I thought I bought you gloves," he chastised.

She tugged, and he immediately let her go. "Maybe I don't want to wear gloves," she countered, surprising herself.

He cocked his head at her tone. "Suit yourself."

"I like to feel what I'm doing," she explained.

"Don't want you gettin' blisters," he retorted. "I didn't bring you here to work for me."

They stood no more than a yard apart, their breath coming in and out at the same time. She could have asked him then, *Why exactly did you bring me here?* It wasn't just to give her the truck so she could drive herself to Texas, was it?

There were memories in this house that haunted him. He didn't want to be alone.

"Will you tell me something?" she asked him.

"What?" His regard turned wary.

"Will you tell me how your mother died?"

He just looked at her, pulse throbbing at the base of his neck. "You want to talk about the past?" he challenged quietly.

She got the feeling that she would have to be just as candid about her own history, which she'd rather forget. "Maybe it would help," she conceded.

"Hanta virus, probably," he said, keeping his answer short. "It swept through the Midwest in the late eighties but it wasn't identified until the nineties, after several people died. Comes from contact with rat droppings. She used to sweep the barn."

"Did the baby have it, too?" Sara asked, horrified.

"No, but she was born too early 'cause my mama was so sick."

Sara searched for the bottomless grief Chase must have felt at the time. His face was a mask. "How old were you when they died?" she asked, shaking her head.

"Fourteen when the baby went. Fifteen when Mama died."

She thought of Kendal, who'd looked at her in terror yesterday. *I don't want you to die.* Surely Chase had felt the same way about being abandoned, left with a stepfather who'd been less than fatherly. "I'm so sorry," she whispered, feeling tremendous compassion for Chase the boy.

"Your turn," he countered almost angrily but not threateningly. "What did Garret do to make you leave?"

Sara swallowed, willing the past to stay where she'd left it. She let out a huff of air. "He controlled everything—all of my free time. He cut me off from my friends and family. Made me use his credit cards instead of cash, so that he could keep tabs on my spending. He took away my driver's license when I got in an accident. Nothing I did ever met his expectations. When he strangled Kendal's rabbit, that was the last straw."

Chase's expression reflected disgust and sympathy. "Did he hit you?" he asked her bluntly.

"No." Garret's blows were always mental and emotional, which in some ways was worse than physical because they left no trace; left her wondering whether what had happened was possibly her fault; made her think that she could try harder the next time and he wouldn't react the same way.

She'd wasted eleven years of her life wondering if the invisible scars were really there.

But now that she was far away, and her perspective was clearer, the abuse was so blatant that she could never go back into that environment again.

Chase raised his hand, and Sara barely caught herself from flinching. He hesitated just a second then lightly cupped her jaw and stroked her cheek with the pad of his thumb.

He didn't say anything. He didn't need to. It was a gesture of comfort. Sara's nerve endings tingled with disproportionate pleasure.

It would be a mistake to lean on Chase any more than she already had. Garret had taught her not to trust what seemed to be. How could any man be as solid and considerate as Chase seemed to be?

"I thought I'd cook the sausages tonight with stewed tomatoes and zucchini," she volunteered, testing him.

He glanced in puzzlement at his watch. It was early afternoon. "You hungry already?" he asked her.

"No," she answered, succumbing to a smile. "It's just . . . never mind."

He crossed his arms and frowned at her. "I didn't bring you here to cook for me either," he added, chastising her again. "But I ain't gonna turn down a home-cooked meal if you're offerin' one up," he added wryly.

"I'm offering," she reassured him. She even looked forward to it.

"Okay then. What time?"

"Six o'clock?"

"I'd best get crackin', then." With a grimace for his thumbnail, he left the kitchen, taking the bag of ice with him.

At six-twenty, the setting sun put a golden patina on the scarred surface of the kitchen table. Three plates stood empty in front of the table's three occupants.

"I'm all done, Mom," Kendal declared, putting down his emptied milk cup. "Can I go outside and play?" He'd been waiting all day to catch crickets at dusk and put them in the box he'd filled with grass and twigs.

Sara glanced at Chase, who was sopping up the remainder of his tomato sauce with bread. Catching her eye, he glanced at Kendal. "Keep an eye out for bobcats," he recommended. "They like to come out right before sunset."

"I will," Kendal promised. After taking his plate to the counter, he pushed through the screen door, letting it slam behind him. "Sorry!" he said, reappearing on the other side.

"Chase doesn't need another thing to fix," Sara chided,

before Chase had a chance to rebuke him. She was conscious of the SEAL's thoughtful gaze as he chewed his last bite of bread.

"Sorry," Kendal said again before darting away.

"Thanks for the meal," said Chase, pushing his plate away. "You're a fine cook."

She wasn't sure what to say in response to his compliment. She'd intentionally cooked a meal she'd never made before. There was room for improvement in her book, having burned the ends of the sausages. Standing up, she hesitantly began to collect their dishes.

"There's no rush," he told her, and she immediately sat down again.

Silence fell between them, but it wasn't awkward or tension-filled. Chase eased back in his chair. "Wish you could relax with me," he admitted unexpectedly.

"I am relaxed," she protested. But she wasn't, not really. She was too aware of everything about him, from the breadth of his shoulders to the way he'd held his fork with his left hand. She hadn't realized he was left-handed.

"You should maybe know that little things don't bother me," he offered, "like a screen door slammin' shut or a corner of a sausage gettin' burned. There's bigger things to stress about than that."

"I agree," she said fervently. "I'm sorry, I'm just . . . trained to worry, I guess."

"Don't apologize," he said, his gaze warm on her flustered face.

"Sorry," she said, before realizing that she'd done it again.

He smiled faintly, but then his gaze shifted toward the

living room, and she knew that every one of his five senses had just kicked into alert mode.

"What is it?" she whispered, straining her ears. Was that a rumbling sound she detected?

He shot out of his chair and moved soundlessly into the other room. Sara followed with caution, curious to identify what she was hearing. Through the big window at the front of the house, she spied an older-model El Camino, stalled on the curve in the driveway, half-concealed by prairie grass. The once-white car had a headlight missing. Rather than approach the house, it remained where it was, idling menacingly.

"Go get Kendal," Chase said on a very serious note.

Sara didn't question him. It was obvious from his demeanor that he felt the vehicle was a threat. She raced out the back door, wondering wildly if Garret had found her already. Only he'd never in his life drive an old beater like that. "Kendal!" she called with quiet urgency.

She found him on his knees by the barn wall, cupping an insect in his hands. "Honey, you have to come in right now."

"Why?"

She grabbed his elbow and hauled him to his feet. "Because Chase says so, that's why."

She found Chase exactly where she'd left him. The car still loitered. Every few seconds, its motor revved as if the driver were issuing a threat.

"Who could it be?" Sara whispered, keeping a protective arm around her son.

"Don't know exactly," Chase replied.

The cold quality of his voice had her glancing at him. This was Chase the warrior, she realized, with a shiver.

The focus in his eyes had turned them arctic, a far cry from the Caribbean blue they'd been just moments before.

"I want you two to step into the hall, away from the windows," he instructed. "Go on."

"What are you going to do?" Sara asked, drawing Kendal with her as she backed up.

"Scare 'em off," he said.

Be careful. He was out the door in an instant. She watched through the living room window as he leapt athletically over the porch rail and dashed toward his car, keeping his head low. He stuck his key into the passenger door and unlocked it. Diving inside, he withdrew his gun from beneath the seat. She'd almost forgotten it was there. Thank God he'd kept the car locked.

He checked the SIG briefly, snapping off its safety. In one fluid movement, he leapt up and fired over the top of his car toward the interlopers.

From where she stood, Sara couldn't see if he'd hit the other car or not. But a short while later, she thought she heard the El Camino backing up.

"What's going on, Mom?" Kendal whispered, trembling in her arms.

"I don't know, sweetheart. Maybe the squatter wants to get back in. Chase'll scare them off."

Chase pushed through the front door just then, strapping a holster over his shirt. Obviously, he meant to carry the gun on his person.

Seeing her look of dismay, he added, "It's safer on me than it is in the car." He stalked past them, shouldering his way into Linc's study. He drew the blinds, then flicked on the overhead light, pausing before the gun cabinet to consider its contents.

Sara was quick to guess his thoughts. "You think they're after the guns?" she asked, braving the musty odor of the room to join him.

"Just a hunch," he said, giving the doors a shake, but the lock held. "Be right back," he said, abandoning them to stride through the house and out the rear door.

"Sure is a lot of stuff in this room," Kendal commented, bending to peer at the piles of magazines. "*National Socialist Movement Catalogue,*" he read carefully as he picked one off the top of the pile.

Socialist? Sara turned to take it from him. "Oh, my goodness."

The catalogue sold every type of Nazi paraphernalia imaginable, from sound recordings of Hitler's famous speeches, to T-shirts proclaiming white supremacy, to Nazi flags. She put it down with disgust. "Don't touch any more," she warned her son.

Chase reappeared bearing a metal filing saw. Working it into the crack between the cabinets, he sawed away at the lock while Sara took closer stock of the room. "Chase," she hedged, hoping it wouldn't make him angry, "your stepfather was a white supremacist."

"I know." He put the saw on the desk and pulled the cabinet open, plucking out a rifle. Handling it with casual precision, he checked it for ammunition.

"Honey, why don't you play in Chase's old room for the rest of the evening," Sara suggested to Kendal.

"Oh, Mom!" Kendal protested, sounding truly put out. "I wanted to catch some crickets."

"There's plenty in the closet to play with," she insisted. She'd peeked in there this morning, seeing collector's cards, old comic books, and toy cars.

"Fine," he relented, stomping down the hall to disappear into the next room.

Sara went to stand next to Chase as he took out the next rifle. "This isn't anyplace for a child," she said quietly.

His hands stilled. "Never was," he retorted. "Not after Linc moved in."

"Maybe you should call the police," she suggested, postponing what she really had to say.

"I will," he promised. "Don't need a bunch of cops gettin' a look at you right now."

"We should probably leave then." There. She just came right out and said it, even though a large part of her quailed in protest. Leaving Chase meant putting herself in the real world, alone. It meant vulnerability, and a loneliness that she didn't anticipate.

Chase put the gun back in the cabinet. With a sigh, he turned to face her. "I told you, it's not safe to use public transportation. Let me fix up the truck. I'll work on it tomorrow."

"How long will it take to get it running?" she asked him, turning toward the window.

"I don't know," he said almost irritably. "Couple days, at least. In the meantime, I'll keep this room locked."

Sara nodded, relieved that leaving right away was impossible, anyway. Besides, Chase still needed her help here.

"Do you think those people are going to come back?" she asked, peeking through the blinds.

He'd reached for another gun. "Most likely."

"Maybe you should leave those guns outside for them to take."

He went perfectly still. "I don't put guns in the hands of terrorists," he replied.

"Of course not." She realized that she had spoken thoughtlessly. Chase had made a career out of beating back terrorism. He wasn't the type to give in to bullies. She ran a sweeping gaze over the room. "I just can't believe all of this." There were actually Americans who believe in the supremacy of the Aryan race. "It seems so un-American."

"Pretty fucking unbelievable," Chase muttered, opening the chamber of the rifle in his hands. "Sorry," he added, shaking pellets into his palm.

"Loaded," Sara commented with dismay.

He dropped the pellets into his pocket and reached for the fourth rifle. Watching him manipulate the machinery with such practiced ease drove home the differences between them. She was from a privileged background. He'd had to fight for everything he had. It was inevitable that they would go their separate ways soon.

"I'm going to see what Kendal's doing," she said, heading for the door with a heavy heart.

With a mutter of disgust, Chase replaced the pamphlet on Linc's desk and rotated his stiff neck. It was nearly dawn. He'd stayed up all night, puzzling through the propaganda that littered the room, unable to shake his suspicion that the guns in the cabinet were intended for some ultimate battle.

According to the trifold pamphlet he'd just read, Linc and his cohorts were members of the Fists of Righteous Americans, a subgroup of the National Socialist Party. They'd gone to the trouble of publishing brochures to increase their ranks—although, in order to become an officer, you had to be a direct descendent of one of the first white pioneers to settle in Oklahoma. Every member had to shave his hair right down to the scalp.

The FOR Americans advocated violent removal of the dark-skinned immigrants—Mexicans, blacks, and Arabs—who "usurped the white man's hard-earned positions in the job market, corrupted the language, and lowered the standards in schools."

"Son of a bitch," Chase growled, pushing to his feet. He prowled around the cramped office, pausing before a plaque that declared Linc Sawyer honorary member of the FOR Americans. A swastika symbol was etched beneath his name. Linc hadn't been an officer because he'd hailed from Kansas.

Chase faced the room with a scowl. Obviously, he needed to alert the authorities, but not until Sara was safely launched for Dallas, and he wasn't in any special hurry to launch her, either. While she was certain that Garret would not uncover the secret of her birthmother, Chase was not so cavalier.

On the other hand, given the fervor of the skinheads to get their hands on their guns, this wasn't the safest place for mother and son to stay. All he wanted for them was a respite from their troubles, peace of mind. But he couldn't give her that, not with the skinheads posing a menace.

Obviously, Chase needed to get Linc's truck running so that she could be on her way, leaving him here to face his demons. How ironic was it that, even dead, Linc was messing up his life?

"Fucker," he muttered, considering the guns. No way in hell was he going to let them fall into the hands of

Linc's close-minded friends. He'd disassemble every one of them if necessary. But until he found the time for that, he'd hide them.

Kendal was hiding again. "Kendal!" With a sigh of exasperation, Sara pushed through the screen door at the rear of the house and called her son.

The roar of a sit-down mower muted her cry. Chase cruised into view, cutting a swathe through the prairie grass at the driveway's edge. Catching sight of her, he cut the motor and rolled to a halt. Sara approached him, fighting to keep her gaze from dropping to his gleaming, sun-kissed torso. In deference to the heat, he'd shucked his shirt, leaving him naked from the waist up. Though the house was slightly cooler, she wished enviously that she could do the same.

"Have you seen Kendal?" she asked, raking the open space for any sign of him.

Chase seemed more intent on remarking the streak of ash that grimed her cheek. "You been playin' in the fireplace?" he asked her.

"Sweeping," she corrected him. "Where's Kendal. I told him to play inside this morning."

"You can't keep a boy indoors, Sara," Chase admonished gently. "Ken's over there by the tree line." He gestured with his head.

Sara stood tiptoe to peer over the grass that was as yet uncut. "What's he doing over there?" she asked anxiously.

"Bein' a boy, I reckon," Chase replied.

She looked back at him and sighed. "You think I'm overprotective, don't you?"

"It ain't gonna hurt to let him wander a ways," he drawled.

"I'm worried about those squatters coming back," she explained.

Chase smiled faintly. With the gun peeking out of the waist of his camo pants, he looked infinitely capable of defending them. "Don't be."

She glanced at Kendal one last time, giving her cheek a self-conscious swipe. "Will you keep one eye on him?" she asked.

"You bet." Chase's warm, blue gaze lingered on her flushed face. "Take it easy in there, will you?" He glanced at the porch where the carpet was slung over the porch rail.

"I'm having fun," she assured him, surprised that she was actually telling the truth. Who would have thought that sweeping out a hearth choked with ashes, beating a rug, and scrubbing oak floorboards could be enjoyable? "How about you?" she asked. "Are you going to cut the whole field?" She cringed for the sunflowers standing in full bloom.

"Just edgin' the driveway for now," he told her. "Gotta get more gas before I mow the field."

She nodded her understanding. "You want some lemonade?" she asked him.

Before he had the chance to answer, Kendal emitted a wail, then another one. With a gasp, Sara started toward him.

Chase leapt from the mower and sprinted ahead of her. As Sara chased him across the field, struggling through the tall grass, possibilities raced through her mind: Kendal had been bitten by a snake; stung by a bee; twisted his ankle.

By the time she caught up to Chase, Kendal had stopped crying, although it was probably his fear of angering Chase that had him biting his lip. To Sara's consternation, she saw bright red blood dripping from Kendal's left hand. "What happened?" she gasped.

"He's usin' tools that he doesn't know how to use," Chase retorted grimly. "Take your shirt off," he added, helping Kendal to pull it over his head, "and wrap it around your finger."

Sara helped him while trying to assess how badly he'd cut himself. Her gaze fell to the small box of tools at Kendal's feet. She guessed by their shape and size that they were tools for whittling. Kendal had probably found them in Chase's closet. "Oh, honey," she admonished, darting a worried look at Chase's set face. "You should have asked first."

Chase bent down and closed the box. "Come into the house," he said shortly. He led the way, carving a path back across the field.

He left Sara in the kitchen to wash and tend Kendal's cut while he went to retrieve a first-aid kit from his car. Sara was relieved to see that the nick in Kendal's finger wasn't so deep that it required stitches. Wrapping it in a paper towel, she turned to accept the bandage that Chase handed her.

They stood there in an uncertain knot as Sara waited for the bleeding to stop. Kendal stared at the door like he couldn't wait to dash outside again. Both he and Sara waited on pins and needles for Chase to start lecturing.

Sure enough, he was the first to speak. "You still want to learn to whittle?" he asked.

Kendal lifted a startled, questioning look at him. "Yes, sir," he murmured.

Sara held her breath, ready to defend her son if the need arose.

"You think you should have asked first before you took the tools?"

Kendal tucked his chin to his chest. "S-sorry," he stammered.

A tense silence stole around them.

"Apology accepted," Chase finally answered, cutting a measuring look at Sara. "With your mother's permission, I'll show you how to whittle tonight."

Kendal shot her a pleading look.

"That's fine with me," Sara said, in a voice breathy with relief. "Just be careful," she added.

"Take care of that finger," Chase said to Kendal. And then he turned away, slipping out of the rear door with barely a sound.

As it tapped shut, Kendal and Sara shared a look of mutual wonder. Neither of them needed to say out loud what they were thinking: *Chase wasn't anything like Garret.*

Chapter Seven

Kendal watched Chase unscrew the nut that held the cover down on the truck's carburetor. Morning sunlight blazed through the cracks in the barn's eastern wall, laying a stripe of gold across Chase's scarred knuckles.

"You ever work on engines, Ken?" Chase had asked when Kendal wandered into the barn that morning.

"No," Kendal had replied, trying to back away.

"Grab that stepladder. I could use your help."

With a heavy heart, Kendal had toted the ladder to Chase's side. Last night, Chase had taught him how to whittle pine, and even though he was clumsy, following Chase's directions with difficulty, the man had never yelled at him. It wasn't wariness that made Kendal drag his feet. It was his reluctance to leave. He didn't want Chase to fix the truck.

With a dull mind, he listened to Chase explain what the various components of the engine were. The realization that he was expecting him to keep the truck running after they left made his stomach hurt.

"Old filters get clogged," Chase was saying. "All this

black stuff gums it up, and the engine can't breathe. When it starts to cough, you spray the filter with this." He snatched up a can that rattled as he shook it. "Here, you try."

Kendal took the can reluctantly. He had to stand tiptoe on the rickety stepladder.

"A little more," Chase prompted. "I'm gonna leave an extra can in the glove compartment. Go ahead and put the lid back on."

Kendal slid the cover into place. Given the Band-Aid on his finger, it took several attempts to thread the nut onto the bolt and screw it down tight.

"Done," said Chase. He moved to the front of the engine, making it necessary for Kendal to pick up the stepladder and follow him. Chase removed a black cap and pulled out a long, metal stick. "This here's the oil gauge."

It took a second to realize that Chase was saying "oil" and not "all."

"Old cars and trucks burn oil, so you got to check the oil level. Like this." He snatched up the rag that lay on the fender, swiped the stick, then stuck it all the way in and out again. "The oil level ought to be between these marks." He showed it to Kendal. "What do you see?"

"There's not enough," Kendal guessed.

"Right—10-W-40," Chase instructed, holding up a plastic bottle. "I'll leave two of these in the glove compartment along with the filter spray."

His baritone drawl reminded Kendal of a cat's purr.

He watched as Chase poured amber liquid into the opening. It went *gallup, gallup, gallup*. Kendal's gaze slid up Chase's arm toward the muscle made evident by the cutoff sleeves of his T-shirt. He wondered if he'd ever have muscles like that.

Or a tattoo like that. He'd seen it a number of times, but for the first time, he noticed that the skeleton with flowing, black hair was holding a baby, and his thoughts flashed to the gravestones outside. It was then that he made the connection.

If that was Chase's mother, then the one with the headdress had to be his grandpa, which meant that the big one was Chase's father, who'd died when he was a boy.

"Somethin' you want to ask me, Ken?" Chase asked, intercepting Kendal's stare.

Kendal jerked his gaze away. "No, sir."

Chase just looked at him with eyes that were the same deep blue as the sky here.

"How old were you when your dad died?" Kendal heard himself ask. He hoped it wasn't one of those questions you weren't supposed to ask.

"Five," Chase said easily.

"Did you miss him?"

Chase shrugged. "Missed him later. When I was old enough to realize that he wasn't comin' back."

The answer made Kendal uncomfortable. He didn't want to miss his father—*ever*. "I don't miss my dad." He looked down at the dirt floor, embarrassed to have said such a terrible thing.

"Well, I don't miss my stepdad none," Chase replied, as casually as if they were discussing the weather. "He was mean."

"Yeah, mean," Kendal repeated, relieved that Chase understood.

"My grandpa told me to forget the bad stuff, though," Chase added. "Makes a man angry."

Kendal felt angry every time he thought about his father.

"So I work on remembering the good stuff. Ol' Linc taught me how to fix things, like this truck," Chase added. "If it weren't for him, things would break, and I'd have to pay other people to fix 'em."

Kendal thought of something good that his father had taught him, like the importance of good grades.

Chase reached into his pocket and pulled out a set of keys. "See if the truck starts," he said, holding them out.

Kendal balked. "I never did that before."

"First time for everything," Chase replied. "Use the key with the square head."

" 'Kay." With his mouth dry, Kendal took the keys. Putting the stepladder away, he climbed into the driver's side door, fumbling to insert the proper key into the ignition.

"Give it a turn," Chase called out, "and hold it there till the engine cranks over."

Holding his breath, Kendal turned the key. The old truck coughed three or four times before giving a throaty roar. He snatched his hand back. *Cool.*

But the truck was running.

And his heart sank. Just when he was getting used to this place, they were getting ready to leave it. He didn't want to leave. Sure, it had been scary when they first got here, with the stranger running out of the house, then finding the headstones under the tree.

But since then, he'd grown to like it. He liked how the sky was bigger here, but it was so quiet that you could hear a hawk screaming way up. And in the evening, when the sun set, the whole sky turned orange, and the prairie grass looked like it was on fire.

No one demanded the impossible. His mother didn't scurry around looking tense. The only scary thing was those squatters wanting their guns back, and as long as Chase was here, they wouldn't dare get close.

Leaving was a bad idea. Kendal knew it in his bones.

"Why do I have to go to bed so early?" Kendal complained, flopping back against his pillows.

"Because you're grumpy," Sara told him. "You've been staying up late looking for nocturnal animals, and you haven't had enough sleep."

Her son was determined to spot a bobcat prowling about the ranch. For the past two nights, he'd paced the area around the house, directing a high-powered flashlight into the prairie grass, hoping to catch the reflection of a wildcat's eyes, but no luck yet.

Tucking the covers up around him, Sara kissed his cheek. "Good night, sweetheart."

"I'm not tired," he insisted, even as he issued an enormous yawn.

With a smile, Sara crossed the living room into the kitchen. She spent a few minutes tidying up from their evening meal. It was a peaceful chore that she enjoyed performing. How different life was without the weight of Garret's demands to oppress her! The front door stood open, and through the screen, she could hear the crickets chirping. Chase was on the front porch, as was his custom, sipping a beer.

For the past few nights, Sara had left him alone with Kendal, teaching him to whittle on the pine they'd collected from the tree line. Pine was soft wood, perfect for building skill with the various whittling tools.

This evening, with Kendal in bed, and with her time here dwindling, Sara felt compelled to join him. Who knew if it would be their last moment alone together?

The poignant thought had her asking through the screen door. "Mind if I join you?"

He sat on the top step, his face tipped toward an indigo sky. "Naw, come out. Why don't you grab a beer first?"

"That's all right." She stepped into the cool outdoors, savoring the sweet smell of wild grasses as she determined the best place to sit. There weren't any chairs. The porch itself, though recently swept, was crowded with empty ceramic pots. She had no choice but to sit on the step beside him.

Glancing at the sky, she sought what was holding his attention. The sky was deepening to cobalt by the second. Here and there, stars leapt off the canvas to twinkle as brilliantly as diamonds, and the moon, which was nearly full, gleamed like a platinum disk. Crickets and nightingales played a musical accompaniment, as fruit bats whirled and flittered in a dizzy dance.

"This is the only place in the world where the stars blink on so quick," Chase divulged, breaking the comfortable silence.

The sorrow-tinged note of his voice had Sara glancing at him. He kept his eye on the sky, regarding it as he must have done when he was just a boy. She kept quiet, sensing that he might say more if she didn't ask, just listened.

"In Malaysia, you're lookin' at the moon from a different angle," he added. "There ain't a man in the moon. Over there, it's a rabbit."

"A rabbit?" she repeated, peering up at the waxing moon to seek it.

"Sure. You can see it here, too. Just have to turn your head like this." He tipped his head to the right.

Sara did the same, and sure enough, there was a rabbit, complete with ears and a powder puff tail. "Oh, my gosh," she laughed with delight.

"You should see the sunsets in Borneo," he added. "Unbelievable."

"The only place I've ever been outside of the States is France. I studied abroad one year in college. I'm envious that you get to travel," she admitted.

Chase cut a look at her. "Envious?" he repeated, with a cynical twist to his lips. "Don't be."

She knew in a heartbeat that the places he'd been would frighten her in the same way that Garret had frightened her, probably worse. "Can you talk about your work?" she asked him, hoping to satisfy her curiosity once and for all.

"What do you want to know?" he countered warily.

"Well, what do you do? You look so different from the other SEALs."

"I have a no-shave chit."

"Why?"

He fixed his gaze on the deep green bottle in his hand. "My work involves concealment," he explained. "I'm not supposed to look like a SEAL."

"Are you a spy?" she asked quietly.

She thought she'd guessed rightly, but he didn't answer right away. "I watch people," he agreed, taking a swig of his beer.

But it was more than that. "I don't understand . . . unless it's top secret."

Several more seconds elapsed. "I'm a sniper," he admitted. "My job is to protect my teammates by eliminating hostiles who interfere with the objective."

At this chilling explanation, the moon abruptly dimmed. The stars lost their shine. It seemed awfully dark under the eaves of the porch. Sara shivered. She thought she'd known who Chase was, but the man sitting next to her was a stranger. "Hostiles are terrorists, right?" she asked, wanting to reconcile him to the warmhearted man she'd come to know.

"Hostiles are enemies of the state. They can be arms smugglers, drug lords, or terrorists," he explained.

"Oh," she said, trying to get her mind around the fact that he killed for a living. Even if it was necessary in order to hold back the tide of evil, it was his job. My God, if she'd thought that Garret, a lawyer, was dangerous, then what did that make Chase?

She drew a deep breath. "I think I should go in now," she said.

He made no apologies. "Suit yourself," he said. Lifting the bottle to his mouth, he took another long pull.

"Good night," she added, squelching the urge to run.

At the door, she glanced back.

He had to be absolutely confident that the persons he was shooting were guilty of horrific crimes, and that *not* shooting them would result in greater bloodshed. But even so, didn't his conscience spawn nightmares that kept him up at night?

Maybe that was why he never seemed to sleep.

Numb with shock, Sara tottered toward Marileigh's bedroom. She and Chase were from totally different worlds. That had never seemed more obvious than it did tonight.

When Sara awoke the next morning, the first thing she thought of was Chase's occupation. In the light of day, it didn't seem quite as horrific; after all, someone had to check the spread of evil while protecting the interests of the free world. But Kendal's voice reached her ears, and realizing he was alone with Chase, she leapt out of bed mistrustfully.

She found them at the breakfast table slurping oatmeal. Kendal had brought the whittling kit to the table. Catching sight of her he blurted, "Mom, today I'm gonna whittle hardwood!"

Glancing at Chase's wry smile, it was impossible to think of him as a killer. "I thought you had a million things to do today," she pointed out.

"I'll stain the house this afternoon," he said, with a shrug. "Ken's gotten so good with pine, it's time to take the next step. Finish your oatmeal," he told the boy. "Then we'll take a walk and see what we find."

Half an hour later, Sara watched them tramp across the dew-glistening field toward the tree line. She had no reason to believe that Chase was a danger to her child. On the contrary, he was everything that Kendal needed right now. But he was possibly a danger to her, she admitted—not in the way that Garret was. His pull on her went deeper, down into the essence of her being.

At least she knew the truth about him, and the truth would keep her vigilant.

Launching herself into her self-appointed tasks—

scrubbing mildew from the tiles in the hallway bathroom— Sara overheard Chase and Kendal's return. The twosome hunkered down on the porch steps, as was their custom. They spent the next several hours with their heads bent over their tools. Chase's soft-spoken instructions reached Sara's ears as she traveled through the living room to fetch her rubber gloves, and then a second sponge.

By midafternoon, Kendal was skilled enough at whittling hardwood to attempt his first solo carving. But the best medium for that was cedar, and the only cedar on the ranch, according to Chase, grew deep in the woods beside the stream.

"Let's get some!" said Kendal, quivering with excitement.

Sara was not immune to it. "Fine, but first we need to eat the sandwiches I made."

Following lunch, they set out on their quest, leaving Jesse to guard the house in case the skinheads decided to look for their rifles. Down the driveway they went, seeking the path that led straight to the creek.

Over the course of eighteen years, Mother Nature had reclaimed it, casting a tapestry of foliage over any path that might have existed. Somehow, Chase had no trouble discerning which way to go.

Stepping beneath the bower of trees was like entering a world of enchantment. Having grown up in a suburb of Washington, DC, Sara had limited contact with nature. The kaleidoscope of forest colors, the sloughing of leaves overhead, and the carpet of tender ferns charmed her. As she trailed Chase and Kendal deep into the woods, a peacefulness stole over her.

Not even the realization that Chase's gliding walk was

a skill honed from his profession could disturb her deep contentment.

He shot out a hand, and she startled to a stop, only to realize that he had spotted a deer. The doe stood half concealed in shadow, her eyes wide, ears twitching, tail raised like a flag. With a bleat of warning, the animal took off, crashing through the undergrowth to seek her herd.

Chase smiled to himself, and Sara realized that he valued life and beauty, something a conscienceless killer would not.

Unbeknownst to him—or perhaps he just pretended not to notice—Kendal began to imitate his walk.

About a hundred yards later, Chase stopped again, and the boy crashed into him. "Listen," he said, and Kendal tipped his head to one side, his gaze intent.

Sara could hear it in the distance: the sound of rippling water. She knew, with a tingle of respect, that nothing escaped Chase's notice in the forest, from the snapping of a twig, to the darting of a squirrel, to the sweat dampening her pink T-shirt on the underside of her breasts.

His warm gaze made her tremble with awareness. Sniper or not, he held powerful sway over her senses.

"I hear it," Kendal breathed, with excitement.

"This way," Chase said, nodding in the right direction.

They came upon the stream abruptly. Pristine water trickled over sandstone rock before pooling in a basin of deep red soil. The water was so clear that the pebbles on the bottom caught and held the sunlight. Overflowing the basin, the water gave a lazy turn through a cove of elderberry trees before disappearing from view.

"Oh, wow!" Kendal breathed, kicking off his sneakers.

He waded gleefully into the stream, leaving Sara and Chase standing on the shore, watching.

Sara took in Kendal's delight with a sense of poignancy.

"Not many places like this in Dallas," Chase observed.

"No," she agreed, with a pinch of doubt. But there'd been no doubt yesterday when she spoke with her birthmother for the first time, using Chase's cell phone. Their previous communication, six months' worth of e-mails, had made the call more than comfortable. Sara had hung up, convinced that heading to Dallas was the right thing.

So, why was she feeling ambivalent today?

"Look, Mom, a crayfish!" Kendal cried, having caught it in his hands.

"Out here we call 'em crawdads," Chase imparted. "Come on," he added, dropping the saw he'd brought with him in order to take off his boots. "Let's cool off."

He had to pull a mean-looking blade out of his boot first. Sara'd had no idea it was there. Added to the gun that peeked out from under his left arm, he looked every inch the dangerous man that he was.

She slipped off her sandals and stepped up to the bank to dip a toe into the water. Goodness, it was cold!

"Come on," Chase said, stepping in boldly.

She hesitated, and he held a hand out to her.

Sara's gaze slid from his hand to his watchful eyes. It became a test of wills to see who would look away first.

"Trust me, Sara," Chase said.

He'd said that back when she'd agreed to let him cut her hair, and that had turned out fine, hadn't it?

Besides, she was leaving soon. What harm could come

from holding Chase's hand, so long as her eyes were wide-open?

She extended her hand tentatively. He caught it, clasping his fingers firmly over hers. A thrill chased up her arm, speeding her heart rate, sending a wave of pleasure through her.

It wasn't just the temperature of the water that made her nipples tighten as she stepped into the stream.

"Let me see that critter, boy," Chase demanded of Kendal, pulling Sara with him.

Cold water crept up past her knees. By contrast, Chase's hand felt wonderfully warm, slightly rough from the physical work he performed.

"I want to keep it," Kendal said, gazing at his crustacean in rapture.

"Oh, no, honey," Sara said on a breathy note. "It'll die if you take it from its habitat."

"I want to keep it," he repeated on a petulant note.

"It belongs here," Chase said firmly.

Kendal looked as if he might argue. But then he caught sight of them holding hands, and he lowered the crayfish into the stream without argument.

Flustered, Sara tugged her hand free. It wasn't right to send Kendal the message that she and Chase were lovers. That could never be.

"I got a mission for you, Ken," Chase said, with a conjecturing glance at Sara. "Head upstream and see if you can find us a good cedar tree."

Kendal turned toward the miniwaterfall behind him. "Okay," he said, turning to plod upstream.

As Kendal scrambled up the tiered rock, Chase bent

down and scooped up a handful of water. "You thirsty?" he asked Sara. "It's clean enough to drink."

There wasn't a hint of deadly sniper in the mischievous little smile that tipped the corners of his mouth.

She edged away from him. "Er, no thanks."

"It'll cool you off pretty good, too." And that was all the warning she got before he upended the water over her head.

She stifled a shriek, and with speed that surprised even her, she responded in kind, throwing a handful of water at his chest. Laughter burst out of him, a rich, infectious sound that made her laugh as well.

Her laugh became a shriek, as he scooped her into his arms, holding her just like a baby. Caught utterly off guard, all Sara could do was to throw her arms around him.

Holding her aloft was obviously an effortless feat for him. Strength and heat surrounded her, making her want, irrationally, to melt into him. She glanced toward Kendal, who had stopped to gawk at them. "Put me down," she requested with reluctance.

But Chase still held her captive. His gaze had fallen to her lips, and his smile had been replaced by something far more focused.

"Put me down," she repeated, more seriously.

With a tightening of his jaw, he dropped one arm, and her feet slid back into the water. He removed his other arm from around her back. "I wouldn't hurt you, Sara," he muttered.

"I know that," she reassured him.

But he was already turning away, snatching up the saw he'd left on the shore. He abandoned her with the water swirling coldly around her calves and her heart feeling empty in her chest.

What the hell did I expect? Chase berated himself. He'd gone and told her what he did for a living because he wanted honesty between them. Did he really think she'd just shrug her shoulders and tell him *no big deal*?

How could she? She'd never been in his shoes. She hadn't traveled the crossroads and byways that had led him to where he was today. God forbid that she ever walk through that valley of death and despair.

But she was drawn to him, in the same inexplicable way that he was drawn to her. He'd been taught that honesty was the best policy between friends, which was what they'd become. Only, in this case, it was serving as a wedge.

Fine. He couldn't balance on the beam of friendship for long, anyway—not when he'd rather have Sara as a lover, which was wishful thinking anyway. Even if she was attracted to him, she was way too much of a lady to have sex for pleasure's sake. And that was the only reason Chase ever had sex.

"Whatcha got, Ken?" he asked, tamping down his frustration.

Kendal rubbed the knob growing out the side of the largest cedar tree. "I want this bump," he said.

"You got it." For the next five minutes, Chase directed his energy toward sawing the bump off the tree. "When you take something from the earth, you need to leave a gift," he said, imparting to Kendal the wisdom of his Creek ancestors.

Kendal patted down his pockets. "All I have is an old Indian penny that I found in the barn."

"Leave it here," Chase instructed.

Kendal left the penny balancing on a knobby root.

With one last glide of his saw, the lump fell into Chase's hand. He passed it to Kendal, not letting go until the boy looked at him. "I want you to handle this wood before you cut into it. Feel it with your eyes closed. Don't whittle at all, until it tells you what it wants to be."

"I won't," Kendal swore, his eyes so similar to Sara's that Chase's stomach tightened.

"And don't whittle on your way to Texas," Chase added, on a sterner note, "or you'll cut yourself again."

The reminder that they were leaving soon cast a shadow over Kendal's face. Chase felt for him. He understood the grip the ranch had on a boy's heart.

"Can I come back and visit?" Kendal inquired.

"I won't be here," Chase reminded him. "I've got a job to get back to." The reality of his reenlistment had never seemed so harsh.

"Come on," he said, catching himself from brushing a twig off Kendal's flattop. "Let's go show your mama what you've got."

Chapter Eight

The familiar crowing of a rooster roused Sara to a sky the color of a ripe persimmon. Beyond the faded curtains at Marileigh's window, a mockingbird ran through its repertoire of songs.

This is the day we're leaving.

She lay paralyzed, unwilling to move just yet.

There was something so restful about this place. Every morning that she'd awakened to the rooster's cry, she felt more and more certain that her break from Garret was a lasting one. There was no indication, at least in the local newspapers, that the hunt for her and Kendal had gone national. The hope that she was free made her spirits soar.

Free to live her life the way she wanted, without re-crimination, condemnation, or control.

Dallas had always been her final destination. She couldn't wait to meet the mother she'd been parted from at birth. She couldn't wait to see what she could make of her life without Garret stifling her.

So why wasn't she jumping out of bed, racing to pursue her dreams? Was it the strange pull that Chase had on her? Or was it the peace she'd discovered here and was loath to let go of?

Whatever the bond, she had to break it, like a hatchling cracking through its eggshell to greet the world.

As Sara tossed their meager possessions into the back of the truck, Kendal climbed into the cab and slammed the door shut.

"Good-bye, Chase." Sara turned to Chase at the last second and offered him a quick, impersonal hug. Tears sprang inexplicably into her eyes, especially when he banded his muscular arms around her and squeezed her hard.

That night on the motel balcony in Memphis, when she thought that he might feel like a pillar or a haven? She'd been right. His embrace was all that and more.

She could have stayed there forever. Instead, she pushed herself free. It was pointless to suffer last-minute regrets. She climbed inside, and Chase shut the door.

He rounded the truck to speak to Kendal through the lowered window. "Hey."

Kendal looked up from the thread he was unraveling from his T-shirt.

"Take care of your mama," Chase charged him, putting on a stern face.

Kendal just looked at him, half-wary, half-hungry for more.

"And remember what I said," Chase added.

" 'Bout what?"

"Remembering the good stuff," Chase replied.

Kendal gave a solemn nod, leaving Sara to wonder what conversation she'd missed this time.

With a parting thud on the passenger door, Chase stepped back. "Start her up," he said.

Sara cranked the engine. It settled into an irregular rumbling that had Chase cocking an ear to listen. He said something to Kendal that Sara couldn't catch.

"What'd he say?" she asked him, as she clicked her seat belt into place.

"He told me to check the oil soon," Kendal answered.

"We should be okay," she reassured him. "Grandma Rachel gave me directions. It's pretty much a straight shot. We'll be in Dallas in about four hours."

She tried to infuse optimism into her tone. But as she lifted a hand in farewell, her gaze locked with Chase's, and a tide of emotion swelled in her.

Tears blurred her vision as she pulled the gearshift down into the drive position. Chase had insisted on giving her lessons this morning. She relied on her kinesthetic memory to circumnavigate the potholes in the driveway.

Mastering her tears, she glanced at Kendal, who'd wrapped his arms around his midsection. "Mom, I'm getting carsick," he complained.

"Honey, we just started driving," she answered with frustration. "We're not even on the turnpike yet."

"But my stomach hurts."

"Well, so does mine," she retorted, truthfully. And wasn't it ironic, she thought with a sad shake of her head, that leaving Garret after spending a decade with him had been easier than leaving Chase after barely a week?

Chase closed the front door but he wasn't able to lock it, not without a key, which was as elusive as the key for the gun cabinet had been. The only way to keep the house secured while he was gone was to leave Jesse guarding it. He'd drop by the hardware store on the way back from the courthouse and pick up new sets of locks for the front and back doors.

Meanwhile, the skinheads were free to waltz right in, if they really wanted to tangle with Jesse.

They wouldn't find the guns, though. Chase had wrapped them in plastic yesterday and tossed them under the house in the dank crawl space.

He stalked to his car, itching to get away. With Sara gone, memories from his past seemed to jump out of the closets. Voices echoed in each of the rooms. His skin crawled with uncharacteristic agitation.

He thought of Sara and Kendal, beginning their road trip to Dallas. What if the old truck broke down? What if something happened to them? Worse than that, how were they going to make it in the cold, cruel world with the authorities looking for them?

His skin prickled with anxiety.

And it'd be hours yet before they'd call to say that they were safe.

"I forgot my wood!" Kendal exclaimed, startling Sara from her glum thoughts. She had just turned up the ramp that put them on Highway 51.

"What wood, honey?"

"My cedar! I put it on the front porch, and I forgot it there." He pressed a fist to his stomach.

"Maybe Chase put it in the back."

Kendal twisted in the seat to peer through the window

into the truck bed. "It's not there," he declared. "We have to go back."

"Honey, we're already on the highway."

"No, I can't leave it! Chase gave it to me. He told me to hold it and feel it with my eyes closed!"

Kendal's agitation was rattling her equilibrium. They were approaching the next exit. It wouldn't kill Sara to turn the truck around so that her son could get his wood. "Calm down, honey. I'll just get off here, and we'll go back."

Strange that pointing the truck towards the ranch had an immediate calming effect on her nerves. *You're just going to pick up Kendal's wood,* she chastised herself. *Going back changes nothing.*

But she couldn't quell the lifting of her spirits as she turned into the driveway. They rumbled out of the woods into the clearing, and Sara's anticipation burst like a bubble.

Chase had already left. His car was gone.

"Hop out and get your wood, honey," she said, trying to ignore her disappointment. There was Kendal's lump of cedar sitting on the porch ledge.

He did so, leaving his door ajar. She listened to his shoes crunch the gravel drive. It occurred to her, with a spiking of her senses, that the house was too quiet. Jesse ought to be barking.

"Kendal!" she called, on a worried note, but he didn't hear her. She pushed out of the truck, scanning the area with the sudden certainty that they weren't alone. To her horror, her gaze fell on the fender of the El Camino, barely visible from the front of the house, because it'd been parked near the kitchen door. *Oh, no, not this!*

"Kendal, get back into the truck!" she cried hoarsely.

He hefted the cedar in his arms, turning to regard her with confusion.

But it was too late. The screen door slammed open, and two young men with hair shaved to their scalps sauntered onto the porch to smirk at them. Sara rounded the truck to protect her son.

"Well, lookee who we got here," drawled the lankier of the two men, hooking his thumbs through the belt loops on his tight jeans. "It's Chase's woman and his kid."

Sara didn't bother to set him straight. It probably behooved their situation if these fellows thought that she was married to a Navy SEAL.

"Linc never said nothin' 'bout Chase havin' a kid," said the shorter of the two.

"Maybe it ain't his. Hey, lady, what'd yer ol' man do with the guns?" demanded the taller skinhead. He descended the porch steps and swaggered toward them.

"I don't know," said Sara quickly. "He hid them. He didn't tell me where."

"Right," said the skinhead, raking a crude look down her scantily clad body. Sara felt a stab of regret for the dowdy clothes she'd left behind.

"I think you best recall where he hid them, or you're coming with us, till we get 'em back," he warned with an ugly smile.

"You leave my mom alone!" Kendal shouted, stepping around Sara to protect her.

"Look," Sara countered, wrestling Kendal behind her again, "I don't know a thing about those guns. All I know is that you're trespassing on private property."

"Oooo," said the skinhead, mocking her bravado.

"Well, it don't make sense that Linc left the ranch to Chase in the first place. And in the second place, it's our personal property that we want back. Those rifles ain't his to hide."

"I *don't* know where they are," Sara repeated, grateful for the anger that kept her fear at bay.

The lanky skinhead shared a conspiring look with his companion. "In that case, we're just going to have to take you for a trade," he decided.

"No!" said Sara, shaking him off as he went to reach for her. She backed away, holding on tight to Kendal.

The skinhead rolled his eyes in annoyance and casually produced a handgun. He leveled it at Sara, who froze with sudden, chilling terror.

She sensed that it was loaded. Worse than that, she sensed by the awful silence surrounding the ranch house that it'd already been used. On the dog.

"Now," said the skinhead, wagging his head with self-approbation, "I got yer attention, don't I?"

Sara stared at the barrel, dreading the thought of a bullet blowing out of it and punching her through her heart. The IQ of the man holding it worried her even more.

"There's no need for that," she heard herself say. Over the course of her marriage to Garret, she'd learned to placate the adversary. "Put the gun away, and I'll come with you."

"*I* say the rules, lady," the skinhead reminded her. "Both of you are comin' with us." He jerked his head toward the side of the house. "Get in the car."

Sara held her ground, though her knees quaked. "You need my son to tell Chase where to bring the guns," she reasoned, heart pounding painfully.

The men shared another quick look. Apparently it took two of them to come up with a single decision. "Fine," agreed the taller one, knocking Sara aside and grabbing Kendal by the scruff. "If you call the cops," he warned, giving him a shake, "or if Chase calls the cops, we're gonna kill yer mama, you got that, kid?"

Kendal nodded, too terrified to speak. He cast his mother a wild-eyed look. *I don't want you to die.*

"Everything's going to be fine, honey," Sara managed to reassure him. "Tell Chase that these men want their guns back. He's to bring them to . . . Where are you taking me?" Heavens, who was in charge of this abduction?

"The ol' Reeves place," said the skinhead apparently in charge. He spat on the ground to assert his authority and waved the gun at her again. "We want all eight guns within five hours, boy, or your mama's gonna be sproutin' up daisies come springtime. Come on, lady." He grabbed Sara's elbow and slung her in the direction of his car.

Sara kept eye contact with Kendal. "Just give Chase the message when he gets back," she called. The phone lines in the house weren't working, so Kendal would have to wait. There wasn't any way to call Chase. "It's going to be okay, honey," she added, just before the skinhead shoved her around the corner, taking her out of Kendal's sight.

"What'd you do with the dog?" she demanded as the shorter man opened the passenger door of the banged-up vehicle.

"Shot him," he said, giving her a push before he climbed in after her.

With numbness creeping over her, Sara settled into the

middle of the bench seat, only vaguely aware of the springs poking out from under the filthy seat cover.

Surely the skinhead was joking.

Because if Jesse was dead, and Kendal found him that way, it wasn't going to be okay. Not even if Chase brought the rifles to the Reeves place and got Sara back, unscathed.

Chase saw Linc's truck, with its doors left open the minute he broke through the tree line. *What the . . . ?* He accelerated abruptly, curious to see what had brought Sara back to the ranch.

But then the stillness of the scene penetrated his consciousness, summoning his sixth sense. As he braked to a halt behind the truck, his trained eye caught sight of tire tracks in the grass, marking the flight of a third vehicle.

Concern jostled to the forefront of his emotions. He reached for the gun he'd stowed under the seat while filing for a deed at the city courthouse. He stepped out of the car and scented the air, hearing at the same time a terrible silence.

Jesse should be barking.

Concern congealed into dread. *Oh, fuck, no. If those skinhead bastards hurt my dog or—God forbid—Sara and her son—I'm going to wreak holy havoc on them.*

He tamped down his spiraling fears, channeling them into focused energy.

Releasing the safety on his gun, he mounted the porch steps without eliciting so much as a creak. A breeze blew over the back of his neck as he opened the screen door and nudged the inner door open. His gaze fell on Kendal, who lay on top of Jesse in the entryway, both of them unmoving.

The scent of death was unmistakable. Blood had oozed out from under the dog to stain the carpet.

"Ken," Chase called, bending down to put a tentative hand on Kendal's shoulder, relieved to find it warm.

The boy jumped with a strangled scream. He looked at Chase through expanded pupils, his face the color of glue.

Chase clicked the safety of his gun back on and jammed it into the back of his cargo pants. "Ken," he said again, glancing at Jesse, who'd been shot in the head. "Hey," he said, giving him a little shake. "Where's your mama?"

"They took her," Kendal said, in a voice that was raw from weeping.

"Who's they?" Chase asked, though he already knew. He had to keep himself from crushing Kendal's slender bones.

Linc's son of a bitch cohorts.

"Th-they told me to tell you"—the boy broke off to drag air into his convulsing lungs—"to bring the guns to the Reeves place or they'll kill my mom, too."

"The Reeves place," Chase repeated, hearing the second half of the threat but refusing to dwell on it. In his mind's eye, he pictured the farmhouse where the skinheads wanted to do the exchange. It stood in the middle of a field without any trees around to offer cover—crap.

"And we can't call the police," Kendal added. His face crumpled as he bowed with renewed anguish over the dog.

"Listen, Ken. I won't let anything happen to your mama, you hear me?" He pried him off the dog again.

"We're going to take Jesse outside in the grass where he'd like to be. And then I'm going to get the rifles and we'll take 'em to get Sara back. Help me roll the carpet up."

Sniffling and staggering with shock, Kendal none-theless gave a hand in rolling Jesse's body in the ruined carpet.

With a heavy heart and knowing Jesse's death was going to hit him later, Chase carried Jesse outside, head-ing automatically toward the pecan tree where he'd buried everyone else he'd ever loved.

He lowered the carpet in the grass with Kendal fussing over it. Stalking toward the little door that gave access to the crawl space, Chase reached inside and retrieved the rifles.

Kneeling right there in the grass, he jammed as many of the components as he felt he had time to, disabling five of the eight weapons. Then he gathered them in his arms and stood up, wondering what he should do with Kendal. "Come on, son," he called, striding toward his car.

Kendal hurried after him, sniffling but responsive.

Five minutes later, Chase pulled up in front of Ray and Linda Mae Goodner's sprawling ranch house. "You're going to stay here with a friend of mine," he said.

"No," Kendal protested, gripping the car door with the tenacity of a cat up a tree. "I have to get my mother."

"I know how you feel, Ken," said Chase, in the lulling tone he reserved for dealing with victims of violence. "But this is somethin' that I have to do alone. I can't bring you with me."

Kendal grabbed Chase's arm and gripped it fiercely. "You'd better bring her back!" he shouted, anger spitting from his green-gray eyes.

Chase took heart from Kendal's rage. "You bet I will," he swore. *After I rearrange their body parts.*

He pushed out of the car to escort the boy up to the Goodner's front door, but Linda Mae was already bustling toward them. She took one look at Chase's set features, and her smile fled.

"This is Ken," Chase said, shutting the passenger door with the heel of his boot. "I need you to watch him for me. Linc's friends are keeping his mother till I give them their guns," he added tersely.

"Oh, Lord!" cried the woman, stepping up to Kendal with motherly concern.

With a reassuring pat, Chase relinquished Kendal to Linda Mae's care. He headed back to the driver's seat.

"Should I call the police?" the woman inquired.

"I will," Chase said, glancing at Kendal's worried face. "Afterward," he added, dropping into his car.

As he peeled away, he glanced into his rearview mirror to see Linda Mae ushering Kendal inside. She'd do and say all the right things to keep Kendal sane in the next hour or so. Chase's job, meanwhile, was to ensure that he kept his promise to Kendal and brought his mama home alive.

The Reeves place was an abandoned farmhouse back when Chase was just a kid. Teenagers used it as a place to escape their parents, to smoke and drink. It had fallen into serious disrepair since then, listing to one side as a result of the constant, southerly winds.

The sagging roof stood at the verge of collapse. The clapboard siding, which had once been white, had peeled away, exposing old, dried wood underneath. With many of the windows broken or boarded shut, the house looked to Chase like a skeleton as he surveyed it from a distance of two hundred yards, beyond the scope of peering eyes.

Welcome to the headquarters of the FOR Americans, he scoffed inwardly. They used to be holed up in Linc's office. Now this was all that was left to them.

He eyed the stormy, purple sky, wondering if he should wait for nightfall or just drive up to the front door, hand them their weapons, and get Sara the hell out of there—assuming they would even let her go. But they were racists, he reassured himself, not murderers. Chances were they'd let her walk in exchange for the weapons. Only Chase wasn't satisfied with just compromising their rifles. He wanted to rip their fucking hearts out.

Dammit, I should never have brought her here!

This was the last thing she deserved after dealing with the likes of Garret. She deserved peace and quiet, not fear and threats.

He'd never forgive himself if Linc's buddies hurt her.

With no choice but to play it by ear, Chase ducked back into his car. He donned his holster and slid the SIG into place. The blade that he carried in his left boot was his backup weapon. He could peg a man in the heart with a flick of his wrist.

The MP5, which he'd taken out of the back of his car, was propped on the floor of the seat beside him, in case he was driven into retreat. Two extra magazines were stowed in the pockets of his cargo pants. It was time to draw the line.

As he eased the car out of a copse of trees and onto a rutted road, he could feel the warrior within him coalesce.

He could feel the rocks on the road through the steering column. The skylarks diving for insects over the fields seemed to fall in slow motion. And a cicada buzzed over the hood of his car, moving like a CH-46E Sea Knight helicopter.

By the time he pulled up before the clapboard farm-house, the sky had taken on a bruised hue, with rain clouds sweeping closer. Chase got out, leaving the MP5 right inside the open window. He reached into the backseat, scooping up the eight rifles, five of which would never work again.

Feeling eyes on him, he marched toward the rickety front stoop and rapped loudly on the crooked front door.

Sara's heart pounded with the dread of impending violence. Like a true-blue hero, Chase had come for her, knocking on the door with purpose that had her holding her breath.

If he thought he could storm inside and teach these men a lesson, though, they might all wind up dead.

The morons who'd abducted her weren't the problem. Les and Timmy, as she'd heard them call each other, didn't have the brainpower to overcome a trained Navy SEAL, not even with the nine-millimeter gun that Les toted.

It was their leader, Will, who worried her.

For the last hour or so, she'd made his acquaintance. And she'd discovered that her amateur skills in psychology couldn't begin to sound the depths of the man's complexity. He'd been an Army Ranger during the Vietnam War, the equivalent of a Navy SEAL. Obviously, at sixty, he wasn't in his prime, but what he lacked in speed in agility, he made up for in experience. She'd heard enough stories to know.

In old Will's mind, the war was ongoing. He'd insisted on showing her his arsenal of weapons. He owned a box-ful of hand grenades purchased from a crooked cop. He had mortar rounds for a machine gun that was being shipped UPS. He even had a shoulder-mounted missile launcher made by the Russians, which he admitted to her didn't work.

Will had a passion for history, too, only it wasn't the version Sara was familiar with. It was Will's version: a litany of how the White Man had been wronged.

He'd sat on an upended crate across from her folding chair trying to recruit her to his cause. The Sterno burner, which he'd lit to combat the encroaching gloom, threw light onto the undersides of his cheekbones, leaving his eye sockets in shadow.

By nature, Sara abhorred anger and violence. For a decade she'd gone to great lengths to keep from agitating Garret. She played the same passive game with Will, lull-ing him into thinking that she agreed with his twisted point of view.

When he shot off his seat at the brisk knocking, she gasped in terror, wishing there were some way to fore-warn Chase of the danger he was facing.

She forced herself to speak up, smoothing the wobble from her voice. "Perhaps I should meet him at the door. He could leave the rifles on the porch," she suggested.

"And then what?" Will countered. "Let you go? So you run to the police?"

"I wouldn't do that," she told him, truthfully. "I told you, I'm leaving for Texas."

Eyeing Chase through a knothole in the boarded-up window, Will cracked his knuckles and thought.

The brisk knock came again.

"I'll get it," Les volunteered, materializing out of the shadows of the back room, gun in hand.

Will stopped him with a single word. "No." He turned his head and looked at Sara. "She's going to answer the door."

Sara's relief evaporated in the next instant when he added, "And if she doesn't persuade him to leave the guns on the porch, we'll shoot 'em both. Go on." He jerked his head.

Chapter Nine

Sara rose on legs that jittered. As the skinheads retreated into the shadows, she crossed to the door and opened it, coming face-to-face with Chase, who carried more than half a dozen rifles over one shoulder. He managed to look at her and past her all at the same time, his eyes translucent in the gloom.

"Hi," she said, getting his full attention with her overly bright tone. "Just put the guns down here, and we can go."

She could feel the adrenaline radiating out of him. He was more than braced for a confrontation; he was itching to thrash the enemy soundly, only she stood squarely between the opposing forces. "Put them down," she repeated, imbuing her words with deeper meaning, "and we walk away." *Alive,* she added mentally.

To her vast relief, he leaned over. The rifles clattered onto the wooden stoop. He straightened, grabbed her hand, and pulled her with him toward the car, keeping his body between hers and the house as he opened the passenger door to let her in. Rounding the car, he lifted his submachine gun off his seat and dove inside.

He was backing down the driveway before his door was even shut.

Over her galloping heart, Sara listened to the whine of his engine as they picked up speed. He found a place to spin them around, and they shot away from the farmhouse with efficiency that left her breathless.

Chase didn't slow down until they'd driven several miles. He pulled off the road, suddenly, yanked up the hand brake and reached for her, his hands hot on her upper arms. "Tell me the fuckers didn't hurt you," he demanded roughly.

"I'm fine," she reassured him, though every muscle in her body ached from all the tension. "Where's Kendal?"

"Staying with Mrs. Goodner, my neighbor. I'm going to take you there now."

She could feel the rage still shimmering in him. "You're not going back, Chase," she said, sensing that was exactly what he intended to do. "I met the leader of the group—Will. He's a former Army Ranger and a Vietnam vet," she told him quickly. "He's convinced that he's fighting a war. You can't go back. There are three of them and only one of you. Someone's going to get killed."

There was just enough daylight left for her to see Chase's jaw muscles jump as he released her and sat back.

"Call the police," she urged. "Forget about me; you have to call the authorities. Will has plans. Something about a . . . a lesson to teach the liberal duffers to look after their own kind." She shook her head in bafflement. "Whatever that means."

Chase tugged off the elastic that kept his hair in a ponytail. It fell to his shoulders in wavy locks, giving him a savage look. He went perfectly still, as if meditating on the hunt to come.

"Please, Chase," Sara begged. "I don't like violence. And I don't want you to get hurt." Tears sprang to her eyes.

He glanced at her and cursed. "You just want me to walk away?" he asked on a disbelieving note. "They killed my dog," he growled. "They broke into my house; they fucking terrorized you and Kendal, and you just want me to turn my back on that?"

The confirmation that Jesse was dead made her waver. "Don't tell me Kendal was the first to find him," she begged.

"Yes, he was," Chase bit back. "Does that change things for you?"

Sara wrestled with conflicting impulses. On one hand, imagining what her son had suffered today, she wanted nothing more, as a mother, than to teach the skinheads a lesson they would never forget. She was tempted to unleash Chase on them.

On the other hand, if he were hurt in the process, how much more awful would that be?

"Just call the police, Chase," Sara begged. "Please. Let them handle it."

A fierce frown settled on his forehead. Sara held her breath. It was a defining moment. She would see for herself what he was made of. He reached abruptly over her knees and snatched the cell phone out of the glove compartment. Watching him press the illuminated numbers, Sara released a silent sigh of relief.

"Nine-one-one, do you have an emergency?"

In a concise message, Chase relayed the whereabouts

of the FOR Americans, with the added warning that they were armed. He refused to give his name, saying only that he preferred to remain anonymous. That, of course, was for her benefit. He didn't want the police swarming the ranch, asking questions.

"Let's go get Kendal," Chase said, when the call was done. His tone was calm, his scowl was gone. By all appearances, he was ready to put the experience behind him.

"Thank you," she whispered, collapsing weakly against her seat.

Sweat poured from Chase's body. His thighs burned from pumping underneath him as he tore up and down the half mile driveway in the dark, hoping to relieve his pent-up energy.

Jesse was dead. They'd buried him under the pecan tree just before the rain came pouring down.

Rainwater trickled down Chase's cheeks in lieu of the tears he was unable to cry. He wished he could, if only to relieve the pressure in his chest.

Kicking off his squishy running shoes, he pushed through the front door, moving quietly to keep from disturbing Sara and Kendal. But there was Sara, sitting cross-legged on the sofa, waiting up for him. He shut the door against the gentle murmur of the rain.

She was wearing the nightshirt she'd bought in Memphis. She didn't have a drop of makeup on her clean-scrubbed face, and her eyes looked puffy and red-rimmed in the lamp glow. For some reason, she was more appealing to him than ever.

"You okay?" he asked, his back still to the door.

"I wanted to talk to you," she explained.

With an excess of testosterone still in his bloodstream, it was not a good time. He wanted vengeance and sex, and he wasn't too picky as to which came first.

But Sara had been through hell because of him. The least he could do was put her mind at ease. "Let me shower," he stalled. Snatching fresh boxers and his sweatpants from his duffel bag, he headed for the bathroom.

A cold shower helped to settle some of his inner seething. He left his sodden clothes in the laundry closet and returned to the living room in his sweatpants. At the same time, Sara emerged form the kitchen bearing two steaming mugs.

"Chamomile tea," she said, her gaze skittering over his naked chest. "It's been in the cabinet for a while, but I don't think tea goes bad, does it?"

Her nervous question had him plucking a T-shirt from his duffel bag. He jammed his arms through the sleeves and tugged it down to accept the mug she passed him. He never drank tea, except in Asian restaurants. "Thanks."

He sat on the end of the couch, unnerved when Sara eased down next to him. She smelled like soap and sundried cotton. She sipped her tea, strangely quiet, considering she'd said she wanted to talk.

He took a swallow. "How's Ken doin'?" The boy had cried for hours, which was one of the reasons why Chase had left the house. It'd reminded him of his mother crying.

"I slipped him some Dramamine," she confessed, with a self-deprecating grimace. "I guess I'm a bad mother."

"You're not," Chase assured her. He emptied his mug, burning his throat to distract himself from her proximity.

She had no idea how tightly wound he was. "Is that what you wanted to talk about?" he asked. The faster they ended this discussion, the safer she'd be.

"Actually, I just wanted to thank you," she told him, unexpectedly

"What the hell for?" he growled. He blamed himself for the whole fiasco.

"For not going back. I know you wanted to." Her green-gray eyes shone with faith—faith he didn't deserve since he was still considering it. The night wasn't over yet.

"Tell me again what happened," he demanded, needing to make up his mind. She'd sketched an outline of the events for Linda Mae's benefit, but who knew what details she might have left out?

With a sigh, she relayed their reasons for returning to the ranch in the first place. She retold how they'd surprised the skinheads who were searching the house for the rifles. As she mentioned her distress at leaving Kendal behind, her eyes filled with tears.

Fuck, he wanted to comfort her, but then he'd have to touch her. "I want you to tell me if those bastards hurt you," he insisted, watching her closely. "Don't cover up for them."

"Les and Timmy jostled me around a little," she conceded, dashing the moisture from beneath her eyes, "but no harm done. And Will just talked to me. God, did he give me the creeps!"

It gave Chase the creeps to hear the skinheads' names on her lips. She should never have experienced what she'd gone through today. Kendal, either. It was Chase's fault that they'd wound up smack-dab in the middle of a racial conspiracy.

He threw himself off the sofa to prowl around the living room. "This is all my fault," he admitted, hating himself.

Her eyes flashed like a prelude to a summer storm. "Don't you dare blame yourself, Chase McCaffrey. We were leaving, remember? It's our fault that we came back."

"I should never have brought you here, to a place like this," he qualified.

"What do you mean a place like this? There's nothing wrong with this place."

"It's common," he retorted. "There's nothing here but work to be done and backwards-thinking people like Linc and his cronies."

"You're here," she countered. "And there's nothing backward about you."

That pulled him up short. "You gotta be kiddin' me." How could she say that when she knew what he did for a living? He was as backward as a treed possum.

"I'm not," she said, defending him vehemently. "You've made all the difference to me and my son. Tonight you could have started World War III, but you walked away. That's not backward, Chase. That's heroic."

Huh? He stood there wondering if he'd heard her right, but then his hearing was beyond perfect.

She jumped off the couch, and he backed up, terrified of being tested in the state that he was in. She stopped squarely in front of him with her hands clasped.

The smell of her made him light-headed.

"Thank you," she repeated gently. "That's all I really wanted to say. That, and I'm sorry about Jesse."

He flinched as she went up on her toes, pressing a warm, soft kiss on his cheek.

The reminder that his dog was dead kept him from taking advantage. If that happened, she'd find out just how unheroic he could be.

He watched her turn away. She collected both their mugs and took them to the kitchen. Passing him one last time, she cast him a sweet, sad smile. It did nothing to ease his lust.

Once she was safely out of range, Chase threw himself down on the couch and scowled.

He'd never been accused of heroism before.

It had a way of humbling a man.

Reaching for the lamp, he snapped off the light. Surrounded by darkness, he instantly missed the loyal company of his dog. His chest hurt, but the tears refused to come.

Frances Yates cut through the wedge of cantaloupe with the side of her fork and lifted the morsel to her mouth. Since her daughter's disappearance, she'd lost weight she couldn't afford to lose. Her doctor had chided her just yesterday, but, honestly, how was she supposed to maintain an appetite when something awful had befallen Sara and her only grandson, Kendal?

Marvin, who sat across from her, his back to the golf course of their retirement community, seemed to be experiencing the same struggle.

When the doorbell rang, it came as a relief to have to get up from the table. "Another well-wisher," Frances shouted to Marvin, who was deaf. She rose painstakingly to her feet, careful to watch her equilibrium.

Marvin dabbed his chin with a napkin, getting up to follow her down the hall.

Frances opened the door, expecting to be greeted by a flower arrangement or a familiar face, projecting sympathy. Nearly everyone within their gated community had dropped by to offer encouragement and consolation. It took Frances a second to recognize her son-in-law, looking less than fastidious. His navy blue jacket was wrinkled, and his hair was windblown.

The only reason he would have come to Florida in person was to deliver terrible news. "Oh, heavens, no!" Frances cried, putting a hand to her chest and stumbling against her husband, who'd followed her to the door. "They were found," she guessed.

Bartholomew's dark eyes narrowed as he took in her dismay with strangely apathetic eyes. Those same eyes scrutinized Marvin, whose hand curled protectively around Frances's frail arm. "No," he said, looking past them, into the foyer.

"What's going on?" Marvin shouted.

"I don't know," said Frances, remarking Garret's peculiar behavior. "Please, come in." She gestured toward the living room, and Marvin stepped back so that his son-in-law could duck under the lintel and enter their dwelling.

Garret took a seat on Marvin's favorite reading chair, his posture rigid. His dark eyes darted here and there as if looking for something.

Marvin helped Frances lower herself onto the sofa and took the seat next to her. "Do you have news for us?" she pressed. He'd spoken to them via phone forty-eight hours after Sara and Kendal's disappearance, but not since then, though they'd left a number of messages.

"No," he said, in a flat voice. "None. The authorities are questioning whether it was an abduction, after all."

"What else would it be?" Frances asked in confusion. "Perhaps their abductor wasn't looking for money." *Perhaps he merely wanted to abuse them and kill them and dump their bodies elsewhere.* "Oh, dear," she moaned, suffering a dizzy spell that was made all the worse by her vertigo.

Bartholomew regarded her dispassionately. "I should be going," he announced, coming abruptly to his feet.

"But you just got here," she protested. "Can I get you anything to drink?" she offered, thinking she ought to have asked earlier.

"No. Thank you." He headed straight for the door. "I came to see how you were holding up," he muttered with his back to them. "Sorry that I don't have better news for you."

Frances and Marvin both struggled to their feet, chasing Garret to the door to see him off. He was already down the steps, heading toward a nondescript rental car. "Thank you for your thoughtfulness," Frances called, lifting a hand in farewell.

He didn't even turn to acknowledge it.

She watched him wrench his car door open, stoop to climb inside, then roar away.

"Strange," she murmured, pondering his odd behavior.

"What did you say?" Marvin asked.

"Didn't you find his behavior strange?" she asked him, loudly.

"Yes," he agreed with a disapproving frown. "He behaved as if he expected to find Sara and Kendal here."

An arrow of insight pierced Frances's consciousness, speeding her heart. A sudden dizzy spell had her groping for her husband, who caught her in his arms. Heavens, had Bartholomew been implying that Sara and Kendal ran away?

Oh, thank God! For if they had, then they were still alive!

But why hadn't Sara come to them if she needed help?

Venturing onto the front porch, Sara discovered that the rain had moved on, trailing cooler weather behind it. With no fall clothing to put on, she hugged herself for warmth, even as she watched Chase drag a plywood contraption along the grass that edged the driveway, leaving lines in the heavy dew.

What is he up to? she wondered.

The door creaked open behind her, and she turned to see a puffy-eyed Kendal greet the new day. His gaze went first toward the hump of earth beneath the pecan tree where Jesse lay. But then he spotted Chase setting the structure on its base by the curve in the driveway. "What's he doin?" he asked.

A giant bull's-eye had been painted on a sheet of plywood with the stain Chase was using to coat the house. "Maybe he wants to practice shooting," Sara suggested.

Together, they watched him retrace his steps. His gaze caught and held Sara's and her pulse quickened with awareness and admiration for his heroism.

"Mornin'," he called, snatching up a rifle that was hidden in the grass. He turned his back on them, aimed his gun at the target, and fired eight shots in quick succession, hitting the center of the bull's-eye every time.

Sara and Kendal gawked in amazement.

And then Chase was crossing the driveway toward

them. "Your turn," he called to Sara, giving her a familiar, challenging look.

She shook her head. "Oh, no."

"Come on down," he invited, absolutely serious. "You're not goin' to Dallas till you know how to protect yourself."

They were planning to leave for Dallas later today. That didn't leave much time.

"Why can't we just stay with you?" Kendal demanded, wresting Chase's attention.

The question rocked Sara briefly on her heels. If that were an option, then it would probably be her first choice, she realized. "We can't, honey," she answered on Chase's behalf. "Chase has to go back to his job, you know that."

"Why can't he quit?" the boy cried, on an emotional note. Without waiting for an answer, he spun around and flew into the house, slamming the door behind him.

Sara winced. "Sorry," she said to Chase, who frowned at Kendal's outburst. "There have been so many changes. He's just looking for some solid ground."

"You want me to explain the terms of my enlistment to him?" he offered.

"Maybe that would help," Sara agreed. Curiosity got the better of her. "What, uh, are the terms?" she asked.

"I reenlisted three months ago, while I was overseas. I have four years left till retirement," he said, with a grim set to his jaw.

Four years! The chilly breeze licked over Sara's bare arms. What were the odds of a sniper's getting killed in that span of time?

"Come on down here," he invited again.

"No," she said, eyeing the rifle. "I really don't think it's a good idea."

"It's a lightweight semiautomatic buck rifle that Linc used to hunt with." He hefted it to show her how light it was. "You won't have any problem handlin' it."

"It's just not my thing to shoot people," she said without thinking.

He went perfectly still. "It's not my thing either, Sara," he retorted, with a flicker of anger in his eyes.

She hadn't meant it like that, and yet, what he did for a living put a gulf between them—though it wasn't so much what he did as *where*, and for how long.

"I need to feel better 'bout sendin' you off alone," he explained. "Please, just do this for me."

Well, when he put it that way, she really didn't have much choice, did she?

With a sigh of surrender, Sara descended the steps and followed him across the driveway to the place where he'd shot those eight bull's-eyes, at least twenty-five yards from the target.

"This rifle can shoot up to a mile," Chase informed her.

"Mmmm," Sara hummed, pretending to be impressed.

"This is how you release the magazine to chamber a new one," he added, handling the gun with daunting competence. "This rifle will give you eight consecutive rounds per clip. Here's how you empty the magazine." He showed her. "Go ahead and take it out."

Feeling as inexperienced as a baby, Sara released the empty magazine. He took it, handing her a new one. "Slide it in till you hear a click. This here's the safety," he continued, touching the lever by her thumb. "Keep it on till you plan to shoot."

No problem.

"You ready?"

"Not really."

Ignoring that, he positioned her into the proper front-and-back stance. He lifted the butt of the rifle against her right shoulder. "Bend your elbows. Loosen up your shoulders; I don't want any tension in 'em."

It was his proximity that was making her tense. If he touched her much more, the rest of the lesson was going to be a complete waste of time.

"Sight down the barrel and center the crosshairs on the bull's-eye. You doin' that?"

"Yes," she said, shutting one eye and squinting through the lens with the other.

He bent down to inspect her aim. "Go ahead and release the safety. Then squeeze the trigger."

Tamping down her awareness of him, Sara flicked the safety off and squeezed the trigger.

Boom! The rifle kicked, ramming against her shoulder and sending her flying back into Chase's arms. "You didn't say it was going to do that!" she accused, whipping her head back to glare at him.

He chuckled at her outrage. "So, now you know," he said reasonably. "Try again. I think you hit a squirrel."

With a groan for her shoulder, she readied herself a second time.

"Check your stance."

Sara widened her stance before sighting down the barrel again. She squeezed her eyes shut and pulled the trigger.

Boom! She staggered back a couple of steps.

"You got to keep your eyes open," Chase chided, with a smile in his voice.

"I can't do this," she said, not referring so much to shooting the rifle as to standing so close to him and not melting into his arms.

"Sure, you can," he argued, unaware of her private dilemma. He positioned her back in the proper stance. "This time keep your eyes open."

Sara blew out a breath, widened her stance belatedly, and peered through the scope to fire again. *Boom!* "I missed."

"Try again."

Boom!

"I think I hit something."

"Yep, the ground. One more time."

Sarah whimpered. Her shoulder felt bruised where the rifle butted it. *Boom!*

"Maybe you need some help," he conceded, stepping closer. With that short notice, he fitted his larger body, front to back, against hers.

Sara's senses screamed. *This is going to help?*

"Ready?" He murmured the question in her ear, sending a rush of anticipation through her.

"Yes," she breathed.

"Focus on the target."

She could scarcely see out of her heavy-lidded eyes, yet alone pinpoint the center of the bull's-eye. All she could focus on was Chase's warmth, his cedarlike scent, and the zipper of his jeans pressed intimately against her backside.

"Pull the trigger."

She did, with a burst of excitement similar to the onset of an orgasm.

Boom! Crack!

She heard the bullet rip into the target. By then she'd been driven too deep into Chase's arms to care. She had no idea where the gun went, only that it disappeared. Chase caught her chin, angling her lips toward his. And suddenly he was kissing her with so much focused hunger that her rational faculties ground to a halt.

There was a reason why she ought not to welcome the heat of his palms burning a path toward her breasts. She couldn't remember what it was. Desire pooled with a warm gush, accompanied by a desperate craving for more.

She twisted in his arms, crowding closer, hips pressed to the unyielding column of his zipper.

A single, rational thought penetrated her sensual haze: *Kendal might be watching out the window.*

What message would it send to see his mother kissing Chase like there was no tomorrow? The wrong message. The message that she and Chase had a future together.

Didn't Kendal realize that Chase was ephemeral? All it took for Chase to disappear was for Uncle Sam to crook a finger. It had been just like that in the past, with Chase gliding in and out of Sara's life, ever elusive.

It was that realization that made her drag her lips from his, even as she issued a moan of regret.

He kept tight hold of her, his breathing fast and deep. "Come in the house with me," he urged, his eyes so blue she could hardly look at them.

"We can't," she reminded him. "Kendal's in there."

"Stay one more night, then."

She considered the futility of intimacy. "It's pointless, isn't it?"

"How's it pointless to make a memory worth keeping?" he retorted.

Worth keeping, yes, but not worth the heartbreak that would come after. The world needed Chase. She had no right, no way to keep him.

"I can't," she repeated.

Her decision rendered him mute.

"Let me go," she added, with the tiniest concern that he might not.

But he did, instantly. He turned away, bending to snatch up the gun that was lying at their feet, his scowl thunderous.

Sara watched with an apology stuck in her throat.

Suddenly, Chase's head whipped toward the tree line. The muscles in his back flexed. "Car's comin'," he warned.

She couldn't hear anything, but she didn't waste a second in hurrying toward the house.

It was bad enough that Linda Mae Goodner couldn't get enough answers to satisfy her curiosity last night.

Sara couldn't afford to show her face to everyone.

From the shadow of the porch, she noted the white police cruiser with blue and gold decals creeping around the bend in the driveway. A sense of foreboding rose up in her.

Surely her true identity hadn't become public knowledge already.

Chapter Ten

Chase angled the buck rifle over his shoulder and waited for the Broken Arrow Police Department cruiser to pull up beside him. He recognized its single occupant as Dean Cannard, a former high school classmate and peer.

The two men took stock of each other before Cannard broke the silence. "Mornin'," he said. "Good to see you again, Chase. Been almost twenty years, now, hasn't it?"

"Eighteen," Chase answered, stepping over to the driver's door to extend a hand. "You look the same." Cannard's dark good looks had made him popular in high school. Chase, on the other hand, had been a rangy loner, respected for his wilderness skills.

"You've changed," countered the man taking in the breadth of Chase's shoulders. "I heard you came back to claim your land."

"Yep." Chase nodded, noting from the corner of his eye that Sara had shut herself inside the house.

His terseness left Cannard no choice but to get to the point of his visit. "The BAPD got a call last night that took us over the Reeves place. Ran into a couple a skin-heads totin' rifles. They said they got 'em from you."

Chase allowed himself a sneer. "They left them here in Linc's study," he admitted. "I disabled most of 'em after they shot my dog. Did you arrest them?"

"I brought them in," Cannard confirmed. "But all I could charge them with was trespassing. It ain't illegal to carry rifles in this state. Had to let them go this morning."

Chase ground his molars in disgust. He should've gone back there last night to teach those boys a lesson, regardless of Sara's persuasions. "How many did you arrest?" he asked, suddenly suspicious that Will, the leader, had gotten away.

"Just two," Cannard confirmed. "Les Wright and Timothy Olsen. You know either one?"

"No," Chase said shortly.

"They happened to mention a lady friend of yours, though," the cop added, notching Chase's tension tighter. He reached into his shirt pocket and produced a ring. "This belong to her?"

It was Sara's wedding band. He wondered how it had come to fall off her finger. "Might," he hedged, holding out a hand to receive it.

"I'd like to talk to her, if you don't mind," Cannard requested.

Refusing him would look suspicious. Chase managed a careless-looking shrug. "She's inside," he said. "Why don't you come in? Linc's friends left some stuff that you might want to look at."

Getting out of his car, Cannard followed Chase into the house. As he stepped inside, he let out a low whistle.

"Place looks a good sight better." The comment told Chase that he'd visited a time or two while Linc was living.

Sara had withdrawn into his mother's bedroom. Chase went to get her. "You left this behind last night," he said, handing her the ring, which she took back with a grimace. "You want to tell me how it fell off?"

"Tim was going to . . . tie me to a chair, but Will called him off."

His temper flickered that she hadn't mentioned that last night. Of course, he definitely would have wreaked some havoc then. "Sergeant Cannard wants to talk to you," he said quietly. "Just tell the truth 'bout what happened, but not much more."

With a nervous nod, she left the room before him. When she greeted Dean Cannard, she sounded composed. "Sergeant," she said. "I'm Serenity Jensen."

Chase turned the corner just in time to catch Cannard's stunned look. Either the man recognized Sara or he thought she was cuter than hell.

"Detective Sergeant," he corrected her with a grin that had made the girls in high school fan their faces. "I'm not in the uniformed division right now. I work investigations."

The man was obviously hoping to impress her. Unluckily for him, being an investigator wasn't going to win him any points.

She took a seat on the edge of the hearth, across from the sofa where he, too, sat down. "Thank you for bringing my ring," she said. "It must have fallen off."

He regarded her with genuine concern. "I take it you were there against your will," he fished.

Sara glanced at Chase. "The skinheads came here looking for some rifles that belonged to them. When they couldn't find them, they took me as incentive for Chase to bring the rifles to them. They left my son behind to communicate the message to Chase. That was after they broke in and killed the dog. "

Cannard's dark gaze shifted to Chase, who was standing in the entryway just in case Kendal decided to amble out of his room to see what the stir was about. No need for Cannard to get a look at both Sara and her boy. "That's when you disabled the weapons," Cannard deduced.

"Five out of eight," Chase corrected him. "I didn't want to take too long."

Cannard nodded thoughtfully. "So you took the rifles over there, and they handed Ms. Jensen back peaceably?"

"Pretty much," Chase agreed.

"I'm surprised you didn't beat the crap out of 'em—if you'll excuse the expression," he said to Sara. "I heard you're a Navy SEAL," he added, proving that Mrs. Goodner's grapevine had been functioning without a glitch.

"Thought I'd leave that to you," Chase replied, with just a hint of accusation.

"The law is the law, McCaffrey. I couldn't hold 'em long for trespassing 'cause the Reeves place is abandoned. On the other hand, if Ms. Jensen's willing to press charges, I'll arrest 'em for breakin' and enterin', abduction, and even cruelty to animals."

Chase took note of Sara's discomfort. In order to press charges, she would have to enter her name into court documents, and she didn't have her new ID yet. "She's about to leave the area," Chase said, offering a plausible excuse.

"I saw the loaded truck," Cannard answered, proving himself observant. "Where're you headed?"

"Texas," Sara said, intentionally vague.

The detective's gaze went from Chase to her and back again, as he clearly tried to assess their relationship. After all, he'd just handed Sara back a wedding ring.

"There's another way to do this," Chase suggested. He stepped back, opening the door to Linc's study. "Have a look in here."

Pushing to his feet, Cannard approached the messy room. He stepped inside, assessing the amassed media and paraphernalia with a quick and discerning eye. "Jesus," he said, plucking up one of the FOR Americans pamphlets and skimming through it.

Sara came to stand at the open door. "The leader's name is Will," she divulged. "He volunteered that he's a former Army Ranger who served in Vietnam. I think he's very dangerous," she added.

Cannard considered the information with a frown. "Holding meetings and spreadin' propaganda ain't a crime, either. It's protected by our Constitution. Unless you're willing to press charges, there's nothing I can do about any of this," he added, giving her a compelling look.

Sara squirmed. "I'm sorry. I'm leaving today," she repeated. "I don't have time to get involved. Chase could still press charges."

But obviously Cannard wasn't as interested in inviting Chase down to the station. He looked at the piles of literature, instead. "Mind if I help myself to some of this stuff?" he asked.

"Hell," said Chase, "take it all."

"Can't fit but so much in my car," Cannard answered, with a wry glance. "You want to give me a hand with this?"

By the time he departed half an hour later, the collections in Linc's study had dwindled to more reasonable proportions.

"Do you think he suspects?" Sara asked, as she and Chase stood on the front porch watching the cruiser disappear.

"No," he said with confidence, "though he does wonder why you're holdin' out on him." He glanced at her, his gaze lingering with a stab of regret on the soft pink curve of her lips. The kiss they'd shared had been the sweetest thing he'd ever lived through. "Guess you should head out soon," he said, hating the words as they came out of his mouth. "Not that I want you to."

With the sunlight reflecting off the porch step, her eyes looked more than ever like those Malaysian waterfalls.

"I'll miss you," she admitted, glancing away shyly.

The confession put pressure on his chest. "I'll miss you, too," he said, gruffly. He'd said that once or twice to women he'd been lovers with, but never to one that he'd known only as a friend.

"I'd better talk to Kendal," she said, turning regretfully toward the door.

He halted her. "I said I would," he reminded her.

Her grateful nod made the daunting task seem a little easier.

For the second time in a week, Sara pointed the truck toward Highway 51 and then the Muskogee Turnpike, grateful that this time Kendal didn't mention any stomach cramps. Chase must have explained that his terms of enlistment were unequivocal. He had no choice but to go back; just as they had no choice but to go forward. That reality didn't keep Sara's heart from hurting though.

Something brimming with potential had been cut short with her departure.

Potential? she scoffed at her own naïveté. Potential for what, loneliness? Disillusionment? Did she honestly think that deepening her intimacy with a sniper would result in anything else?

No, it was better to leave Oklahoma now, before she became any more invested. Still, it was all she could do to keep her eyes from straying to the rearview mirror until the mailbox at the head of the ranch fell from view.

The old truck seemed to run better in the cooler weather. Sara edged her speed up to sixty miles an hour. A cool breeze blew through the truck's half-opened windows, bearing in a scent she'd grown to love. There wasn't a drop of humidity in the air, so that the sky above them was a huge blue canvas, stretched from one flat horizon to the other. It was an excellent day to put her plans back on track. Texas had always been her final destination.

Where, then, was her enthusiasm?

The farther Broken Arrow fell behind, the more uneasy she became. The skinheads, Les, Timmy, and most especially Will, were still at large, spreading their message of hate and amassing weapons—for what? To target innocent people. If she'd agreed to press charges, it would at least have thrown a wrench into their plans, if not put an end to them completely.

But how could she press charges when she herself was a woman on the run, as yet without identification? And would her new name and social security number, when she finally held them, hold up to any sort of scrutiny?

With a sigh, Sara found a cheerful tune on the radio and glanced at Kendal, who sat unmoving with the lump of cedar in his lap.

He'd been carrying it around all morning. *Listening to it,* he'd earlier explained. There was enough to look at, like dried up cow ponds and despondent-looking bulls jostling for shade under rare trees, but Kendal stared unseeing down the highway. His fingers moved over the wood's surface like a blind man reading Braille.

"Are you okay, Kenny?" she asked him, using the name Chase had suggested he be called by.

"Sure," he said, though it sounded as though he were miles away.

Minutes later, he startled her by exclaiming, "I hear it!"

"Hear what?"

"I know what to carve," he clarified, with a hint of enthusiasm, the sound of which was a balm to her ears.

"Well, aren't you going to tell me?" she prompted.

"Nope, I can't," he retorted, turning it over to examine its underside. "Besides, it's for Chase."

"Honey," she said, her heart constricting with regret, "we're not going to see Chase again," she said gently.

He flashed her a rebellious frown. "You don't know that," he retorted. "No one knows what's gonna happen."

For some reason, his words made her shiver. "That's true," she conceded, mollifying him.

If only they *could* see Chase again. It would make the future seem less daunting, less uncertain.

After all, he'd given her a whole new lease on life. And despite what he did for a living, he'd always be her hero.

✦ ✦ ✦

With buzzards circling the cloudless sky, it seemed like an appropriate time to tackle Linc's study. Sara and Kendal were gone. There were no distractions to prevent Chase from getting the unpleasant business done and over with.

First he removed the window with the broken pane, intending to take it to the glass shop, later. Then he dragged the garbage bin around the house, setting it right outside the window hole.

Back in the office, he sifted through old magazines, some of which dated back to the years that he'd lived here. He lobbed them through the window, straight into the bin, to take to the recycling plant when he was done.

As with Sara's initial departure, the silence in the house was deafening. The walls seemed to whisper to him, snatches of conversations from his past; the sound of his mother grieving over the baby's death. God, she'd wept for weeks!

More than once, he caught himself walking toward the door to leave. But if he did that, the work would never get done.

The more propaganda he discarded, the angrier he became. The skinheads had killed his dog. The fuckers had put their hands on Sara, making her struggle enough to lose her ring, though she hadn't told him that—oh, no.

Because *that* would have tipped the scales. He'd have gone back to the Reeves place at nightfall, caught all three men by surprise, and beat the living shit out of them.

Why hadn't he done that in the first place? He'd let Sara talk him out of violence, just like she'd talked him into helping her escape the clutches of her maniac husband. It wasn't so much what she said, though, as how she'd looked at him.

Jesus.

And now he felt strangely lost without her, like everything was swinging out of his control, when it wasn't. He was doing exactly what he'd set out to do—cleaning up the homestead so he could rent it out.

That part of the plan hadn't changed; nor had his intentions that Sara would head for Dallas in a truck that she could keep. She'd had one false start, but she was gone for good this time, with the promise to call him from a rest stop halfway there.

Only, he hadn't gotten a call yet. Maybe that was the reason he was feeling so edgy this afternoon. He'd invested a lot in Sara. He didn't want something happening to her now, or to Kendal, when she was so close to freedom.

But—fuck—he wasn't lying when he said he'd miss her. He missed Ken, too.

He missed his dog.

With a shouted curse, he slung a wad of pamphlets out the window. Half of them scattered onto the grass. Swear to God, if he ever came across the men who'd shot Jesse, he was going to wring their necks. His hero status be damned.

A vibrating at his hip jarred him from his fury. He snatched up his cell, eager to hear Sara's voice. "Sara," he rapped.

Hesitation on the other end. "No, sorry, this is Dean," said Detective Cannard. Too late, Chase realized that the call was from the local area code. He grimaced at the oversight and perspired briefly for having used Sara's real name. "Go ahead," he said, wondering what the man wanted.

"I've been looking through the stuff you gave me," Dean volunteered. "Turns out that I won't need Ms. Jensen to press charges. There's plenty here that constitutes a crime: conspiracy to murder, for one thing."

"Glad to hear it," said Chase, thinking maybe the skinheads would get their comeuppance, after all. "Well, you know what I mean." Of course, he wasn't glad to hear of any type of conspiracy.

"There's even a mention of ANFO," Dean added. "You know what that is?"

"Ammonium nitrate with fuel oil," Chase confirmed, with a spurt of consternation, "explosive as hell." And all it took to come up with the lethal combination was fertilizer and car oil, both readily available, especially in an agricultural area.

"It's the same stuff Timothy McVeigh used in the Oklahoma City bombing," Cannard confirmed. "According to the minutes recorded at a meeting of the FOR Americans three weeks ago, the group has five hundred pounds of fertilizer mixed with fifteen liters of fuel oil, ripening in a truck somewhere. They plan to use it on Columbus Day."

Columbus Day. Chase turned toward the calendar that was still hanging on the wall. He flipped the page. That was a week from today. "What's the target?" he asked.

"I can't find that information."

"Sounds like Homeland Security ought to know about this," Chase suggested. "I have a friend in the FBI. If you want, I'll give her a call."

"We have our own FBI contacts," Dean countered. And

given the tone of his voice, he wasn't too thrilled with them.

"This one's a woman. She's smart and pretty, and she won't try to take over the department."

"What's her number?" said Dean. His chair creaked as he presumably reached for a pen.

Chase had to look it up on his cell directory. The thought of Hannah joining the BAPD's investigation brought him out of his sour mood.

So did Dean Cannard's unexpected offer. "Listen, one of our Special Ops Team members just pulled his back. I don't suppose you'd like to fill in for him?"

Chase had plenty of work to complete around the house, but the chance to avenge Jesse's death and escape a home filled with hurtful memories was too tempting to pass up.

"I'd like that," he said without a second's hesitation.

"Well, great. We're gonna meet on Thursday at two in the afternoon, Conference Room B."

"See you then." Chase snapped his phone shut with a renewed sense of purpose. Now he had some real motivation for getting his work done.

At the knock on her office door, Betsy Bartlett, Head Administrator at the Refugee Center, Norfolk, looked up from the federal forms she was perusing. Her secretary hovered in the presence of a stranger, whose angular features and thin mustache struck Betsy as vaguely familiar. He wore the uniform of a Navy officer. "Yes, Amber?"

"This is Mr. Garret," Amber began.

"Captain," he corrected her in a doleful voice.

"Sara's husband," Amber explained, although Betsy had just guessed that for herself.

"Captain Garret!" she cried, pushing immediately to her feet. She rounded the desk with both hands extended. "Please allow me to extend my condolences," she said, thinking of Sara and how much she'd been missed. "It just hasn't been the same without Sara here."

The captain's handshake was limp and faintly damp.

"What can I do for you?" Betsy asked, releasing him. Surely he was beyond despair at having lost, not just his wife, but his son, also.

"I'd like to collect Sara's things," he explained, his eyes too murky to impart any emotion in particular.

"Of course," Betsy answered, thinking of the few personal items Sara had left on her desk. "Would you care to follow me?" With a professional smile, she escorted Captain Garret out of the administrative offices and down the hall to the teachers' workroom, a large area shared by seven English instructors.

"This was Sara's desk," she said, stopping at a cubicle that was kept neat and tidy with only a few knickknacks, gifts from grateful immigrants—pencil holders and notepads, magnets, and a paperweight. "The police were here earlier this week," she divulged, "Looking for pictures of Kendal. They never did find any."

Captain Garret's eyes were glued to Sara's computer. "Could I have a look at her files?" he requested.

"Her files?" Betsy repeated, thinking it an odd request.

His head rotated in her direction. "I don't believe my wife is dead, Mrs. Bartlett," he told her. "If there's any way to find her alive, then no stone ought to be left unturned."

Oddly, Betsy's first instinct was to protect Sara's privacy. "I'm afraid her account is password protected. There's no way to access it."

"Your IT administrator has access," the captain insisted smugly.

Betsy sighed. That was true. And if there was any possibility that Sara's whereabouts might be made known by opening her personal files, it was her legal obligation to do so. "Charles," she called across the room, to a man working under another desk. "Do me a favor and get Sara's account running on this computer," she requested.

The heavyset man plodded over and squeezed his backside into the desk chair. Powering up the computer, he typed in his administrative password to open Sara's account. "There you are," he said, rising.

"We'll give you some privacy," Betsy offered, withdrawing.

Making her rounds throughout the center, she returned to the workroom several minutes later and was immediately struck by the difference in Captain Garret's demeanor. Gone was the long, mournful face. He was bent over the desk, gaze intent, fingers flying over the keyboard as he composed an e-mail, of all things.

Seeing her out of the corner of his eye, he promptly sent the letter, and before she could chastise him for taking liberties, he emptied the highlighted items in the open folder. "Captain Garret!" she called, bustling over. "What on earth are you doing?"

"What do you mean?" he countered, standing up to loom over her. "My wife's e-mail isn't anyone's concern but mine."

"Well—" He had her stymied there. "I hope you found

something of interest," she said, falling back on her concern.

"Not particularly." But the gleam in his dark eyes said otherwise. "Thank you all the same, Mrs. Bartlett," he replied. "Have a good afternoon." Swiveling on highly polished shoes, he strode from the room, leaving behind the personal items he'd supposedly come to collect.

"Well!" Betsy stared after him, utterly bemused.

Chapter Eleven

Pouring herself a bowl of cereal in her mother's minisicule kitchen, Sara heard a key slide into the lock at the door. It was just past six in the morning, the time when Rachel returned home from the hospital where she worked as a night shift delivery nurse. Her cat, a Russian Blue named Mosby, sprinted to the door to greet her.

With Kendal sleeping on the couch between them, Sara and her mother greeted each other wordlessly. Rachel deposited her purse on the coffee table and scooped up her cat as she crossed the room. "You're up early," she commented in a hushed voice.

"How was work?" Sara asked.

"Eventful." With a tired sigh, Rachel eased onto one of the two seats at the tiny dinette table. The window beside her overlooked the narrow plot of land in Willow Woods Trailer Park. "Eleven babies were born last night. Must be the full moon."

Sara transferred her bowl of cereal to the table to sit across from her. "Goodness, it must be."

"Trouble sleeping?" Rachel asked her, with a search-ing look.

"Not really. Back at the ranch, there was a rooster that woke me up at the crack of dawn every morning. I guess I'm still in the habit." As she chewed her cereal, hearing it crunch between her teeth, she was conscious of her mother's close regard.

During the first forty-eight hours of their reunion, all they did, it seemed, was stare at each other. Sara had been astonished to discover how much she resembled her birth-mother, right down to the second toes on their feet, toes that were slightly longer than the first.

They'd bonded on sight, unconditionally, in a way that bordered on psychic. But with seventeen years between them, their relationship was more sisterly than that of par-ent and child.

"What's on your mind, Sara?" Rachel asked her gently. "You're not still worried about being a burden to me, are you?"

Sara had mentioned that misgiving within minutes of her arrival. She sent Rachel a fleeting smile and shook her head. "No," she admitted. "It's a couple of things."

"Like what?"

"Like the school that Kendal is supposed to attend. It's huge," she added, with a tug of dismay. "He's shy around large groups. I feel like he's going to be swallowed whole."

Rachel nodded her understanding. "And what else?" she prompted.

Sara rubbed her forehead. "I don't know."

"Yes, you do," said her mother coaxingly.

"I miss the ranch," Sara admitted. "It was peaceful there—not that it's awful here or anything. It's just . . .

there was so much open space, so much quiet." And the trailer park where Rachel lived was just off the beltway, where the traffic circling the city of Dallas created a muted roar that never went away.

"And you miss Chase," Rachel guessed, prompting a startled look from Sara. Never once had she hinted of any deeper feelings for Chase than gratitude.

"Is it that obvious?" she asked, aghast.

Rachel smiled a little smile. "Only if you've been in love before."

Sara balked at the word *love*. She couldn't love a man who, in a week's time, might be on the other side of the world annihilating terrorists. "Missing him is pointless," she said, endeavoring to convince herself. "Even if I went back, he'd leave, and I'd still miss him."

"But you'd be living in his home. And you'd have hope that you'd see him again."

Perhaps she would, four years from now, when his enlistment was over. Then again, maybe not, given the memories that had kept him away in the first place.

Rachel's gaze shifted, taking on a faraway look. "You know, I thought that it would ruin your father's life if he learned that he'd gotten me pregnant. All he ever talked about was going away to college. I didn't want him quitting school to take care of me, so I didn't tell him. I wanted him to live his dreams. And to this day, I regret not giving love a chance. Sometimes it overcomes amazing odds."

Sara's heart contracted. "Do you think Chase would rent the ranch to me?" she asked, saying aloud the thought she'd been pondering lately.

"Why don't you ask him? Maybe he doesn't want you completely out of his life."

Hope buoyed her spirits. "But what about you?" she asked with worry. "I don't want you to feel like we're abandoning you."

"Oh, Sara," Rachel replied, her eyes soft with love. "Your adoptive mother raised you right. You have such a good heart. What matters most to me," she replied, reaching across the table to grasp her hand, "is your happiness. Do you think I could be happy keeping you here, knowing that you and Kendal are miserable?"

"We'd make pretty lousy housemates," Sara agreed. Especially Kendal, who'd done nothing but mope and carve obsessively at his hunk of cedar.

"Call him," Rachel encouraged with a tired smile.

"I will," Sara promised, experiencing a sudden case of the jitters. What if he turned her down? "Later," she added, "after I think about the best way to word it."

"Okay," said Rachel, sounding satisfied. "On that note, I'm going to bed." She rose to her feet and stretched.

Sara noted the wrinkles and stains on her nurse's uniform with respect. "Hey, Mom," she said, using that term for the first time ever.

Rachel sent her a startled look.

"Thank you," she said.

"Oh, baby, you don't have to. That's what moms are for." With suspiciously bright eyes, Rachel turned toward the rear of the trailer, leaving Sara clinging to hope.

Hearing a car come barreling up the driveway, Chase had to smile. He could tell that it was Hannah—Special Agent Lindstrom—who'd called his cell phone half an hour ago to say that she'd arrived at Tulsa Airport, and could he give her directions to the ranch?

Pushing his way out onto the front porch, he grinned at the sight of her behind the wheel of a cherry red Mustang, a rental car. Hannah had a thing for Mustangs. They were a reflection of her personality: American-made, with power-ful engines and a love for speed.

As she parked behind his car, Chase closed the space between them. She'd barely killed the engine before she was out of the door, throwing her arms around him.

He actually staggered back a couple of steps. Hannah was almost as tall as he was, with short, flame red hair. She could shoot a gun as well as any SEAL he knew and face down danger with a smirk on her face. Flamboy-ant and fearless, she was the perfect match for the six-and-a-half-foot Luther Lindstrom, lieutenant junior grade in Chase's platoon, and the most decent guy he'd ever worked with.

"Westy! Oh, my God, this place is so you!" Hannah exclaimed, pausing long enough to take in the house, the barn, and the big pecan tree, where her gaze snagged briefly on the headstones.

And then she was looking him over through dancing, green eyes. "Button-up shirt, jeans, big buckle, and the ubiquitous cowboy boots. Welcome home, Westy! This goatee is *so* much better than the Grizzly Adams look," she declared. She looked him straight in the eye. "How was Malaysia?" she asked, not having seen him since before he left on assignment last year.

"Hot, sticky, and crawling with lowlife scum. I'm sorry I missed your wedding," he added, with real remorse.

"I'm sorry we couldn't wait for you to get back," she replied.

"So what's it like, working for the FBI?" he inquired, flicking a glance at her juniper green pantsuit. She managed to look professional and sexy all at the same time, not that he was looking.

"Great!" She pivoted to collect her briefcase. "I'm on Valentino's field team, so I travel a lot, but never overseas, which keeps Luther happy. Right now we're setting our sights on a diamond smuggler," she added, slinging the strap of the briefcase over her shoulder.

"You're sure you've got time to catch a bunch of skinheads?" he asked her. If he were Luther, he'd be chafing to have his wife to himself.

"The Boss has given me a week to check this out," she reassured him. "And by that, I mean Valentino, not Luther. He wanted me home yesterday."

"This'll all be over in a week," Chase said grimly. "Come on in the house."

"Oh, my God, this is so quaint," Hannah exclaimed as she stepped into the cool living room—the central air had been serviced just this morning. Her gaze flitted over the couch, with its freshly laundered cushion covers, the gleaming hardwood floor, and the big bay window that Sara had scrubbed to a shine.

"Thirsty?" Chase inquired, turning toward the kitchen. He pulled open the pristinely clean refrigerator and poured them two tall glasses of lemonade.

"Thanks," said Hannah, chugging hers down as she checked out the kitchen.

Chase's cell phone rang. With a cartwheeling sensation

in his stomach, he recognized the number. "Excuse me a sec," he said.

"Sure." Hannah turned her back on him to survey the land through the kitchen window.

Chase strode into Linc's study, which held nothing in it now but a desk, empty gun cabinet, and an armchair in the corner. "Hey," he said, answering the call from Sara.

"Hi," she said, sounding hesitant. "How's it going?"

"Good. Can't talk much now," he admitted. "Hannah's here."

"Oh," said Sara. He'd told her yesterday that the FBI was getting involved in the quest to catch the skinheads, and, for that matter so was he.

"What's on your mind?"

"Maybe it should wait," she said uncomfortably.

He could sense her indecision as surely as if he were feeling it himself. "No, tell me," he urged, hoping it wasn't about Kendal, who'd withdrawn into his shell again, according to Sara.

He overheard her indrawn breath before she asked very quickly, "Is there any way you'd consider renting me the ranch?"

The walls around him seemed to jump closer. Chase slid his butt onto the edge of the desk to anchor himself. "You want to live here?" he asked, feeling a strange mix of astonishment and hope.

"I think Kendal would be happier in a small-town environment," she explained. As she spoke, he detected a throbbing note in her voice that betrayed a certain amount of desperation. "I mean, I totally understand if you don't want us there. You don't have to say yes, Chase, I just thought I'd ask."

Sara at the ranch. It wasn't the first time he'd considered the idea. "But . . ." He caught himself.

"What?" she asked on an anxious note.

"You sure you belong in a place like this?" he asked her. "I mean, it's a far cry from where you came from." He pictured the neighborhood where she'd lived with Garret.

That silenced her for two seconds. "I'm not the pampered miss that you think I am, Chase. My roots are as humble as yours are. If you're worried that you'll be responsible for us in any way, you won't," she reassured him. "And, of course, I'll pay the full rent, which I hope I can afford," she added belatedly.

Her feisty reply made his lips twitch. He liked it when Sara stood up for herself. "When're you figurin' on coming up?" he asked.

"What about tomorrow?"

The thought of her and Hannah crossing paths unsettled him. "You should wait till the skinheads are apprehended," he suggested.

"But that's part of the reason that I want to come back," she confessed. "I want to help with that. I'm the only one who knows what Will looks like."

Chase grunted his acknowledgment.

"And then there's Kendal, who's missed so much school now. I wanted to enroll him before Columbus Day."

Yeah, and his leave time was also dwindling. If he meant to spend any time with Sara, it was best that she came back soon. Obviously, he was going to have to tell Hannah what he'd done.

"Well, come on home, then," he invited, with a rush of anticipation that he didn't care to ponder too much.

"I will. See you then," she promised, hanging up.

Chase put away his cell phone with a self-mocking smile. As before, he just couldn't seem to tell her, *No*.

Members of the Special Operations Alpha Team, convened in Conference Room B at the Broken Arrow Police Headquarters around a long, rectangular table. Chase was introduced by Dean Cannard as a former resident of Broken Arrow, currently a counterterrorist Navy SEAL, who was standing in for their missing team member. Given the closed looks of the fourteen other SOT members, he was going to have to win their acceptance.

Hannah, on the other hand, had been warmly received. She sat at the head of the table, one ear cocked to the conversation, fingers poised over the laptop in front of her. Using a wireless connection, she had established real-time communication with FBI analysts at headquarters.

"Les Wright and Timothy Olsen can't be located," admitted the SOT leader, Captain Lewis, sitting back in his chair and crossing his arms. "The leader of the group goes by the name Will. Detective Cannard's found no mention of his last name in the evidence that we've gathered."

Hannah looked up from her laptop. "He's the former Army Ranger?" she inquired.

"That's the rumor," the captain corroborated.

"I'll have my analysts access the American Veteran's database," Hannah offered. "If there's a Will living in Broken Arrow and receiving pension benefits, then he's probably your man."

Captain Lewis flicked a glance at Cannard. "Good idea," he answered.

"And as for Les Wright and Tim Olsen, I've requested tax information from the IRS on both of them," Hannah added. "It never hurts to look at employment history."

"Excellent. We're talking about a group of at least ten members, none of whom can be located for questioning right now. All we have is a reference to a truckload of ANFO and the promise of a demonstration on Columbus Day. We need to bring some of the members in. I have our uniformed division out scouring the city for them."

"Let's talk about potential targets," Hannah suggested, keeping Chase from having to open his mouth.

Detective Cannard leaned forward to put in his two cents. "Well, I've reviewed all the evidence at our disposal; I've even had a couple of officers here look at it, but we can't find mention of the target anywhere. Given the racial bias of this group, it could be a federal building, as in the Oklahoma City bombing. It might also be an ethnic neighborhood or a school, or even a local company that's given jobs to minorities and laid off too many white workers. Who knows?"

A reflective silence stole over the table.

"The members of the group know," said Hannah, garnering everyone's attention. She gave them a cool smile. "You put up flyers all over town with Les and Timothy's pictures on it, and offer a reward. Does anyone know what Will looks like?"

Dean Cannard's gaze slid expectantly in Chase's direction. Hannah followed his gaze with a curious look.

"We may have to subpoena Ms. Jensen to give us a description," Dean said on an apologetic note.

Chase couldn't give him the excuse that Serenity was

gone, not when she was on her way back, even as they spoke.

"Who's Ms. Jensen?" Hannah asked, with a frown.

"Friend of mine," said Chase, earning a long, curious stare from her. Now that Sara had identification corroborating her new name, he supposed it wouldn't hurt if she gave a statement. "She's been out of town. I'll bring her in tomorrow."

Hannah put a thoughtful finger to her lips.

"See if you can get a composite sketch from her," Captain Lewis instructed Cannard, who gave a nod.

Chase was conscious of Hannah's burning regard throughout the rest of the meeting.

At last, the group disbanded, and she and Chase headed into the sun-baked parking lot, headed for the red Mustang. She'd insisted on driving, not because of her unlimited mileage but because she loved flying along the hilly back roads at way over the speed limit.

"Okay, Chase," she said, tossing her briefcase into the backseat, "spill the beans."

He waited until their car doors were shut and she was backing them out of the parking space. "You remember Sara Garret, the lawyer's wife at Jaguar's court-martial?"

She shot him a funny look. "Yeah, she and her kid disappeared a few weeks back."

Chase kept quiet, waiting for her to figure it out.

"Oh, no," she exclaimed with predictable horror. "Oh, my God, Chase!"

"Don't lecture me," he warned her. "You don't know what her life was like, what he did to her kid."

His words rendered her silent for a long, long while.

That didn't slow her speed, however. The Mustang screamed down the country road, turning the pastureland on either side into a green blur. Chase lost his stomach on a couple of hills as the car caught air.

"Chase," Hannah finally said, with a rare quaver in her voice, "that case was labeled an abduction. An Amber Alert was issued nationwide. Do you know what that means?"

He'd intentionally not given it much thought.

"It means," she continued with intensity, "that the FBI has jurisdiction over the case, which means that I have every right to arrest you right now."

"It wasn't an abduction," Chase insisted. He didn't suffer a moment's doubt that Hannah would arrest him.

"That doesn't mean that Garret won't press charges." She shook her head, shooting him a few more looks, each one more incredulous than the last. Unexpectedly, a smile seized the edges of her mouth, turning her frown into a grin.

"What's so funny?" he demanded.

"I never thought I'd see it," Hannah declared.

He had an inkling of where she was going with this.

"You're in love!" she cried, with a shout of laughter.

Chase's heart seemed to freeze over at the suggestion. He glowered at her, causing her broad grin to fade. "Don't say shit like that," he warned her. If she were any woman other than Hannah, he wouldn't talk that way. But Hannah, to him, was one of the guys, as good a friend as Luther was.

Her smile disappeared. "Come on, Westy, lighten up," she countered. "Everyone falls in love at some point in their life."

"Not me," he insisted, hardening himself further. "I

don't want you sayin' it again, especially not around Sara. She knows what I do. She doesn't need to be misled by some cock-'n'-bull notion that I'll be there for her. Besides, what would she even see in a redneck like me?"

"Are you kidding?" Hannah retorted, giving him a candid once-over. "You have to realize what a catch you are."

"I'm not a catch," he said, incredulously. "I'm a sniper. Everyone knows that snipers are psycho, especially the ones that've spent as much time in the field as I have."

"So maybe it's time to quit," she suggested gently.

"I just reenlisted," he articulated on a growl. "I can't fucking quit."

There wasn't a hint of humor left in Hannah's pitying look. "Just remember what you told me back when I was falling in love with Luther," she advised him.

He hated it when his advice was thrown back at him. "What?"

"Some things can't be planned ahead of time. You take them as they come," she tossed out, imitating his drawl.

And of course, she remembered that word for word. With a grumble of annoyance, Chase set his jaw, refusing to talk the rest of the way home.

Chapter Twelve

Sara quelled the impulse to jump out of the truck and run up to Chase the way Kendal did.

"We're gonna get a puppy!" he shouted, circling Chase like Indians circling a wagon train.

"I said to *ask* him, not tell him!" Sara chastised, reaching into the back of the truck. It was all she could do to behave like her heart wasn't leaping at the sight of him and her spirits weren't soaring.

"What's all this?" he asked, his gaze sliding to the boxes in the truck bed. He didn't greet her with the enthusiasm she'd privately hoped for.

"My mother took us shopping," Sara explained. "I tried to talk her out of spending money, but she said she'd gone forever without a daughter or grandson to spoil. She even bought Kenny a television."

"I'll get that." Chase took the unwieldy box out of her hands. As their fingers brushed, pleasure licked over her; but if he felt it, too, he hid it well.

Feeling strangely hurt, Sara grabbed a smaller box that was filled with some of her new fall wardrobe. She followed Chase into the house, taking comfort from the home she'd worked so hard to clean. It'd had been so heart-warming to see the ranch again, not as a temporary resting point but as a place to put roots down.

"I thought maybe your FBI friend would be here," she said, moving past Chase to the bedroom that would now be hers.

"She's stayin' at a motel in town."

Sara paused halfway down the hall and hefted the box higher. It occurred to her belatedly that Chase might have preferred to be left alone with Hannah. The agent was married to Chase's best friend, but that would account for his lack of warmth right now.

Disturbed by the thought, she deposited the box on the bedroom floor and went back to the truck for more. Kendal was carrying his TV into the house. "Be careful with that," she told him.

Going in and out several more times, she passed Chase again and again, never managing to time it right so they would be together. Their gazes met briefly. Each time he was the first to look away.

Finally, she blocked his path. "Are you sure you want me here, Chase?" she asked, her emotions in a wild flux. This wasn't how she'd pictured their reunion.

He gave her a long look, one that remained oddly detached. "'Course I want you here," he told her. "I just got a lot on my mind right now, tryin' to stop the skinheads before I have to head back East."

She nodded, her heartbeat faltering at the reminder of his impending departure. "When do you have to leave?" she asked him.

"Pretty much right after Columbus Day."

She nodded, digesting the information as unemotionally as possible. Chase wasn't the man for her. If only her head could persuade her heart of that.

"I need you to come downtown with me tomorrow and give a statement to the police. We need that physical description of Will."

"I can do that," she agreed, grateful for the new ID that she carried everywhere she went. Thanks to Chase, she also had a college transcript from Dartmouth College. "But I need to register Kendal for school first."

Kendal had fake transcripts from a school in Vermont and a copy of his shot records.

"No problem," Chase said, summoning a smile for her that wasn't entirely reassuring.

She let him step around her, taking the box he held into the house. To comfort herself, she regarded the sunflowers in the field, most of which had gone to seed. The nights had gotten cooler, and soon the sycamore trees, the first to turn, would flush scarlet.

Taking a long, deep breath, she savored the scent of prairie grass and dry air. *I'm going to be happy here,* she told herself. *With or without Chase.*

Kendal wanted Chase to walk him to the head of the driveway in order to meet his bus on his first day of school.

"Better ask your mother," Chase said, thinking that this was probably the only time he could actually put Kendal on the bus, since Monday was Columbus Day, a school holiday, and he'd be leaving for Virginia on Tuesday.

Sara, who'd fussed over Kendal's new school clothes

and packed his lunch box, looked momentarily non-plussed. "Well, of course, honey, if it's okay with Chase."

Chase, who was planning to mow the rest of the field this morning, got up from the breakfast table. "Sure it is," he said, eager to get out of the house. If he stayed in here alone with Sara, he was bound to betray his agitation. She was getting way under his skin.

At quarter to eight, he and Kendal stepped off the front porch to encounter an autumnal chill, the kind that stimulated the brain and made you actually want to go to school.

The sun set the tops of the trees on fire, warming Chase's face as they forded the driveway. He abandoned thoughts of Sara long enough to glance down at his bright-faced companion. "Not scared or anything, are you?"

While registering Kendal yesterday, Sara had expressed her relief that Country Lane Elementary School was the same size as Kendal's previous school.

"'Bout school?" he scoffed. "Nah, school's easy."

"You think?" Chase had dreaded school.

They stepped beneath the trees, where the thinning leaves overhead filtered through sunlight. "There's lots of things worse than school," Kendal added philosophically.

"Like what?"

"Like my father finding us."

Chase's stride almost faltered. "He won't find you here," he said, sending him a reassuring look.

But Kendal was watching his feet glide through light and shadow. "I wish you'd stay," he said quietly.

The words pegged Chase right in the chest. "We talked about this already," he said roughly.

Kendal swung his backpack off one shoulder and fumbled with a zipper, his steps slowing. "I made you some-thin' to take with you," he announced. Taking a palm-sized object out of his bag, he handed it to Chase.

It took Chase a second to recognize where it'd come from. What used to be a sizable hunk of cedar had been whittled down to a miniature box turtle.

He stopped to inspect it, turning it over with amaze-ment. The high, rounded shell bore hexagonal markings, each painstakingly delineated. Ken had even remembered to carve out three toes on the rear legs. "Wow," Chase said, touched by the gift.

"You said they were your favorite."

And he remembered that? "You sure you want to give it to me? Why don't you give it to your mama?"

"It's for you," said the boy, with gravity.

Okay. "Thanks," he said again, cradling it gingerly.

"Turtles carry their homes on their backs," Kendal added, meaningfully. "When you look at it, I want you to think about your home."

Jesus. "I will," Chase said, his voice thick. "Better walk fast," he added, glancing at his watch.

They arrived at the head of the driveway just as the bus came into view. As it pulled away, Chase watched Kendal's face grow indistinct in the rear window. His chest felt full and tight.

If he'd known three months ago that life was going to take this strange little detour, he wouldn't have reenlisted. Even back then, he'd hesitated before signing his name, wondering what he could do with his life that didn't entail living out of a duffel bag. The answer was nothing.

That was then. Right now he could think of plenty of things he'd rather do than jump out of a helicopter into some godforsaken country in order to thin the population. And every one of those things was right here on this ranch, where Sara and Kendal were.

Dean Cannard had just walked into his office when Chase McCaffrey and Serenity Jensen showed up at his door. As with the last time he'd laid eyes on Serenity, she enchanted him. There was something familiar about her, probably because she looked like Meg Ryan. He went for blondes in general, especially slim, pretty blondes with intelligent eyes and a manner of speaking that betrayed a high level of education.

"Well, hey there," he greeted them, waving them in. "Sorry 'bout the cramped quarters. Have a seat."

As they lowered themselves into the mismatched ladderback chairs, he reached for the phone. "Let me call Al, my lead crime scene investigator. He acts as our in-house artist."

Al promptly joined them with a sketch pad and pencil in hand. "Some departments go with computerized composites, but I still think that the hand-drawn ones are more accurate," he explained.

As Serenity described the leader of the FOR Americans, one feature at a time, Dean was content to study her. He liked the gentle way she spoke, with no hint of any kind of dialect. It'd been days since the skinheads had held her for ransom, but she remembered every detail of Will's face, from the sparse hair on the top of his head to the sickle-shaped scar on his square chin. She was observant, like he was.

He wondered if he'd ever have the chance to woo her.

That depended, of course, on exactly what her relationship with Chase was.

There wasn't any doubt that they seemed connected, even when they avoided eye contact, never touched. But they had nothing in common that Dean could see. Sara was obviously upper-class. Chase was still a good-ol'-boy, rough-and-ready and also extremely dangerous, given his military training.

"Where are you from, Miss Jensen?" Dean asked, prompted by his curiosity. He was conscious of Chase's blue gaze rising from the sketch-in-progress to skewer him.

"Er, Vermont," she answered, "near the New Hampshire border."

"You don't sound like you're from New England," he pointed out.

"I've moved around a lot," she explained.

She wasn't letting him know much, was she?

"You going to settle down here now?" he pressed.

Chase was definitely glaring at him.

"Yes," she said brightly. "I fell in love with Chase's ranch." She immediately blushed in the wake of her words, which sounded an awful lot like, *I fell in love with Chase*.

"Then you changed your mind about Texas," he guessed, enjoying himself. There was nothing like a mystery to intrigue him.

"I guess I did," she admitted. "Will's eyebrows were bushier than that," she said to Al, who angled the tip of his pencil to fill them out.

Dean waited until the drawing neared completion. He'd never seen the suspect before. If he had, he probably would've recognized him, as he rarely forgot a face. "So, when're you headed back East, Chase?" he inquired.

The Navy SEAL took his time answering. "I have a week of leave time left," he said with a steady stare.

"Takes, what, three days to drive that route?"

"A little less."

Dean caught back a chuckle. The man's jealousy was palpable. Too bad he was going to be so far away from Serenity for months at a time. From what Dean could tell about the woman, living on an isolated ranch wouldn't be easy for her. She'd need a man to lean on.

He'd give her two months to pine for her Navy SEAL. And then he'd ask her out to dinner.

"Okay, so what have we got?" Captain Lewis asked the group gathered around the conference table on Saturday morning. Hannah, curiously, was late. Chase had tried to call her cell phone but it was busy.

"Detective Cannard?"

Dean Cannard whipped out the composite sketch that Sara had helped put together yesterday. "This is the leader of the group," he announced, giving everyone around the table a good look. "Every officer in the uniformed division has a copy, and they're scouring the city for 'im, but we still have no last name, don't know who he is."

"What about the other two clowns?"

"Les Wright and Tim Olsen are nowhere to be found," Cannard admitted, with an edge to his voice.

Two bomb squad personnel from Tulsa had been called into the meeting, along with the fifteen SOT members, Chase included. They all sat there looking at each other.

Columbus Day was two days away. The suspects were at large, and the clock was ticking. Chase suffered the premonition that FOR Americans was going to get away with whatever bad shit it had planned.

Hannah burst into the dampening silence like a musical symphony. "Sorry I'm late," she said, bustling in with her laptop slung over one shoulder and papers in hand. Her pantsuit today was the color of a freshly cut watermelon. Nineteen pairs of eyes blinked at her as she handed the papers off to Captain Lewis.

"What's this?" he asked.

"We have a positive ID on Will," Hannah announced. "Do you mind passing out these copies? They're the reason I'm late. Willard Douglas Smith is his full name. He is a decorated veteran of the Vietnam War and a member of the Seventy-fifth Ranger Division. He retired in 1992 in Broken Arrow—at least, that's where his pension benefits are sent, to a PO Box address. I'm afraid I wasn't able to find a street address."

Chase hid a smirk behind his hand. Yeah, but she'd found a hell of a lot more than Cannard, who was staring down at the paper in his hand, looking chagrined.

"As for Les Wright and Timothy Olsen, the IRS faxed me their last year's tax returns. Both men worked menial jobs. Tim didn't even make enough income to pay taxes. I've requested five years of returns for Willard Smith. If he worked at all, we'll have a record of his employers, who might be of help in locating him."

Captain Lewis waited respectfully for Hannah to finish. "This is excellent," he admitted. "We'll disseminate this information to the public right away. We should have Willard apprehended in no time. SOT members, you're on call for the remainder of the holiday weekend. I'll keep you posted if anything changes. Flint and Sievers," he added to the bomb squad duo, "I'd like to talk with you a moment longer. Dismissed."

Chase was the first man out of his seat. "I've got to go," he said to Hannah.

"I'll walk you to your car," she said, snatching up her laptop. "Be right back, sir," she said, to Captain Lewis.

Chase glanced at his watch. This morning's meeting had lasted only twenty minutes, but he didn't like leaving Sara at the ranch alone, not even with phone service installed, especially not with the skinheads still at large.

"So, how's it going at the ranch?" Hannah asked, matching his long stride as they headed toward the exit.

"Fine," he said shortly. He'd struggled for two nights straight with the burning desire to sneak down the hall and slip into Sara's bed. But the fear that Hannah was right, that he really was in love, had kept him paralyzed.

Hannah eyed him sidelong. "You can't even leave her for half an hour," she pointed out. "How're you going to leave her for months at a time?"

He came to an abrupt halt, causing her to step back warily. "I told you not to talk about that."

"It's not going to go away."

The aching hunger inside him *had* to go away. He couldn't operate like this in the field. He had to be cool, completely unemotional. He turned toward the exit. "You're invited to dinner tonight," he said, switching topics abruptly as he pushed open the door for her.

"Really?" Hannah asked. "Isn't that going to make Sara uncomfortable?"

"Serenity," he reminded her. He didn't answer her

question until they were clear across the parking lot, out of range of anyone who might overhear. "She doesn't know that the FBI gets involved with Amber Alerts," he explained, sending her a warning look. "And she isn't going to find out from you."

"Gotcha," said Hannah, with a wink.

"See you at six," said Chase, dropping into his car.

He left Hannah standing on the curb, contemplating his haste with a lopsided grin.

Chapter Thirteen

Hannah arrived at Chase's ranch at promptly 7:00 P.M., which was quite a feat, she acknowledged, giving herself a mental pat, because it was pitch-black already, and there wasn't a single streetlight on any of the roads headed out of town, only the welcoming light on Chase's front porch.

As she knocked on the door, Hannah tried to wipe the little smirk off her face. But then she recalled how often Chase had smirked at her when she'd gone through the wringer, falling in love with Luther a year ago. Payback was such a bitch.

He pulled the door open. Seeing her expression, he gave her a warning scowl. "Behave yourself."

She was hit with the wonderful aroma of chicken enchiladas. The woman coming out of the kitchen taking off oven mitts couldn't be Sara Garret. "Hello," she said, with a shy smile. "I remember you."

It took Hannah several seconds to realize that, yes, she *was* Sara Garret. The eyes and the cheekbones were the same, but that was all. "Holy Toledo," she exclaimed, "you look completely different!" From the hip-hugging, bootleg jeans, to the flattering knit top to the blond tips of her short, spiky hair. "No wonder Chase is crazy about you."

"Dinner ready yet?" he interrupted on a testy note.

"I just need to set the table," Sara rushed to assure him.

"I'll do it," he said, relieving her worried look.

Minutes later, they sat down at the scarred kitchen table, joined by Kendal, a quiet, watchful boy, who vaguely resembled the photo that Hannah had peeked at on the FBI Web site for lost and missing children.

Watching the threesome eat, Hannah couldn't help but notice how comfortable they seemed with each other. Chase kept Kendal's milk cup filled. He made a point of praising Sara's cooking. She, in turn, handed him the salt without his asking. It was like they'd known each other for years.

And yet, Chase had been adamant that Sara was too good for him, from a different world. Hannah set out to prove him wrong. "So, Sara—Serenity," she caught herself, with an apologetic smile, "forgive me if I get too nosy, but what is it that you plan to do for a living?"

"Pretty much what I did before," she replied, "which was to teach English to speakers of other languages. I've checked with the local library, and they said they're fine with letting me use their facilities for tutoring."

"That's great. So you majored in English in college?"

"Linguistics," Sara corrected her.

"She has a master's degree," Kendal piped up, speaking for the first time.

Oh, dear. And here she was trying to bridge the gap. Undaunted, Hannah plowed on. "Linguistics," she mused, glancing at Chase. "You speak several languages, don't you, Westy?" she asked him.

Sara eyed Chase with surprise. "You do? What do you speak?"

Given the wry gleam in his eyes, he knew exactly what Hannah was up to. "Enough Malay to keep myself from getting shot. Basic Thai," he added. "I used to speak Bosnian, but that's rusty."

"And you went to language school for . . ." Hannah left it to him to fill in the blank.

"French," he finished.

"He speaks French like a native," Hannah boasted. "You should hear him."

Sara looked at Chase like he had horns growing out of his head. "I went to France as an exchange student my junior year," she volunteered. *"Pouquoi as-tu besoin d'apprendre le francais?"* she added, asking him why he'd needed to learn French.

"Not everyone likes Americans," he answered succinctly.

"This past year he pretended to be a French botanist while cozying up to an arms smuggler with a passion for plants," Hannah divulged, noting Sara's intense interest. "Is it okay for me to tell her that?" she asked, sending Chase a wide-eyed look.

Chase just frowned at her.

"A botanist," Sara marveled, with a visible shudder for the danger inherent in such a mission. "I didn't realize that your concealment had to be so complete."

"It was a special assignment linked to a CIA-related endeavor," Hannah explained. "Not his usual thing."

"I knew a lot about plants already," Chase admitted,

shifting the focus to his cover. "'Course the varieties in Southeast Asia are different from the plants I grew up with," he acceded with a shrug. "But it wasn't that much of a problem learning what I needed to know."

"I love to garden," Sara confided. "I was thinking that all those pots on the step could be put to good use, if you don't mind," she asked him.

He stabbed at his food. "Why would I mind?" he answered.

Sara's smile lit her up from the inside. Chase glanced up and stared.

Watching him wrestle with his attraction was probably the best entertainment Hannah had enjoyed in years. She couldn't wait to tell her husband that Westy, the baddest boy in SEAL Team Twelve, had fallen hard.

But the evening wasn't over yet. They retired to the living room, where Kendal popped a video about bobcats into his VCR. He'd checked it out at the library. Hannah seated herself intentionally in the armchair, leaving Chase and Sara to share the sofa. She sat at one end; he at the other.

But every glance, every nuance of their body language, betrayed nerve-plucking awareness of each other.

An hour later, Hannah decided to let nature take its course. Chase trailed her into the kitchen, where she carried her glass. "You're not leavin', are you?" he asked with a hint of desperation.

"Yeah, it's getting late. I need to pester some IRS people who left the office early on Friday. I still don't have those tax returns for Willard Smith that I requested."

"You could stay a little longer," he suggested.

She put her hands on his shoulders, thinking he was

certainly a lot shorter than Luther was. "You'll be fine without me, Westy," she reassured him. "Stop fighting it," she added on a whisper. "That only makes it worse."

The muscles flexing under her hand were every bit as dense as Luther's, though.

With a sisterly pat, she let him go. Bidding Sara good night, she thanked her and Kendal both for an enjoyable evening.

Chase escorted her out to her car, notably quiet.

"Check in with me tomorrow," Hannah invited, slipping behind the wheel. She couldn't wait to find out how his evening ended.

"Take it slow on the way home," he replied. "Watch for deer."

She backed up, executing a swift U-turn. A final glance in her rearview mirror showed Chase still standing in the driveway, looking as tense as a loaded gun.

Hannah chuckled.

Sara tucked a sleepy Kendal into bed. They discussed the possibility of a play date tomorrow with Kendal's new friend, Eric. She left his room, confident that he would be happy here in Broken Arrow, even after Chase was gone.

Hearing Chase in the shower, she slipped into her own room to prepare for bed. She had just donned the pale pink nightgown Rachel had bought for her and was heading to the kitchen for a glass of cold water, when Chase emerged from the bathroom, towel girded around his hips.

They collided—slinky polyester meeting warm, moist skin—and jumped back.

"Sorry."

A tense silence ensued as they eyed each other under the hall light. A water droplet slid from Chase's collarbone, over a dense pectoral muscle, and down washboard abs, drawing Sara's gaze down to where the towel covered his lean hips. His half-naked splendor made her head spin. She reached for the wall, needing it to keep her balance.

"Good night," Chase said, but he seemed incapable of turning away.

She thought of the kiss they'd shared before she left for Texas. For days after, she'd recited all the reasons why she couldn't kiss Chase like that again. Oddly enough, she couldn't recall a single one of those reasons right now.

With an impulsive step, she closed the space between them, rolled up on her toes, and kissed his cheek. "Good night."

His response was far more demonstrative. In a lightning move, he hooked an arm around her waist. He hauled her against him, caught her lips with his, and kissed her hard.

With a groan of relief, Sara kissed him back, blindly, arms coiling around his neck, fingers sliding into his damp, wavy hair. The kiss was a scalding eruption of repressed passion.

It escalated to the next level as Chase backed her against the wall, using the partition to secure her to him as he slid his scorching palms up her body and cupped both of her breasts. "Tell me to stop," he commanded roughly.

"Don't stop," she countered, welcoming the heady plundering of his tongue as he kissed her again.

He grasped her bottom, lifting her higher. His towel shifted. Sara groaned as his arousal prodded her hip.

With a glance at Kendal's closed door, he turned and half carried Sara into her darkened bedroom, kicking the door shut behind him.

There in the cool shadows, he kissed and kissed and kissed her, until her senses were befuddled, and she was too weak to stand.

He eased her onto the edge of the bed. "Be right back," he promised, releasing her.

As he disappeared down the hall, securing his towel as he went, she wondered what he was up to. At the same time, she questioned herself. Was she really going to do this, acting against her better judgment?

But how could she stop now, when every cell in her body, every nerve, every inch of skin cried out for his touch?

Chase reappeared with a fistful of shiny wrappers. He'd closed the door and tossed them onto the bedside table before she realized what they were.

"Oh," she said, wondering how to tell him that condoms weren't necessary.

He didn't seem inclined to talk. He reached for her again, pressing her gently back into the patch of moonlight that warmed her sheets. Then he came up over her, tugging the towel off his hips.

Oh, my heavens.

Her heart pounded with anticipation. She'd never seen anything more erotic than the way Chase looked, braced on his elbows above her, eyes hot with desire, fully aroused.

"You're so beautiful," he rasped, his thoughts obviously running parallel to hers.

He put his mouth to the artery that pulsed warmly at the side of her neck. With nips and licks, he followed the slender column to the curve of her shoulder and lower, pushing down the straps of her nightgown as he went. He peeled back the slinky fabric of her gown, revealing her breasts to the moonlight.

With a groan, he lowered his head. Sara gasped and arched her back, welcoming the scalding heat of his mouth as he worshipped her tenderly, honestly. Her fingers sifted through the untamed locks of his hair, finding it soft, silky to the touch.

Drawing her nipples into peaks, he blew a moist stream of air over them as he lifted the hem of her nightgown past her thighs. His work-roughened hands skimmed her hips, her abdomen, and slipped between her legs to caress the warm, moist fabric in between. "Sara," he whispered with intense feeling.

She couldn't believe it either, that her private fantasies were becoming real, that they were even more powerful than she'd imagined.

She touched him back, smoothing her hands over the breadth of his shoulders, to the furred mounds of his chest muscles, over rock-hard abs, and lower, until she held him in her hands, thinking . . . *Oh, yes, this'll be nothing like it was with Garret.*

But then he was easing away from her, and she realized his intent with a hot flash of anticipation. His tongue slid warmly along her inner thigh, so close that she thought she would die. Then, again, closer still. He dragged her panties over her hips and nudged her legs apart.

She had to fist the sheets to keep the bed from whirling. Intense, heated pleasure spread from the apex of her thighs to her breasts, to every extremity of her body. Chase pressed his palm into the plane of her pelvis. He slipped a finger into her warmth, and then two, his tongue never ceasing its gentle lashing.

A fever swept through Sara, moistening her skin. She looked down at her breasts, gilded with moonlight. Beyond them was Chase, his bright eyes watchful even in the dark, waiting for her to . . . *Oh, my God* . . . to fall apart.

With a sob of bliss, she climaxed.

He brought her gently back to earth. When her eyes fluttered open, he was reaching for a condom.

"You don't need that," she said, hardly recognizing the husky voice that came from her.

At the verge of tearing it open, he hesitated. "You want me to stop?" he asked on a strange note.

"Oh, no. Oh, Chase, I wouldn't do that." She came up on her elbows. "It's just that . . . you can't get me pregnant. I can't have any more children."

Even in the shadows, she saw his searching look. "Complications?"

"Lots of complications," she admitted. "So many that I gave Garret Power of Attorney because I was hospitalized for weeks before my due date. I had no idea he'd use it the way he did."

Chase frowned and waited.

"He told the doctor that I wanted my tubes tied so that it would never happen again," she added. "Garret told me later that he never wanted children in the first place."

Chase didn't move. Sara sensed his anger growing. "I have to say something," he finally grated. "That man had better not come anywhere close to you ever again, or I'll rip his fucking head off."

The lethal tone in which he spoke made Sara's blood run cold. "Don't say that," she whispered, not in defense of Garret but because she didn't want Chase to have to go to jail for protecting her. "He won't find me here," she reassured him.

"No," Chase agreed with a shuddering breath. He reached out and gently stroked the side of her face, "I'm sorry," he added. "I shouldn't have said that."

"That's okay." His vehemence gave her hope that he cared about her, enough to come back to her when his four years were up. His gentle touch had her melting all over again.

He drew her lips toward his and kissed her in a way that indicated that he wasn't going to stop this time.

She thrilled at the silent, possessive message. She wanted to be claimed by him, utterly and completely taken. With a groan of surrender, she fitted her body to his, optimistic that their union would bind them in a deep and mysterious way, keeping him in her life.

Cradling her close, he kissed her as he eased into her welcoming wetness. She could sense his restraint. He was being gentle with her, penetrating inch by slow inch, as if she might otherwise break.

"More," she begged, hips surging to meet him. She wanted to be overcome, to be whisked away to another world, stolen from the past and made his.

Still, he held back, permeating her senses with ecstasy, one layer at a time until, at last, there wasn't any question that she was his. With a cry of relief, Sara gave rein to her sexual expression. After years of repression, nothing felt more intensely satisfying than Chase cradling her, straining to get closer, deeper. Surely, they'd return to this again and again.

It was a homecoming.

He even went the extra mile to ensure that she was with him at the end, sliding a hand between their bodies to coax her over the edge. They tumbled together, bound in a way that defied explanation.

Chase was afraid to move. He was still inside of Sara, subject to aftershocks, following a tsunami of a climax.

The vulnerability that hit him in the wake of that natural disaster had him holding his breath. If he moved, something around his heart would shift like tectonic plates on the earth's crust, bringing more calamity.

Her chest rose and fell beneath him, faintly damp, incredibly soft. "Oh, my goodness," she breathed a note of discovery.

He forced himself to speak. "You okay?"

She gave an incredulous laugh. "Okay? Oh, yes, I'm okay."

He grunted, still afraid to move. He just clung to her.

She smoothed the hair from his face, quietly content to let him hold her. "I have to say something," she finally whispered, mimicking his sentence structure earlier. "And I don't really want to say it but, if something were to happen to you . . . I'd want you to know."

He swallowed convulsively.

"I think I love you," she said on a note of wonder.

He flinched instinctively. In the past, when his lovers said those words, he'd carefully withdrawn his warmth and passion, making it gently clear that he had no heart with which to love them back.

Only this time, he could feel his heart expanding, rising toward his throat. Agony and euphoria raked through, digging through the crust that hardened him.

For no reason that he could comprehend—except that it'd happened right here in his mother's bed—he relived his earliest childhood memory.

It was the night of his father's death. His mother held him in her arms. He remembered her tears falling onto the backs of his hands as she held him close and sobbed.

Years later, he'd been the one to hold her, as Linc covered the baby's grave with dirt.

They'd had each other. Up until the day they rushed her to the hospital where she'd died.

The day they'd brought her body home and put her in the ground next to the baby, Chase realized, with relief, that he couldn't feel a thing.

He'd turned his heart off, flipped the switch.

It was exactly that ability that made him good at what he did. He killed for a living, untouched by torment or remorse.

How could a simple *I think I love you* bring back all the loss and pain that his mother's death should have caused him?

To his horror, it hit him with crushing force, dragging him under waves of despair. A sound like a sob ripped out of him. He hid his face against Sara's neck, mortified.

"It's okay," she soothed. It was as if she understood. "I'm here."

He couldn't make it go away. The grief that he'd buried when he was fifteen years old was suddenly resurrected, prompted perhaps by Jesse's death. The pain was staggering.

Sara held him fiercely, wordlessly, as he choked on his sobs.

After a long, long while, the agony receded to manageable proportions. Chase rolled to his side, and held his breath to regain his composure. Mortified, he kept his eyes closed.

Sara turned to face him. He could tell, even with his eyes closed, that she was looking at him in the moon glow.

He was unable to explain himself, so he pretended to sleep. What did she think of him now? he wondered. Was she brokenhearted that he hadn't returned her words of love? Or did she think that he was certifiable?

He felt her move and quelled his startle reflex when she reached out to stroke his cheekbone and the line of his jaw. She looped an arm around him and snuggled closer.

Still mortified, he didn't think he'd sleep at all. At the same time, a blessed calm stole over him, followed by bone-deep contentment, and he fell asleep in an instant.

Chapter Fourteen

Drugged with the lethargy of sexual release, Sara slept through the rooster's crowing. She opened her eyes to find the room awash with sunlight. Chase was gone, but that came as no surprise. Last night was the first time she'd ever seen him sleeping.

Straining her ears, she sought a clue as to what he was doing. The house remained quiet. A lark twittered in the pecan tree outside.

Sara tossed back the covers. Stepping into her bathroom, she brushed her teeth and hair while gazing dreamily into the mirror and wondering how last night was going to change things, if at all.

Chase would still head back East on Tuesday. He'd still function as the sniper of his SEAL team. His work was dangerous, and he could die.

But surely something had changed. Last night, he'd revealed himself to her in a way that he hadn't before. He'd wept in her arms—something she was certain had never happened with any other woman. That certainty gave rise to tenderness that crested the walls of her heart.

She'd said that she loved him, and though he hadn't answered her with words, his actions had conveyed a depth of feeling that went beyond mere friendship.

So, where was he now? Putting down her brush, she left the bathroom to seek him out.

He was not in the kitchen making coffee. Sara peered toward the barn, but the doors were tightly shut. His car and the truck were both parked out front. Where could Chase be?

The sound of a gunshot rent the peaceful quiet. Sara gasped, spinning in the direction of the sound. The skinheads! Her first thought was that they'd come to the ranch to seek reprisal for fact that the law was now actively hunting them down.

Rat-tat-tat-tat-tat.

The burst of gunfire had Sara stifling a scream. What should she do? The buck rifle was locked inside Linc's truck, mounted to the gun rack. Should she endanger herself by running out of the house to get it, or should she call the police for help, then lock herself in Kendal's room with her son, to wait?

But could Chase hold them off all by himself?

Rat-tat-tat-tat-tat.

Peering in the direction of the gunfire, Sara realized that she was panicking for nothing. Chase stood just beyond the pecan tree, firing down the driveway. She squinted in the direction that he was firing and made out the target that he'd put together the other day, standing way back by the tree line.

He was just practicing his shooting.

Panic gave way to anger. How dare he scare the daylights out of her by holding target practice at seven o'clock on a Sunday morning!

"Mom?" Kendal called from his bedroom.

"Go back to sleep, honey. Chase is just practicing his shooting."

She pushed angrily through the front door, not stopping to analyze that her upset might have more to do with the fact that Chase wasn't doing something tamer, like cooking breakfast. She was about to shout his name when he lifted his submachine gun and fired again.

With a cry of frustration, she rushed down the steps and along the pebbled driveway, wincing as the rocks gouged the bottoms of her bare feet. He had to have seen her. Nothing ever escaped his notice.

"Chase!" she said, as he lowered his weapon to assess his aim.

He turned his head in her direction, and she faltered, rethinking her approach.

He looked angry. Truly angry, though not necessarily at her, because his gaze slid with appreciation to her breasts, which jiggled freely beneath the material of her gown.

She stopped about fifteen feet away from him. "Must you do that at seven in the morning?" she asked him, smoothing the frustration from her voice. "I thought that the skinheads had come here to fight it out!"

He propped the butt of the wicked-looking rifle on the toe of his boot. "The skinheads?" he repeated, arching one eyebrow.

She regarded him more closely. It was obvious to her that he'd donned some sort of emotional armor. It hardened his facial features, making him inscrutable.

Sara's arms stole across her midsection. The cool morning air settled damply on her bare limbs. She stood there, stunned by the aloofness in his gaze, wondering if she'd imagined how close they'd been the night before. "Is that so unreasonable?" she heard herself ask. "They're still at large, right? They must know that we're the ones who told the police about them."

With a nasty smile, Chase snatched up his gun again. "They wouldn't dare come here," he said in a voice that made the hair on Sara's arms prickle. He sighted down the driveway again.

"Don't!" she said with a renewed burst of anger.

He lowered the tip of the rifle but continued to glare at the target like he wanted to annihilate it.

"I wanted Kendal to sleep in today. Just stop it!" With that, she whirled and ran, ignoring the shooting pain of rocks on her tender soles. Tears blurred her vision as she ran up the front steps and into the house. *Stop behaving like nothing happened.*

That was what she'd really meant. How could he withdraw from her so thoroughly, after opening up to her last night?

Moving past Kendal's quiet bedroom, Sara locked herself inside her own room, half-fearful, half-hoping that Chase would pursue her. She threw herself onto the bed, hugging the pillow that Chase had used last night. It smelled like him, like fresh-cut cedar. Hot tears leaked between her tightly shut eyelids.

She had known it would come to this. Chase might be the laid-back, considerate soul she'd always thought him. But, as he'd revealed that night on the front porch, he wasn't like other men. He'd been driven into a profession that few could stomach. He'd reenlisted for another four years. A man like Chase didn't settle down into loving relationships, didn't work a farm, didn't raise a family.

But he could, eventually, when his enlistment is up, insisted a stubborn voice inside of her.

With a sharp sniff, Sara sat up and wiped her cheeks. The Chase she'd fallen in love with wasn't a calculated killer. She remembered how he'd smiled when they'd surprised the doe in the woods. She thought of how he'd taught both her and Kendal to trust again.

He'd never to this day failed her expectations of him.

Which meant that, in time, he *would* come home to them. She had to believe it.

But could she wait four agonizing years for that to happen? That would be foolish. No, she needed some indication from him now—a promise—that he'd come back. Back to the childhood home he couldn't wait to leave in the first place. Such a promise would be hard to coax from him, a man who buried his heart deep inside of himself.

But there was a way. He'd expressed an enormous quantity of feeling the last time they'd made love. Obviously they needed to make love again so he would open up to her. Perhaps then he'd offer the promise of a future she was looking for.

Dean Cannard didn't ordinarily work on Sunday mornings, but with members of the FOR Americans still at large, and wanting to redeem himself in Captain Lewis's eyes, he dragged himself into the office at 8:00 A.M.

The FBI agent, Hannah Lindstrom, had managed in one day to dig up more on Willard Smith than Dean had in nearly a week. In order to uphold his reputation in the department, he intended to find out everything else there was to know about Willard Smith, including his criminal history, if there was one.

With a cup of black coffee within reach, Dean put his fingers to his keyboard, and by midmorning, he'd traced Willard's history from his boyhood in Stillwater, Oklahoma, though his years of service with the Army Rangers. He'd seen twelve years of combat in the Vietnam and Gulf Wars combined and received the Bronze Star for meritorious service. Following his retirement in '94 from Ft. Belvoir, Virginia, he disappeared off the map.

If the man had no criminal record, he was bound to get a slap on the wrist and nothing more when the police apprehended him—provided they captured him before his planned "demonstration."

In the state of Oklahoma, Willard's record was clean. Dean directed his search to Virginia's databases, where he learned that Willard was wanted for using a firearm in the commission of a felony. "Got you now, bastard," he muttered, taking notes.

Clicking on the Web site's homepage, he looked for a point of contact in Virginia. Even as he jotted down a name and number, his eye was caught by a flashing link: AMBER ALERT.

Professional curiosity made him click the link.

Photographs of a mother and son and a composite sketch of their abductor held his attention for a scant second. Closing the screen, he went back to the home page.

Halfway through jotting down the contact number, he hesitated.

Just one minute. He never forgot a face, and he knew those eyes.

With a stab of shock, Dean hit the Amber Alert link again. It couldn't be Serenity Jensen. The woman in the photo had unremarkable hair and blurred features. But the eyes were Serenity's. Or was that possibly a coincidence? Every person in the world had a look-alike, it was said. His gaze fell to the name of the woman: Sara Garret. Her son's name was Kendal.

Sara. That cinched it. Chase had used that name the day when Dean called his cell phone. He'd been expecting her to call him.

Dean had never actually laid eyes on Serenity's son—though wasn't that a telltale sign? She hadn't wanted Dean to see the boy.

Dean focused on the composite sketch of the stranger who'd supposedly abducted them. It had to be Chase McCaffrey, even though the man in the sketch had a full beard.

"Well, I'll be a monkey's uncle," Dean murmured, his heartbeat quickening. He read the news articles linked to the sight, thoroughly distracted from his original search.

Authorities had started off labeling the case a stranger abduction. Since then, they'd backed away from that theory. It was now believed that Sara Garret had run off with her son, enlisting help from the bearded stranger. The case would soon be demoted from an Amber Alert to a mere parental abduction.

Dean was damn glad to hear it. Otherwise, he would be duty-bound to arrest Chase McCaffrey, something he really didn't want to do. Not only had they gone to school together, but the man was way too dangerous to try to arrest. Besides, he needed McCaffrey's help to take down the skinheads.

Dean sat back, reviewing the information at his disposal. For Serenity—Sara Garret—to have run away from her husband, a Judge Advocate General in the Navy, and a captain at that, life had to have been pretty awful. He wasn't about to reunite the two.

The smart thing to do was to keep her true identity a secret—one that he wasn't above using to his benefit at the right time. Once Chase was gone, Dean would reveal that he'd known who she was all along; that he'd protected her identity. That ought to win him a few points.

Maybe once she trusted him, he'd stand a chance to steal her heart.

More than anything in the world, Chase longed for concealment, but there was nowhere to hide. He felt like he'd parachuted into the middle of a war zone with no Ghillie suit for camouflage. He'd be dead before he blinked his eyes.

Firing his MP5 earlier had helped. It had summoned the unfeeling warrior in him, until Sara flew out of the house to berate him.

Glimpsing the disillusionment in her eyes, he'd wanted to banish it. Only he knew what would happen if he did: He'd find himself in even worse condition than he was.

He couldn't let that happen.

For the next four years, he needed to remain what he was before: more machine than man, aloof and detached. Otherwise, he was doomed to fail, to suffer the remorse that plagued other snipers. Resurrecting his buried heart was not an option.

At all costs, he had to avoid a repeat performance of last night. And since he couldn't count on himself to be that disciplined, he had to avoid Sara.

Fortunately, there was still much to be done before heading back on Tuesday. He had to stain the shutters, fix the leaking faucet for the hose, organize the tools in the barn. It shouldn't be too hard to steer clear of her for two short days, especially if the skinheads acted on their threats. On the third day, he'd be gone.

He was kneeling in the weeds beside the house, working a pair of needle nose pliers into the faucet, when Sara appeared on the porch with Kendal in tow. She had her new purse dangling from one shoulder and the truck keys in her right hand.

"Hi," she said. Her gentle smile put him immediately off-balance. Where was the disillusionment he'd glimpsed this morning?

"Where you goin'?" Chase asked, sitting back on his heels. She looked amazing in jeans, sexier than she'd ever looked. She'd put on a little bit of makeup, too. She was going to set the town on fire, going out looking like that.

"I'm taking Kenney to Eric's house to spend the night," she said, swinging the truck keys. "Then I'm going to Lowe's to buy mums for these pots. Remember, you said I could?"

"Sure." He experienced a stab of envy, wanting to go with her to pick out the plants. Envy was followed shortly by panicked recognition of the fact that they would be alone tonight. "I thought we were gonna sleep on the porch tonight and look for bobcats," he said to Kendal, who jammed his hands into his pockets.

"I changed my mind," said Kendal, not meeting his gaze.

With a constriction in his chest, Chase recognized that the boy was protecting himself by withdrawing emotionally, in anticipation of Chase's departure.

"I'll be back in an hour," Sara added, heading for the truck. "Come on, honey."

With the feeling that time was slipping through his fingers, and worried for their safety, Chase trailed after them. Sara turned her gorgeous eyes on him as he sidled up next to her open window.

"Be careful," he said, glancing in to make sure their seat belts were buckled. He suffered an almost overwhelming impulse to kiss them both.

"We'll be fine," she assured him, pulling the gearshift down. And with that, she backed up.

Chase watched her turn the truck around and roar away. He ought to be grateful that she wasn't mad at him or crying tears of unrequited love. She'd gotten herself together, and by all outward appearances, she was going to get by just fine without him. Kendal, too.

That was supposed to reassure him, but it didn't.

Sara peeked out of the office window. The mums she'd transplanted into the pots this morning splashed color onto the front porch. Satisfied with the appearance of the house from the outside, she focused this afternoon on personalizing Linc's office.

She was very much aware that the clock was ticking. Since dropping Kendal off at Eric's, Chase had gone out of his way to avoid her. Obviously, it was going to take extreme measures on her part to coax a promise out of him. He was still in the barn, organizing tools.

She needed a good reason to call him into the house.

Eyeing Linc's desk in the center of the room, she realized she would rather have the desk facing the window, where she could take in the view, only it weighed two hundred pounds, at least, and she couldn't move it herself.

With a prayer for courage, Sara went to fetch Chase.

She was startled to encounter him in the kitchen, chugging down a glass of lemonade. His eyes hit her like lasers as he watched her approach.

"I didn't hear you come in," she confessed. "Um, do you have a spare moment? I could use your help in moving the desk over by the window."

He put the glass down warily, and followed her without a word.

With every nerve in her body tingling, Sara positioned herself at one end of the desk. She waited for him to take the other, and together they slid the desk next to the window. That had been way too easy.

"I'm thinking of converting the gun cabinet into a big bookcase, if you don't mind," she volunteered, keeping him from leaving. "Eventually, I'll have a bunch of textbooks, and I'll need a place to put them. It looks like the hooks come out and I can raise the shelves on the bottom. What do you think?"

He eyed the empty gun cabinet. "That oughta work," he said, avoiding eye contact.

"I'll need a computer eventually, too. But that's still down the road a ways. It's kind of scary starting up a business without a safety net," she added, giving voice to her concerns, encouraging him to talk about the future.

When he glanced in her direction, he was frowning. "I've been thinkin' 'bout that," he admitted gruffly. "I don't want you payin' me rent."

"Oh, I wasn't angling for a handout," Sara protested. "A little moral support would be nice," she added lightly.

"You know you have that," he said evenly.

She just looked at him, willing him to say more.

"Sara, if you need anything, you can call me," he invited gruffly. "My cell phone works anywhere in the world."

She allowed herself a sorrowful smile. "And what about you?" she asked.

He shook his head. "What do you mean?"

"What if you need me, Chase? Are you going to call?"

He didn't answer right away. "Look"—he sighed, breaking eye contact—"I'm going to be gone for the next four years. I can't give you what you deserve in a man."

And that was supposed to convince her to surrender all hope? Not likely. She had more faith in him than that.

"That is so untrue," she said, defending him. "You're the most giving man I know. Whether you're here or on the other side of the world, I can sense what's in your heart. This isn't about your inability to care for me, Chase. This is about your fears and the fact that everyone you ever loved was taken away from you."

He blinked. It was the only sign that her words might have penetrated his emotional armor. His gaze swung toward the door.

Sara made her move. It was now or never.

She crossed to the door and locked it. "You're not leaving this room," she said, releasing the top button of her pale yellow blouse, "until you admit that you're hiding from your feelings."

The ultimatum was ridiculous, considering the ease with which he was capable of overpowering her.

But Sara was certain that the desire roaring through her veins was having the same enthralling effect on him. With trembling fingers, she released all the buttons at the front of her blouse. Beneath his stunned regard, she let it slip from her shoulders, revealing the pale pink bra she wore.

The heat that entered his eyes was unmistakable.

Sara had never seduced a man in her life. But in this case, the reward was worth the risk of rejection.

She released the catch and zipper of her jeans, relieved to discover that she'd donned matching panties. She kept those on as she pushed the soft denim over her hips and kicked it off. "Tell me this doesn't move you," she challenged.

He swallowed hard, but he couldn't manage a single word.

Emboldened by his helplessness, Sara crossed to where he stood. She slid her hands up his torso, over his broad shoulders and down his muscle-corded arms. The control he exerted to hold himself in check made him rigid.

She rolled up on her toes and pressed her lips softly, coaxingly to his. He held perfectly still, not kissing her back, but not resisting her either. His eyes drifted shut, as if he thought he could hide that way.

Sara moved her hands to the buttons at the front of his

camo pants. In a moment he'd have nowhere to hide. One by one, she released the buttons that strained to keep his fly closed. Ruddy color suffused his cheekbones, a reflection of the blush that heated Sara's own face.

Never in her life had she played temptress. But the innate, feminine knowledge came to her now, emboldening her to slip a hand into the slit of his boxers and free him. Ignoring his halfhearted mutter of protest, she sank down onto her knees and took him into her mouth.

His whispered curse was the reassurance that she needed. But glancing up, she found his eyes still closed.

"Look at me," she demanded, banding him with her hand.

He shook his head, no. He couldn't.

"Look at me, Chase," she repeated, more compellingly.

His slit his eyes, giving her a glimpse of the desire fulminating in him. It filled her heart with hope. Setting her mind on his gratification, she prayed it would open the floodgates that it had the last time.

But, all of a sudden, he was pulling away, lifting her to her feet. "Stop," he commanded, seizing her upper arms. "You don't have to do this," he growled angrily.

"But I want to," she reassured him, "because I love you."

His chest expanded at the declaration. He looked like he might explode.

"Make love to me," she pleaded, desperate now, because she sensed the struggle in him, sensed that he might just abandon her here, leaving her without hope, demoralized.

He pulled her abruptly against him, enfolding her in

his arms. With an ear pressed to his chest, she could hear his heart thundering. "We shouldn't," he said.

"But you want to," she pointed out.

"You don't understand what you're asking me. I can't *feel* like this and still do my job."

"You say that as if you have a choice," she marveled, tilting her head back to look up at him.

"That's just the point," he growled back. "I don't have a fucking choice!"

Because the government owned him, she realized. This was her last bid to claim some part of him for herself. "Make love to me," she said again, seeking his lips with hers. She kissed him enticingly, toppling the barricade that he fought to keep erected.

Second by second, she sensed his capitulation. And yet, one stubborn part of him continued to resist, making his kisses rough and resentful. She didn't care. She gave herself all the more sweetly, wrapping one leg around his hips to pull him closer. He half groaned, half cursed at the offering he couldn't resist. He swung her toward the armchair in the corner of the room and pressed her down into it.

And then it was his turn to drop to his knees, scowling at his own weakness. He jerked her hips forward, and she fell back, elbows braced on either of the chair's arms, chest heaving, still wearing her bra.

He didn't take the time to pleasure her, but she knew the reason why. He thought if he did this quickly, it would have less impact on him.

He yanked her panties over her hips and dragged them off. Pulling her hips to the edge of the seat, he positioned himself between her legs and surged deep inside.

Sara swallowed back her cry—not of pain but of emotional overload as she accepted his anger, his helplessness, his resistance, and ultimately his overwhelming need.

He made no attempt to be gentle. His possession was swift and hard and punishing. But if he meant to repel her, he failed miserably. She was with him through the storm, all too willing to experience what she'd been denied for years, the abandonment to lust. Her body convulsed and burned and grew taut at the same time that his did.

The harder his thrusts, the more she strained to meet him. With her heart thundering in her chest, Sara was the first to surrender. She made no attempt to conceal her ecstasy as she rode the crests of rapture. Through her lashes she beheld Chase's astonishment. He hadn't expected her to come at all. Her pleasure was a catalyst to his. With a groan of denial, he buried his face between her breasts and followed her into paradise.

For a long time, neither of them moved. Chase's breath came in and out, raggedly. Sara waited.

In the wake of such a powerful storm, how could he not offer some tangible promise of his return—verbal or nonverbal?

At last he pulled out of her. With his face averted, he adjusted himself, buttoning up his pants. "I'll get some tissues." He used that excuse to disappear from the room while she sought to recover her modesty.

By the time he came back, thrusting bathroom tissue in her hands, he'd retreated once again behind his scowl. "Sorry if I hurt you," he said on a humble note.

"You didn't," she reassured him.

A long, awkward silence followed in which Sara

clutched the wadded tissues in one hand while her panties grew damp. Chase's blue eyes considered her as if she were a weighty problem.

"What do you want, Sara?" he finally asked her.

She didn't have to think about her answer. "I want you to love life again."

He scowled at her vague answer. "How am I supposed to do that?" he demanded.

"By recognizing that you're not alone. We're here, waiting for you."

With a whispered curse, he turned and walked away, giving no indication of whether her bid for assurance had resulted in victory or was an all-out failure.

Chapter Fifteen

Rachel Jensen got stiffly out of her economy-sized car, relieved that her working weekend was finally over, and she would actually have the holiday off.

The sun was just beginning to rise over her trailer, casting warm, golden rays onto the willows that dotted the park. A few of her neighbors were up early, lights shining in their windows. Unlike her, most of them would not have Columbus Day off.

Rachel was grateful for the reprieve. She couldn't wait to sprawl between the cool layers of her sheets and sleep to the hum of her white noise machine, which drowned out the drone of Dallas traffic.

Inserting her key into her front door, she realized, with an unpleasant start, that the lock had been compromised. The door could be pushed open.

She'd been robbed. Oh, no! Thinking immediately of her valuable ring collection, she stepped into her mobile home, never considering that the burglar might still be inside.

He was waiting for her.

At the sight of a tall, dark-haired stranger seated on her sofa, Rachel drew up short.

He calmly pointed a gun at her. "Close the door."

She did. The warm glide of her cat performing figure eights around her ankles created a bizarre contrast to the cold fear that gripped her spine. "Wh-what do you want?" she demanded of him.

"Where is she?" the man asked. His tone was silky, his voice well modulated. Yet he looked rumpled, like he'd slept on her couch for the last six hours.

"Who?" Maybe he'd come to the wrong house. She could set him straight and send him on his way.

The man reached inside the lining of his black suit and produced a platinum ring. "My wife," he said, baring his teeth in what was meant to be a smile.

It was Sara's wedding ring, the one she'd given to Rachel to add to her collection, insisting that it was the least she could do since her mother had spent so much money on them.

Rachel opened her mouth and closed it with a click. What could she say to throw him off the scent? "She's not here," she said, quickly. "I don't know where she is. She decided to move on."

Garret's eyes narrowed. "You're lying," he said, standing abruptly, his head scant inches from the ceiling. "I read the e-mails that you two exchanged. The plan was for her to live with you."

"She changed her mind," Rachel insisted, determined to show no outward sign of fear. Men like Garret preyed upon the weak. She knew because she'd married one such man herself. "We didn't get along."

"Why would she have left you her ring, then?" He closed the small space between them.

"She forgot it here." It was all Rachel could do not to cringe as he cast his shadow over her.

"Another lie," he insisted, without raising his voice. "But then, all women are liars, aren't they? Sara's no different than my mother, and neither are you."

His mother? Oh, yes, Sara had hinted that Garret's problems stemmed from being left in boarding schools while his mother went through a string of failed marriages.

That wasn't Rachel's problem. It shouldn't have been Sara's. "Why don't you go home," she recommended, forcing herself to meet his dark-as-ink eyes. "My daughter doesn't want you in her life."

His pursed lips resembled bloodless earthworms. "Tell me," he growled through clenched teeth, "where she is."

"I told you, I don't know."

His hand shot out of nowhere. The slap that cracked across Rachel's cheek knocked her back against the wall. "Does that jar your memory?" he asked, threatening her again.

Rachel hadn't survived two bad marriages by backing down. "I wouldn't tell you if I knew," she retorted, nonetheless leery of the gun clutched in his right hand.

"Oh, you'll tell me," Garret insisted, capturing her neck in his left hand. With incredibly long fingers, he pinned her against the wall and squeezed.

The pressure in Rachel's temples swelled. Her lungs burned. Still, she glared at him defiantly. She would happily lose consciousness before acquiescing to his tyranny.

With a growl of rage, Garret slung her aside. Her face

hit the door. She rolled as she fell, striking her hip against the desk by the door. The pain that knifed through her was stunning.

The German shepherd, penned outside, two trailers down, began to bark.

Rachel lost consciousness, but only for a second. She was aware of Garret raging away from her. She heard him kick her purse over; heard her keys tumble out. She cracked an eye and saw him stooping down to snatch something else that had fallen out—the accordion-style address book where she kept a record of her closest contacts.

Outside, the German shepherd barked again.

Over the ringing in Rachel's ears, she heard him riffle through the names. "Don't know where she is, hmmm?" he gloated, finding Sara's name with ridiculous ease. "As I said, all women are liars."

She expected him to shoot her. The pain in her hip was so excruciating, she half anticipated the relief that oblivion would offer.

The air shifted. Then, out of nowhere, came a bone-shattering kick to Rachel's ribs. It knocked the air from her lungs, stifling the scream that tore from her throat.

With the dog now barking stridently, Garret turned and slunk out of her home, so quietly that she couldn't hear him over the roaring in her ears.

She lost consciousness again.

She roused to pain many minutes later. It took a moment to recall why she lay on her living room floor, her body broken and uncooperative.

Oh, God, Sara's husband came looking for her! He left with her address.

Rachel had to warn her!

But she was paralyzed. She couldn't move without causing herself unbearable agony.

"Help!" Her feeble voice drove home the extent of her isolation. No one was going to hear her, not even the German shepherd who'd stopped barking.

The only way to warn Sara was to crawl for the phone on the other side of the room.

Digging her nails into the carpet, Rachel pulled. She almost fainted again as her ribs screamed in protest. Determined, she repeated the movement again . . . and again, inching across the room, swimming in and out of consciousness.

I will not give up my baby a second time.

That determination kept her trying.

It came as both a relief and a distraction to be summoned to the BAPD headquarters to await orders in anticipation of the skinheads' demonstration. Chase occupied an inconspicuous seat in the corner of the lobby, next to a potted plant, where he chafed to get under way, only the target had yet to be revealed.

Even after exhaustive measures, the police were reduced to responding to the threat rather than preventing it.

Chase still considered himself an outsider. His partner, a fellow by the name of Robison, had tossed him a load-bearing ballistic vest with pockets full of ammunition, radio, and flash bangs. But beneath the vest, Chase's fatigues were Navy issue with a different camouflage pattern than the fatigues worn by the SOT team. He was content to remain low-profile, as long as he felt that he was avenging Jesse's death.

The team leader, Captain Lewis, paced between Dean Cannard's office and the Information desk, where the phones rang nonstop. Civilians were responding to the wanted posters dispersed throughout town by the uniformed division.

But even now, eight hours into Columbus Day, the police had few solid leads. The skinheads were still at large, and their target was a big fat question mark.

Hannah stood over the fax machine, arms akimbo. Wearing FBI-issue battle dress, including a Magnum holstered to her chest, web belt loaded with ammo, and calf-high boots, she looked like a redheaded version of Laura Croft. Tapping an impatient toe, she waited for the fax machine to spit out paper. At last, an employee at the IRS was sending the requested copies of Willard Smith's tax returns.

Chase recognized the exact moment that Hannah noted something of interest in the returns. She reached for her briefcase, snatching out the papers that she'd copied the other day. She took a second to compare the two. "Captain," she called, causing Lewis to join her in a hurry. "This may be coincidental, but Will Smith and Tim Olsen both worked as landscapers at Indian Springs Golf Course. They either quit at the same time, or they were fired."

The captain shrugged as if to say, So what?

"If their jobs were given to minorities, that'd be an incentive to strike back, wouldn't it?" she proposed.

Lewis frowned skeptically. "A country club seems like a pretty unlikely target," he replied.

A memory popped into Chase's mind, prompting him to speak up for the first time. "What's a duffer?" he asked.

Hannah, the captain, and fourteen SOT members looked over at the seemingly random question. He asked it again.

"What's a duffer?" They all looked at each other. No one knew what a duffer was.

Right then, Dean Cannard popped out of his office, coffee mug in hand. "Duffer? That was in yesterday's crossword puzzle. It's slang for bad golfer."

Chase stood up and tightened his ballistic vest. "They're gonna target the country club," he announced with absolute conviction. "Willard Smith told Sa—Serenity that he was going to teach those liberal duffers to look after their own."

For a second, nobody moved.

Dean broke the silence. "Well, hot damn," he said, glancing at the captain. "That's the break we've been looking for."

Captain Lewis narrowed his eyes at Chase. "You'd better be right about this, McCaffrey," he warned.

Chase just headed for the double doors and the van parked outside.

"Okay, let's go," Lewis shouted, making his decision. "Into the van," he ordered. "Let's stop this thing before it starts."

Chase held the doors for the fourteen other members to file through. Hannah caught up to him, hefting her briefcase. "I'm coming, too," she informed him.

Chase thought of the five hundred pounds of ANFO that the skinheads were purported to have at their disposal. "Keep your distance," he warned. God forbid anything happened to Hannah on his watch. Luther'd never forgive him.

Dean Cannard caught up with them. "Mind if I catch a ride with you, ma'am?" he asked Hannah.

She slanted him a frown. "Aren't you in the criminal investigations division?"

His smile was sheepish. "Yeah, but I get bored sitting behind a desk all day."

"I can relate to that," she muttered. "Sure, come on." With a nod at Chase, she struck out toward her Mustang, leaving Chase to clamber into the SWAT van with the other scouts, snipers, and entry experts. Given their closed looks, they weren't at all convinced yet that the country club was the target area.

Chase eased onto the narrow bench and donned the headset that Robison passed to him. The rear doors clanged shut, and they were off.

His thoughts drifted to Sara. It was his last full day in Broken Arrow. He couldn't stop regret from stitching through him. At the same time, he was grateful for the day's distractions. They prevented him from taking her to bed again, which was all he could think about. Why was it that making love with Sara could terrify and satisfy him at the same time?

It made him worry that he just might be in love. On the heels of love came empathy, then remorse. Moreover, love hurt—more than knife wounds, bullet wounds, or sleeping on mangrove roots. Falling in love would be suicide.

Yet no woman ever deserved to be loved more.

It put him in an awful quandary.

He couldn't save her this time and still save himself.

The radio crackled in his ear, returning his thoughts to the present.

"Heads up, men. We have a situation at the country

club. At least one shooter is firing at golfers on the green. There's a man down on the fourth hole."

Fourteen pairs of eyes swiveled toward Chase, who raised his eyebrows just a tad.

The team leader quickly assigned their tasks. Chase and his partner, Robison, along with one other sniper pair, would flush the shooters from the trees. Scout teams one and two would determine the status of the clubhouse, keeping an eye out for the truckload of ANFO. The five entry guys would remain on standby. In the event that the bomb was pinpointed, Flint and Sievers would be sent in to disarm it.

Chase felt the van veer off 131st East Avenue and bounce into the long drive that led to the clubhouse. It came to a halt.

"Go, go, go!" the team leader shouted.

The snipers and scouts jumped out to find themselves just down the lane from the clubhouse. Chase swept a gaze over the lush terrain. A hardwood forest framed the golf course, providing adequate cover to the shooters.

He signaled to his partner that they would cut through the woods, taking out hostiles as they came across them. Robison nodded.

Chase had been here only once before, as a boy. He waved Robison ahead of him. Together they penetrated the woods at a stealthy run.

They hadn't covered fifty yards when the sound of a gunshot rang out, followed by a woman's scream, then another gunshot. Then silence.

Chase pinpointed where the shots had come from. In his earpiece, he could hear the scouts giving a head count on the number of civilians rushing for the safety of the clubhouse. "Oh, shit," one of them breathed. "There's a closed truck with no plates parked at the food services entry."

The unwelcome news made Chase draw his gun. He sprinted past Robison, who was heavy on his feet, determined to take out the shooter with the least amount of time wasted.

Keeping ten yards between them, they swept the area from which the shooter had fired. On this side of the golf course, vegetation was thick, with plenty of ground cover. On the other side, the woods had been thinned to provide golfers a better view of the glinting Arkansas River.

Chase was the first to spot the shooter. The man was crouched behind a bush, gun pointed toward the green. With a silent leap, Chase tackled him. In the next instant, the man's rifle was ten yards away, his nose shoved into the moss at the base of a tree, and Chase was securing his wrists with a black nylon tie-tie.

Robison snatched up the rifle and emptied it of ammunition.

"Who's out here with you?" Chase demanded in the man's ear. "Where're your friends?" He wondered if this was Timmy or Les. Bearing down on the pressure point on the man's shoulder, he quickly got the answers he was seeking.

There were two other shooters, positioned at forty-five-degree angles around the clubhouse, a hundred yards out.

Chase secured the man's feet so that he couldn't get away. *Let's go,* he signaled to Robison, who left the familiar-looking Remington propped against a tree.

As they went to stalk the others, news floated over

Chase's earpiece that Flint and Sievers couldn't get close to the bomb. An invisible sniper, location unknown, was keeping the entry guys at bay. He'd also shot three civilians trying to leave the clubhouse.

Chase altered direction. Thumbing his mike, he requested Sniper Team Two to pursue the skinheads on the golf course. He was going after Willard Smith, because that was who the shooter had to be.

And chances were it would take a Navy SEAL to catch an Army Ranger.

With Robison crashing through the woods in his wake, Chase raced toward the clubhouse at a silent run. The single-story, brick structure stood in an open area with no other buildings around it, other than an outdoor changing facility at the far end of the swimming pool.

Keeping his squad mates apprised of their location, he and Robison took cover behind an ornamental wall, a brick job that flanked the driveway. Peering around it, Chase immediately spied the three bodies on the clubhouse steps.

Shit. At least one of the victims—a small child—was still alive, making time critical. Not to mention that the fuse in the stockpile of ANFO was probably set to ignite at any moment.

A mental timer started ticking in Chase's head. *Tick, tick, tick, tick, tick.* Chase's heart was beating twice that fast.

He put himself in Willard's position. Where would he be, if he wanted a view of both clubhouse doors, as well as the delivery bay for the restaurant?

He'd be high up in a tree, above it all.

There were only four large trees within range of the clubhouse. Chase scanned them all, his gaze settling on a large oak. He waited, his pulse bouncing off his eardrums. He watched. *Come on, bastard.* And then a branch moved.

It could have been a breeze but . . . no, there it was again. The shooter was propped along a branch about thirty feet up. Chase could just make him out, covered in a green mesh that camouflaged him almost perfectly.

"Sniper located," he said into his mike. "Permission to take him out, sir."

"Request confirmed," the team leader replied, with relief in his voice.

Even though he'd been the spotter, Chase didn't give the shot to Robison, who was the designated shooter. He whipped the SIG from its holster and flicked off the safety, favoring it over the MP5 which would destroy a good portion of the tree. Chase was angling for a little more finesse than that.

He broke from the cover of his hiding place and sprinted in a zigzag fashion toward the oak. He had to get close enough that he wouldn't miss. One shot, one kill was the motto he'd abided by for sixteen years.

Braced for the impact of a bullet slamming into him, he sprinted toward the oak. A round of pellets punched into the soft soil at his feet, letting him know that Smith had seen him coming.

He accelerated in panic, reaching the safety of the oak's broad trunk where he paused, catching his breath. He had the advantage now, and Willard knew it.

What goes up—he thought, preparing to spin around the trunk and fire—*must come down.*

He dodged left, praying that Willard expected him to

come out the other way. He fired with his body still in motion. *Bang!*

An abbreviated roar assured Chase that he'd hit his mark. Willard rolled off the limb where he lay and dropped. He was probably dead before he hit the ground.

With all the skinheads believed to be accounted for, the entry team burst out of their sundry hiding places and swarmed the building.

Chase joined them. *Don't blow,* he prayed, thinking of the truckload of ANFO set to explode at any minute. Sweat drenched him beneath his fatigues and heavy vest, but his training kicked in, as he focused on sweeping the child on the front steps out of harm's way while the entry team stormed past, into the building.

With the young girl in his arms, Chase turned tail, sprinting from the building. His respect for the entry guys soared to phenomenal heights. He could hear them shouting at the civilians to evacuate. The more reluctant members had to be wrestled outside, where the dead couple still lay in a mangled heap on the steps.

Chase glanced down at the fragile life in his arms. The little girl couldn't have been more than five or six. She'd been shot in the shoulder and was losing blood fast.

"Keep going," he urged the civilians scurrying in panicked confusion around him. "Other side of the parking lot."

He laid the girl in the grass. As he hunted through the pockets of his ballistic vest for medical gauze—anything to stop the blood from pouring out of her—he realized he was shaking. Badly.

Maybe it was this unlikely location—the heart of America, where shit like this wasn't supposed to happen. It could have been the tender age of the girl herself. Whatever the reason, this situation was upsetting the hell out of him.

The couple he'd left for dead on the steps were probably her parents. Pressing a square of gauze to the welling bullet wound, he was struck by the cruelty of her circumstances.

He was feeling the girl's weak but steady pulse when Hannah dropped onto her knees beside him.

"Oh, no." She looked behind her at the couple still lying on the steps. "Oh, God."

"She'll live," Chase said in a rough voice, though he doubted she would even want to live when she realized that her parents were gone forever.

Hannah put a comforting arm around him. "I need to see how Flint and Sievers are coming along with the bomb."

No one would breathe deeply until word came that the detonation cord had been severed.

Chase, who'd been listening to the wail of ambulances for what seemed an eternity, waved down the first ambulance to scream up the country club's long lane.

Two others bounced onto the golf course, toward the victims who'd been shot on the green.

"All clear," Chase heard in his mike. "The bomb is rendered safe. The building secured."

A halfhearted cheer went up among the SOT members and bystanders.

With relief, Chase relinquished the girl to paramedics, who packed her shoulder in ice and lifted her onto a gurney. He was still standing there with his heart in his throat when her eyes flickered open and she looked straight at him.

Something in her pretty eyes reminded him of Sara.

Disconcerted, Chase turned away to help round up the skinheads, who were promptly read their rights.

Willard Smith, on the other hand, was being zipped into a body bag.

Trying to shake off his jitters, Chase watched Hannah weave in and out of the milling crowd, making notes into a handheld tape recorder. The sudden vibrating of his cell phone had him reaching into his thigh pocket, heart rate leaping with the adrenaline that hadn't fully receded. Who could be calling him?

He frowned at the familiar number, trying to place it. "This is Chase," he said, needing a clue.

Heavy breathing sounded on the other end.

"Who's this?" he demanded, unsettled by the sound.

"Tell Sara . . ."

The whispered words brought every hair on his head standing at attention, especially when it came to him that the number was Rachel Jensen's.

He covered his other ear in order to hear over the noise around him. "Tell her what? Are you okay?"

"He's coming . . ."

"Who's coming?"

A muffled thud on the other end told him that Rachel had dropped the receiver. "Shit!" Chase hissed, severing the call. He immediately returned it, but the line was busy. Next he dialed the number to the ranch. *"Come on,"* he urged, as the phone rang and rang, "answer the phone, Sara!"

But no one answered.

"Problem?" asked a familiar voice. It was Dean Cannard,

standing directly behind him. He'd just overheard Chase call Sara by her real name.

Ignoring the man, Chase hurried toward Hannah, who was helping an officer identify one of the dead civilians. "I have to get back to the ranch," he said, trying to keep his words from coming out with gunfire urgency. "Can I borrow your car?"

But there was Dean, right behind him. "What's going on?" he demanded.

Chase glanced at him impatiently. "Back away, Cannard. This has nothing to do with you."

The detective wisely took a step back.

"Chase," Hannah admonished. Grabbing his arm, she steered him to one side. "What's the matter with you?"

"Sara's in trouble. I think Garret's found her. Can I borrow your car?"

"Oh, shit," she breathed. "I'm coming with you." She whipped her car keys off the ring on her web belt. She glanced at where Cannard was standing, glowering at them. "He might as well come, too," she said to Chase. "We may need police support."

"I know who Sara is," Cannard added, looking agreeable to Hannah's suggestion. "If she's in trouble, I'd like to help."

I bet you would, Chase thought with a spurt of jealousy. "Let's go," he said.

With Captain Lewis taking puzzled note of their retreat, the threesome raced for Hannah's red Mustang, parked at the country club entrance.

Chapter Sixteen

Sara carried the gardenia plant under one arm, as she and Linda Mae walked the perimeter of the yard, looking for just the right combination of sun and shade. It had been Chase's suggestion that their neighbor be invited over while he volunteered his services with the BAPD.

His concern for her and Kendal was touching, Sara had thought. But considering that he was leaving the next day, she didn't see what difference it made.

"It's so nice that you like to garden," Linda Mae commented. "So did Chase's mother."

Sara eyed the graveyard beneath the pecan tree. "Why don't we put the bush by Marileigh's grave?" she suggested.

"That's a lovely idea!"

Sara set the pot between Marileigh's and Blessing's headstones. Filtered by the leaves of the mammoth tree, the sun's rays would be constant, but never too harsh.

"Perfect," exclaimed the older woman.

Sara dug a hole eight inches deep. "Did you hear a phone ring?" she asked, looking up.

"No." Linda Mae cocked her silver head to listen. "But then my hearing's not the best."

Sara went back to work. She turned the plant out of its pot and centered the root ball in the hole. As she patted the earth down, she imagined that she heard the phone again. "Kendal?" she called, thinking that her son could answer it. Eric's mother had brought him home about an hour ago.

"Boo!" he said, jumping out from behind the tree trunk.

"Oh, my goodness!" Sara put a dirty hand to her chest. "Where did you come from?"

He grinned at her, obviously proud of his stalking capabilities. "You didn't even hear me," he boasted.

"No, I didn't. I guess you're getting good at walking like Chase."

The sound of a vehicle coming up the driveway had her glancing over her shoulder with pleasure that she couldn't squelch. It had to be Chase, who'd been gone for hours. But the maroon sedan that eased out of the tree line was unfamiliar. A trickle of foreboding had Sara coming to her feet. "Let's go inside," she said. "Someone's been trying to call, I think."

Grasping Kendal's hand, she hurried for the front door, aware that Linda Mae was following them with a puzzled expression. On the steps to the front porch, Sara looked back, telling herself she was overreacting. The skinheads were being dealt with today, and Garret would never find her here. She and Chase were both certain of that.

But then the glare that sat on the car's windshield lifted as the sedan passed beneath the pecan tree, and suddenly Sara could see the driver clearly. His height made him instantly recognizable. So did the pinched, angry look on his face as he bore down on them.

Oh, merciful God, it's Garret. He's found us!

While one part of her insisted that she only had to stand her ground and reason with him, another part of her whispered the need to flee and flee quickly. They were well beyond the point of reasonable conversation.

"Quick, honey," she said to Kendal. "Out the back door and into the truck."

As they raced through the kitchen, she could hear Garret addressing Linda Mae, who'd parked herself on the front steps, hindering his entrance.

The truck was in the barn today, but the barn doors stood open. "Run," Sara urged, and they sprinted across the backyard, out of Garret's sight. She indicated for Kendal to clamber through the driver's side door. He did, grabbing his seat belt and locking it into place, his face ghostly pale. Sara spared a glance for the buck rifle. which was mounted to the gun rack behind her. God forbid that she might actually have to use it!

With fingers that shook, she turned the key.

The engine rumbled to life.

Flooring the accelerator, she shot out of the barn and around the house, where Garret stood menacing Linda Mae, his gaunt cheeks mottled with rage. They both looked up, astonished to see Sara roar by, flinging up dust and gravel.

Watching in her rearview mirror, Sara saw Garret run for his car. She accelerated, gripping the steering wheel until her knuckles ached.

She tried to wake herself from what was surely a nightmare. This couldn't be happening. Just when she was certain that her life had started anew and the past would never find her.

With an ice pick of fear stabbing him in the chest, Chase noticed the dust hanging over the driveway as Hannah braked beside Linda Mae Goodner. The woman stood before the house, wringing her hands, eyes wide with fright. She stepped over to Chase as he lowered his window.

"Where's Sara?" he barked.

"She took off in the truck with Kendal—"

"How long ago?"

"Five minutes, maybe. Hurry! That man is chasing them!"

With a nod, Chase signaled to Hannah to turn around.

Linda Mae stepped back, and Hannah flew into reverse, flinging the Mustang 180 degrees to point it in the right direction. Cannard, who sat in the backseat with his knees to his ears, gave a hoarse screech.

"Hold on there, cowboy," Hannah warned him. "Where are we going, Chase?"

"I don't know."

Would Sara have had the sense to drive into town, headed straight for the police station? Or would she automatically take the route she'd traveled several times now, away from Broken Arrow, toward the Muskogee Turnpike?

"Left or right?" Hannah asked him when they came to the head of the driveway.

Chase surveyed the asphalt in either direction. He lowered his window and sniffed the air. "Right," he said, detecting a trace of exhaust fumes left by an oil-burning vehicle.

Hannah accelerated to sixty in mere seconds, flinging the occupants of the car against their seats.

Chase forced himself to consider the worst-case scenario: The truck was slow and easy to overtake. Garret could pass her, force her to stop, walk straight up to her, and shoot her dead.

If he had a gun.

If he was that unbalanced.

On the other hand, the truck was built like a tank. If Sara had the nerve to do it, she could slam into Garret's car and just keep on driving. *Come on, baby.* He knew she had more gumption than she gave herself credit for.

"Let's get a chopper in the air," Cannard suggested, his voice slightly higher than usual. "Once the truck's spotted, we'll get troopers on the road and pull this bastard over." He pulled a cell phone from his pocket.

Chase nodded, grateful now that they'd brought the detective with them. "Thanks," he said over his shoulder. "Take the highway east," he added to Hannah.

He had to brace himself as she took the ramp on two wheels.

Almost immediately, he had reason to doubt his decision. The traffic ahead of them was sparse, and the land stretch flat for miles, but he couldn't see the back of the Silverado.

He must have made a sound of suffering or pain because Hannah put her hand on his arm. "We're going to get her back, Westy," she said, as steady as a rock.

He thought about the young girl who'd lost her parents this morning. Life was unbelievably indifferent when it came to who should live, who should die.

That thought reminded him that Sara's mother had

barely sounded alive when she called Chase to warn him of Garret's approach. Snatching up his cell phone, he dialed her number, only to find the line still busy.

Which meant that Rachel was either dead or unconscious.

He busied himself in the next few minutes making calls to ensure that emergency vehicles were bearing down on her home in Dallas to check on her.

In the backseat, Cannard was also on the phone, choreographing a roadblock with the Wagoner police, into whose jurisdiction they were headed. "Chopper's in the air," he relayed to Chase and Hannah.

Chase felt the tension in him building, a nauseating mix of fear and rage. Emotion never factored into his missions. But this wasn't a mission. This was personal.

Snatching the SIG from the holster on his thigh, he extracted a fresh magazine from his ballistic vest and exchanged it for the one that was no longer full.

Hannah glanced at him sidelong. "You can't shoot him, Chase. Not unless he's threatening Sara's life," she warned.

He slid the new magazine into place and secured it with a satisfying *click*. His promise to Sara hadn't been an idle one. Garret was a terrorist, no different from the hostiles Chase targeted for a living. He might not have orders to take him out, but that wouldn't stop him from killing him, not if he dared to harm a hair on Sara's head.

Sweat slid down Sara's spine as she edged her speed even higher. Her stomach roiled. Every muscle in her body was clenched in fear.

Garret has found me. He's right behind us. Oh, God.

"Where're we going, Mom?" Kendal asked.

She wanted to console him, but she was too shaken to make up a lie. "I don't know, honey," she admitted, licking her parched lips.

She glanced in the rearview mirror at the maroon sedan, still pacing her, regardless of her increased speed. There were only a few other cars on Highway 51, and certainly no police anywhere—of course not.

As was his custom, Garret was keeping her guessing, savoring her helplessness. She wondered what his plan was—to pursue her until she ran out of gas?

She glanced at the gas gauge with its needle showing three quarters empty. That wouldn't take long.

Oh, dear, why hadn't she driven in the other direction, straight to the BAPD Police Headquarters? Now she could only hope to arrive at Wagoner before her fuel ran out, and even then, she had no idea where to find the police there.

Kendal dared a peek over his shoulder. "He's still behind us," he moaned.

"I know, sweetheart." Every nerve in her body, every drop of adrenaline was aware of his threatening proximity.

The whopping of a helicopter's blades crept into her consciousness. With a leap of hope, Sara searched the sky. And there it was, an official-looking chopper hovering over the highway ahead of them.

Yes, I'm speeding! Look at me!

She depressed the accelerator farther, and the old motor sputtered, forcing her to ease off the gas.

Please help! She kept one hopeful eye on the bird. If

she lived to feel Chase's embrace, just one more time, it would be enough.

In her distracted state, she blinked at a road sign that flashed to her right. Had that just read STATE POLICE? Was there a state police building out here, in the middle of nowhere?

"Honey, did you see that sign we just passed?" she asked, as a cold sweat filmed her skin.

"It said the name of some state park," Kendal answered, giving her a fearful look.

"Park? Are you sure it didn't say police?"

"I don't know," he wailed. "We were going too fast."

The exit rushing toward them wasn't marked at all.

At the last instant, Sara took the tight-turning ramp that swept them off the highway. Behind her, she heard the squeal of tires as Garret, presumably, changed lanes to follow.

Sure enough, there he was, shooting onto the narrow country road she'd put them on.

What have I done? Sara thought, eyes widening as she swept them over the rural terrain. There was no sign of any state police anywhere. She'd put them on a country road, and she couldn't turn back, not without pulling in a driveway to perform a U-turn.

The beating of a helicopter's rotors had her searching the sky again. Like a guardian angel, the chopper hovered several hundred feet overhead. Relief wrestled with terror. For whatever reason, she was being watched. Surely a state cruiser would descend on her, making it less likely that Garret would make his move.

But the only other car on the road was Garret's. He pressed closer, surging toward her bumper, then backing away. She could see him, smiling a rather nasty smile as he taunted her, like a cat toying with a mouse.

Without warning, the blacktop under her tires gave way to gravel. Sara's hopes faltered. Oh, God, she wasn't on a dead-end road, was she? The steering wheel grew slick under her sweating palms.

Up ahead, she could see a fork in the road, forcing her to choose one direction over another—a deserted farm, or a trek into the woods.

Not wanting to stop for any reason, she chose the latter, and gravel gave way to dirt as they shot into a sparsely wooded forest.

She could see a lake now, flashing blue through the screen of trees. The helicopter disappeared from sight, but she could still hear it.

The road stretched, long and straight, with no glimpse of a public building anywhere. She roared down it, tires jiggling over ruts, driving faster than she'd ever dared to drive in her life. But then the truck engine sputtered, making her heart stop. It resumed a normal roar, but then it sputtered again. She could feel them decelerating.

"Carburetor's clogged," Kendal said in a strangled voice. He reached for the glove compartment where Chase kept the injection cleaner.

Not that it would do them any good right now. Sara kept a heavy foot on the pedal, but the engine continued to falter.

Please. Oh, please. We can't stop here.

Garret's car was practically on her bumper. She could see him smirking, his eyes glinting as he sensed her plight. To her horror, he eased into the oncoming side of the road and started to pass her.

As the trees to her left thinned, offering a breathtaking vista of the lake, Garret overtook them. Sara glanced at him fearfully. She couldn't see his face, but she could see the handgun lying on the seat next to him. Somewhere, in the back of her mind, she'd always known that he was capable of murder.

It was that knowledge that had paralyzed her for so long.

But not any longer.

With a cry of denial, she wrenched the steering wheel sharply to the left and veered into his path. The heavier truck rammed into the smaller car. Metal scraped over metal, and the car's tires dropped into a ditch on the far side.

With a roar, the sedan leapt out, becoming briefly airborne as it shot between two hickory trees and dove, slow motion, toward the water.

Splash! Sara gaped with amazement as the front half crashed into the lake.

In the same instant, her engine quit. The truck rolled to a stop, and she and Kendal were left with nothing to do but watch Garret's car sink into the astonishingly deep water at the lake's edge.

In just seconds, all that remained visible was the back fender, sticking out.

Stunned by the results of her actions, Sara stared at the bubbles frothing up from the sunken vehicle. On some level, she was aware of the helicopter, hovering now over the lake, its blades agitating the surface farther out.

The bubbling by the shore abruptly ceased. Sara loosened her petrified grip on the steering wheel.

Garret was gone. Under the water.

But not for one minute did she believe he was dead.

She turned to seize the buck rifle off the gun rack.

"Mom, no!" Kendal cried, guessing her intent.

"Stay here, sweetheart," she said, scarcely recognizing her own voice, she sounded so ferocious. "Lock the door and don't unlock it again unless I tell you."

"Please!" He clung to her, sobbing with fright.

"Do as I say!" She peeled his hands loose and locked the door as she climbed down from the truck. Raising the butt of the rifle to her shoulder the way that Chase had taught her, she thumbed the safety and stepped cautiously toward the lake's edge, finger crooked over the trigger.

Fallen leaves crunched beneath her feet, though she couldn't hear them for the beating of the helicopter's rotors.

Straddling the tracks of Garret's tires, she raked the murky water for any sign of him. She could just make out the shape of the car in the water's bluish depths.

Beneath the choppy surface, everything appeared still.

The hope that Garret was dead began to ease the crushing weight of fear.

But then, there he was, head bursting through the water as he gasped in air. Startled, Sara stumbled back. She stepped into the rut left by Garret's tires. She slipped, falling hard. The rifle discharged at the sky before falling uselessly on top of her.

Paralyzed with terror, Sara could only watch as Garret rose from the water, looking like a sodden scarecrow. Water streamed from his black suit as he trudged toward her, murder blazing in his dark eyes, teeth bared, and blood running in a bright red stream down the side of his nose from the cut on his brow.

"You think you can kill me, bitch?" he rasped, closing the distance between them.

Sara grappled with the gun, but with her hands muddied, her fingers slipped, and it was too late. He wrenched the rifle from her grasp, tossing it toward the water's edge. "Get up!" he snarled. He seized her by the hair, hauling her to her feet.

She kicked at him, causing him to tighten his grip. In desperation, Sara peered pleadingly at the helicopter. She could see a shooter positioned in the open doorway, aiming a mounted gun at them, but with Garret holding her so close, the man didn't dare to shoot.

Locking an arm around her throat, Garret backed them toward the truck. "You think you're so smart don't you," he snarled in her ear, as they moved away from the lake's edge. "Did you think I wouldn't find you? I found the e-mails that you sent to your real mother. I should have guessed that you came from trailer trash."

She had to keep him away from the truck. Away from Kendal!

But her feeble attempt to dig her heels in only cut off her airway, making her cough and gasp. He backed her to the driver's door and pounded on it. "Open the door!" she heard him snarl to Kendal.

"No!" he cried in a terrified voice. "Go away, I hate you!"

"Open it, or I'll kill you both."

I'm going to die here, Sara realized, fighting for breath. Already spots were swimming before her, flitting like butterflies among the leaves of the trees around them.

But then a flash of red caught her eye. Garret saw it, too. He swiveled abruptly to stare down the road.

It was a car, Sara realized, hope giving her renewed strength. And not just any car. Hannah's red Mustang was coming toward them. And—oh, please, God—if her eyes did not deceive her—that was Chase in the passenger seat! He'd never let her die.

But then Garret groped in his pocket, and, to her horror, he produced the gun she'd glimpsed earlier. He thrust the cold, wet barrel of it against her temple.

And the Mustang came to an instant halt.

Chapter Seventeen

"Stop," Chase commanded, and Hannah did, breathing an expletive that she'd picked up from him.

He didn't need her to tell him what was on her mind. He had eyes. He could tell that the scene in front of them looked like a classic setup for a double, if not triple, homicide.

One look at Sara's face and he could tell that the fucker was choking her—not enough to kill her, just debilitate her. He had a gun to her head, and she was beyond terrified. Kendal, meanwhile, was staring out the truck window behind him, witnessing something that a child should never see.

"Let me talk to Garret," Hannah promised, with far less confidence than she'd spoken earlier. "I can't believe he's resorting to this."

Chase believed it. Sara wouldn't have run so far and fast if she hadn't sensed that her husband would flip a switch.

All that Hannah might accomplish by talking to the man was to delay the inevitable. Garret had thrown his career down the toilet by his actions today. He'd set out to prove that Sara was his, even if the only way to do that was to take her to the grave. "I have to stop him," he answered, simply.

Hannah knew what that meant. She didn't argue, either, not when Garret had a gun to Sara's head. "Okay, but how?" she asked, glancing at the sparse forest surrounding them. "There's not enough cover; he'll see you. And if he senses that you're going to shoot, then so will he."

Something in the grass by the lake's edge caught Chase's eye. It was Linc's buck rifle. Sara must have dropped it while trying to defend herself.

"Back up," Chase decided as a strategy occurred to him.

"What?"

"Back the car up," he repeated. "Get me out of the fucker's line of sight."

With a questioning look, she pushed her stick shift into reverse and eased them out of the immediate area. The devastation that came over Sara's face was heart-wrenching. Chase jerked his gaze away.

As Hannah backed them up, he went to work unbuckling his ballistic vest, shaking out of it. "Stop here," he said, when he was confident that Garret could no longer see him.

"What are you going to do?" Hannah asked, as he went to work yanking off the holster on his thigh, unlacing his boots.

"I'm swimmin' up alongside him. Sara dropped her rifle by the water's edge. If I can get to it without him seeing me, I can shoot him, and he'll never know. Your job is to keep Sara alive till I get a clear shot."

His boots thumped onto the car floor.

"Swim fast," Hannah urged, freckles standing out starkly on her pale face.

The last time he'd seen Hannah shaken, she'd been rescuing herself from a Cuban prison, while being shot at from behind. "I hope there's ammo in that rifle."

Her nervousness didn't do much for Chase's confidence. "Me, too." Slipping out of the car, he dashed for the shore. He went for a clean entry—diving headfirst into the water and praying he wouldn't gouge an eye on submerged branches. Fort Gibson Lake was deep, and in early October it was frigid.

The chill permeated his fatigues in an instant, but he didn't notice. He was too stunned by the fact that Sara's life could end at any minute. Her husband had outsmarted them both. Not only had Garret found Sara, but he'd chased her into this secluded area for a reason, and it wasn't reconciliation.

No! Chase raged, sending the power of his denial into his legs. He'd give anything for flippers right now and a tank on his back to weigh him down and fill his burning lungs. He broke the surface briefly, assessing his whereabouts, dragging in oxygen.

He could see the bumper of Garret's car projecting out of the water more than fifty yards away. Good for Sara, Chase thought. She'd driven the fucker off the road.

Flipping like an otter, he submerged himself again, making his approach soundless and invisible, the way that he preferred it.

He swam the fifty yards without surfacing again. Sticking his head inside the sunken car, he discovered an air pocket along the roof and used it to replenish his air. He took an extra second to focus himself, to quell the fear that made his muscles want to cramp. A sniper could not hesitate. One slip of the finger, and the wrong person could die.

In this case, that person would be Sara.

The possibility scared him so badly, he thought he might be peeing in the water.

Get yourself together! shouted a voice in his head. It was the voice of Chief Jeffries, hard-ass instructor from SEAL training in Coronado.

Emptying his lungs to one-quarter capacity, Chase withdrew from the vehicle and sank to the bottom, so that he could creep, hand over hand, up the rocks lining the shallow end. Approaching as close as he could without exposing himself, he lifted his eyes out of the water and peered over the grassy bank to locate the buck rifle.

It wasn't as close to the water as he'd hoped.

He could hear Hannah reasoning with Garret to throw down his gun, dangling the carrot of an insanity plea. The helicopter must have moved away to make negotiations feasible.

"Insanity plea," Garret scoffed with innate arrogance. "I assure you, Agent Whoever-you-are, that I know exactly what I'm doing."

"You're a lawyer," she reminded him. "Why not settle this matter by legal means instead of criminal ones?"

"Because the law does not allow for justice," he shouted back. "The criminal here is my wife. I am the law, and I insist on justice being served."

Very slowly, Chase rose from the water to creep toward the rifle. Thankfully, Garret's raised arm blocked him from the man's peripheral view. But Kendal, peering pale-faced and wide-eyed out the truck's window caught sight of him.

Chase put a finger to his mouth. *Don't tell.* He signaled for Kendal to duck down.

Fuck, he'd never killed a man in front of a kid before and never that kid's father. A nauseating chill swept over him. He recognized it as the onset of shock, which was not a good sign. Shock was supposed to come *after,* not during the mission.

To his great relief, Kendal melted out of sight.

Inch by inch Chase slid through the grass. Water streamed silently from his clothing. The buck rifle still lay several feet away. He stretched an arm toward it, hoping it was loaded, that it wasn't jammed. If his own SIG could have tolerated water submersion, then Garret would be dead already.

"You are not the law, Captain Garret," Hannah persisted, speaking to Garret from behind her car door, where she crouched. "You are a lawyer for the Judge Advocate General of the United States Navy, and you have sworn to uphold the law, which makes murder a crime."

"In my house, I am the law," Garret ranted. "I expected fidelity and obedience, and I was betrayed—"

"There are laws bigger than your laws," Hannah interrupted, trying intentionally to keep him arguing, to give Chase just five more seconds.

"Not if the law can't touch me."

Chase recognized the tone of a man on the verge of an irreversible act. With the buck rifle still inches away, he dove for it, fingers sliding into position around the handle as he hefted it, aimed, and fired—*bam!*—straight into Garret's temple, flinging the man off his feet. Sara went with him, and as they hit the ground, Garret's gun discharged.

No! Chase scrambled to his feet. His heart had stopped beating, and his legs felt unwieldy as he sprinted to where they lay. Garret's body pinned Sara's to the ground, yet for the life of him, Chase couldn't simply lean over and thrust the man aside.

Because what if he found Sara dead?

Hannah and Dean caught up to him. They were the ones to haul Garret aside. Sara gazed up at them, eyes staring, mouth open, absolutely silent. But then she coughed and blinked, and Chase's knees buckled.

He hit the ground next to her, grabbed her up into his arms, and rocked her like a baby, moaning "Oh, God. Oh, God."

"Are you hurt?" Hannah asked, flicking him a strange look.

"No," Sara wheezed. "Just lost my breath," she explained, lapsing into hacking coughs.

"I'm surprised his gun fired at all," Cannard commented, noting the water that dripped from the barrel as he examined it.

Hannah shifted her attention to the truck, where Kendal was locked inside. "Hey, buddy," she crooned, stepping over to reassure him. "You're safe now. You want to come out?"

The lock clicked open and Kendal stepped out, falling to his knees, apparently subject to the same affliction Chase suffered. "Mama," he croaked, crawling toward them.

Hannah stepped in front of Garret's body, shielding it from Kendal's view. That sobered Chase right up. He didn't want Sara or her Kendal glimpsing the hole in Garret's head.

"Let's move," he said, coming unsteadily to his feet.

They crossed the road in a huddle, leaving Hannah and Dean to notify the Wagoner police that the threat had been neutralized.

They collapsed as a unit near the spot where Chase had crawled from the water. He put his back to a tree and pulled Sara closer. "You're soaking wet," she whispered, clutching him all the same. Kendal, meanwhile, tried to crawl in her lap.

Endeavoring to overcome his shock, Chase gazed up at the branches overhead. Bright yellow leaves fluttered beneath a flawless sky.

This was supposed to be where the story ended, where boy got girl (and a great kid, too.) If the world could just stop turning, right now, he'd have more than he ever deserved.

But it wouldn't. It would just keep spinning, turning one day into the next, forcing Chase to leave, to answer the commitment that called him back.

Hard, cold reality kept his heart congealed in ice.

He sniffed and looked down, into Sara's achingly beautiful eyes.

"I knew when I saw you, that everything would be all right," she whispered. "Is he . . . ?"

"Yes."

He could tell by the shock in her eyes that it would take time for her to process that reality. "You shot him," she realized.

He flicked a look at Kendal, who regarded him with acceptance, not with condemnation.

"I did what I had to do to keep you alive."

"Thank you," she breathed, tears swimming in her eyes. "I was so afraid. It was worse than my biggest nightmare."

"Yes, it was," he agreed.

"But it's over now," she told herself. He could tell that it would take her a while to accept that also. Next, she'd think that she was free to love him, to have a life with him.

For a second, he allowed himself a glimpse into her fantasy. What would it be like, enjoying home-cooked meals instead of cold MREs because lighting a Sterno meant risking detection? Sleeping in his mother's bed with Sara's soft body tucked against his instead of sleeping on the unyielding ground.

The screaming of sirens chased the vision from Chase's mind. If only it didn't have to be one or the other, but it did. He couldn't be in love and be a sniper. That was never more obvious than this afternoon, when terror had held him in its grip, practically paralyzing him. He'd felt more vulnerable than at any time in his life.

Nothing used to touch him when he did his job. What if he couldn't get that feeling back, that apathy that overtook him just as the enemy stepped into his line of fire?

The thought of feeling this way forever was unthinkable.

With the story of Garret's violent death making the front page of the *Daily Ledger,* Sara decided to keep Kendal home from school. She drove him, instead, to the school administration building on Main Street to explain, straight to the superintendent of schools, the circumstances that had led her to falsifying their identities. She'd asked Chase to accompany them, but he'd said that Hannah needed his help in filling out a report.

The meeting had taken up most of the morning, but the result was just what Sara'd hoped for: forgiveness and understanding on the part of the community.

As she ushered Kendal out into fall sunshine and into Chase's car, she took a second to absorb the atmosphere of the town she'd chosen to remain in. The quaint saloon-style buildings and the churches lining the streets reassured her that, aside from the violent protest of a handful of skinheads, this was a wholesome place for her to raise her son. In this American heartland, they would leave past horrors behind and look forward to happier moments.

Only to herself did Sara admit that her happiness stemmed from her love of Chase, who had yet to mention his departure. He'd kept protectively close all evening. Last night, he'd made love to Sara twice, so tenderly that tears of relief had stung her eyes.

It was only a matter of time before he whispered the words that she felt in his touch: *I love you.* Any moment now he'd ask her to wait for him, which she would gladly do, though four years was an awfully long time. Perhaps he'd be able to visit to ease—not just her loneliness—but Kendal's, also.

The years would seem unending.

And yet, it would all be worthwhile one day, when Chase retired from the Navy. When he came home for good.

Leaving the tree-lined town behind, Sara took the shortest route to the ranch, down Eighty-first Street, through four miles of farmland to Oak Grove Road. Eager to spend every precious minute left with Chase, she zipped into the driveway, sheathed by trees of every color. A sudden sense of isolation crept over her, accompanied by the sudden certainty that Chase was gone.

Panic made her depress the accelerator. Surely his excuse this morning wasn't a lie. He wouldn't leave without saying good-bye! And what about his car?

The trees gave way to grass. There was no way to tell if Chase was in the house or not. She braked by the front porch, jumping out to run up the steps, tear open the screen door, and reach for the handle. The door was locked.

With a heavy heart, she unlocked it, pushed into the house, and called his name.

Just as she suspected, he did not reply.

A sheet of paper sitting on the kitchen counter caught her eye. Sara picked it up reluctantly and read the message written in neat, block letters.

GOT A RIDE TO THE AIRPORT WITH HANNAH. SORRY, BUT I DON'T KNOW HOW TO SAY GOOD-BYE. DON'T WAIT FOR ME, SARA. I CAN'T DO MY JOB IF I'M THINKING ABOUT YOU.

Each abrupt statement tore at the seams of her heart. How could she have been so wrong about him? Not only did he not want her to wait, but he couldn't even spare the time to think about her?

With a strangled cry, she balled the letter in her fists. At the same time, the true meaning of his words filtered through her consciousness. It wasn't that he wouldn't think about her; it was rather that he was *afraid* to think about her, as she'd accused him the other day. Thinking of her kept him from doing his job, ruthlessly and efficiently, the way a good sniper ought to.

The truth was, she'd resuscitated his heart, and now he had to carry it out into the field, where having a heart made him vulnerable. *Oh, Chase.*

"Where's Chase, Mom?"

Sara spun around as Kendal stepped into the room.

Striving for composure, she hid the balled note in her hand. "He had to leave, sweetheart," she said, amazed that she could sound so composed. But Kendal's stunned expression had her reliving her own shock. "He didn't have a choice," she added, her heart protesting the words.

He did have a choice. He could have chosen love.

"But he didn't say good-bye!" Kendal cried, his eyes welling up with tears.

If Chase could see Kendal's pain, he'd be heartsick.

It was that realization that made her defend him. "Some people have trouble saying good-bye, sweetheart, because it hurts so much."

Kendal whirled and fled, slamming out of the doors he'd just entered.

With tears blurring her vision, Sara uncrumpled the note and read it again, hunting for a message of hope.

Don't wait for me. There wasn't any hope in that.

Leaving the note on the counter, she followed Kendal outside, where she sank onto the step she'd shared with Chase that fateful night he'd told her what he did. Not even the pots of colorful flowers could comfort her.

The 747 passenger jet was starting its descent into the Norfolk Airport before Chase opened his eyes. He stretched his arms overhead, grateful for the space to do so. Hannah had bought him a first-class seat next to hers, using her frequent flyer miles.

She shot him an irritated glare. "I didn't think anybody but Luther could sleep on an airplane," she groused. "Thanks for keeping me entertained."

"No problem." Shit, here came the conversation that he didn't want to have. He counted the seconds to see how long it would take for Hannah to broach the subject of him and Sara.

One, two, three—

"Look, I know you're used to your freedom, Chase, but I don't understand your refusal to have a relationship. If Luther and I can make it work, then so can you."

"Luther's not a sniper," he said, very quietly. He didn't have the kind of job to be talked about out loud.

"No, but we spend a lot of time apart. The key is communication. You have a cell phone that works anywhere in the world. So your phone bill goes through the roof. It's worth it, isn't it?"

"It's not about time apart," Chase said, feeling a scowl come on.

Hannah looked at him. "Well, what's the problem then?"

Every bone in his body could feel Sara slipping farther away from him. Where was the relief he was looking for?

Hannah sighed. "You know what I think it is? I think you're afraid," she taunted.

Not her, too. Chase looked out the window. How long was it going to take this plane to land?

"Fine, go into one of your silent sulks," Hannah added,

when it was clear that he wasn't going to talk. "I just hate seeing you alone, that's all."

Sara's words returned to him. *You're not alone. We're here waiting for you.*

Fuck. Swallowing the knot in his throat, Chase turned his head to look at Hannah's profile. "I don't mind bein' alone," he reassured her. It hurt a lot less than being connected. He was counting on that.

She slanted him a pitying look. "Okay, but just remember, you're allowed to change your mind."

Chapter Eighteen

Prajuk Somchai was hard to kill. The man had a rash of bodyguards who kept constant vigil over him. He slept in a high-rise apartment in Bangkok, with no balconies and no taller buildings anywhere in the vicinity.

The four-man squad from Team Twelve had been in the steamy third world city for a week, waiting for the opportunity to terminate the leader of Thailand's notorious Golden Triangle. Killing the heroin king was the first step in crippling the elaborate organization.

PO2 Teddy Brewbaker, who was designated scout, sat out on the hotel balcony, keeping one eye on the drug lord's hideout while dozing in the oppressive heat, subject to car pollution and tantalizing aromas of exotic food. When Prajuk stepped out of his building alone, Teddy fell out of the chair he was sitting in. "Chief!" he exclaimed. And Chase, who had just stepped inside to consume a sandwich delivered by room service, snatched up his Remington to join the black man on the balcony.

Prajuk had obviously given his bodyguards the slip, because he was striking out on his own, thinking that a pair of sunglasses and a baseball cap would keep him from being recognized. Chase raised his long-range rifle to target the man, but the street below was crammed with people. He couldn't risk killing a civilian.

"Let's get him," he said, tossing the rifle aside. He wore his SIG in a holster under his flowered shirt and a camera around his neck. He and Teddy sprinted down the emergency exit and out of the hotel, hoping to catch their quarry.

Pursuing a hostile in broad daylight wasn't their first choice, but coming on the heels of the last messy encounter, it fit the mold.

Not fifty meters out of the building Chase lost Teddy in the crowd—*fuck*! But he could still see Prajuk's orange baseball cap over the heads of the shorter, Asian population. He decided to pursue him, alone. As long as Prajuk remained alive, the mission was at a standstill.

Chase was dressed as a tourist, right down to his Bermuda shorts and sandals. Even if Prajuk caught sight of him, he wouldn't guess that he was being pursued by an assassin.

Chase followed the man into a crooked alleyway, taking precautions to slow his pursuit. He picked his way around the stagnant puddles, drying in the aftermath of the rainy season. Lifting the camera to his eyes, he pretended to photograph the harsher aspects of reality while keeping at a healthy distance from his target.

He hoped to God this wasn't a trap. The heroin king couldn't know that Navy SEALs were working with the CIA to cripple his operation, could he? He turned his camera on a forlorn child sitting on an overturned banana crate. Out of the corner of his eye, he watched Prajuk push through a door into the rear entrance of a cinderblock building. Chase tossed the boy a coin and pursued the drug lord.

He found himself in a deserted stairwell. Sounds overhead had him slipping the SIG out from under his shirt. As he ascended the stairs on rubber soles, a cold sweat cooled a spot between his shoulder blades. He never used to perspire.

But then again, he'd never missed a target until his last kill. It'd taken him three shots to take down the Nigerian arms dealer when the SEALs surprised his yacht at sea.

At the top of the steps, he slipped through a door that gave access to a dimly lit corridor. It was lined with doors draped with beaded curtains. Those and the humid air, perfumed with incense, told him that he'd entered one of Bangkok's infamous massage parlors via the back door.

Where was Prajuk?

It was early afternoon, and the parlor was still quiet. Chase peered through the curtains, finding only empty alcoves. A whispered conversation drew him toward the last room on the right. With his back to the wall, he peeked around the doorframe and found Prajuk disrobing a woman.

Oh, joy. Chase was going to have to wait for the drug lord to fuck his girlfriend. And *then* he could kill him, providing Prajuk left the same way that he'd entered.

Taking a second look, Chase realized that the woman was pregnant. Startled, he glanced up at her face.

It was the wrong thing to do. Her gentle smile reminded him of Sara.

Focus, Chase commanded himself. He had a job to protect the interests of his country. Prajuk's cartel was a threat to world peace. It was that simple.

He turned to leave, but not before the woman's words reached his ears. "Did you feel that, love? The baby moved."

There were times when Chase wished his hearing wasn't so good. He slipped into the stairwell, refusing to picture Prajuk with a baby in his arms.

He tucked himself into the space under the second run of stairs, behind a pile of boxes. The stairwell was an oven. Chase waited, wishing Teddy was with him.

Finally, the door upstairs swung open. Someone, presumably Prajuk, came down the steps, whistling contentedly. Chase's heart thundered. He readied his gun in a slippery hand and waited. The man stepped into view, heading for the door and—*bang!* The force of the bullet slung him against the wall, which he slid down, leaving a trail of bright red blood and little flecks of brain.

Chase tucked his gun out of sight and moved swiftly toward the exit. He hadn't taken three steps into the humid sunshine when he ran into the boy he'd given money to. The kid had bought dried, sugar-covered plums, and he wanted to share.

With a shake of his head, Chase pushed past him, lurching down the alley as swiftly and casually as possible, considering the buzzing in his head.

He wasn't supposed to go into shock. Where was the detachment he was famous for? Racked with shivers, in danger of losing his lunch, he hastened toward the hotel, casting glances over his shoulder.

Still no sign of Teddy. Good, he didn't want the junior SEAL seeing him this way—again. He'd been a nut job after the Nigerian disaster.

He pushed into the hotel lobby, craving its air-conditioning. Luther, the officer in charge, would want to debrief him, but he wasn't up for that. He needed a beer to steady his nerves.

To his relief, the bar was empty. He ordered a tall can of Australian beer, found a booth to hide in, and drank.

What was wrong with him? Where was the apathy, the self-approbation that came from getting the job done? Not here. How could he feel good about killing the father of an unborn baby? Oh, fuck. He hoped the kid with the sugared plums wouldn't find the body.

A waitress sidled up to his booth, and he ordered another beer. He wondered what Sara was doing. He spent a lot of time thinking about that, wondering whether Dean Cannard had made his move yet.

He reached into the pocket of his shorts and pulled out Kendal's turtle, putting it on the table in front of him.

What is with that thing? Teddy had asked him a few days back.

Makes me think of home, Chase had admitted, earning him a pitying look.

"There you are."

Chase gave a start as Luther, the OIC, cast his enormous shadow over the table. Teddy Brewbaker was right behind him. "We've been looking for you."

"I lost you on the street, Chief," Teddy added. "You're as slippery as a wide receiver."

Luther gestured for Teddy to join Chase on the opposite side of the booth, before cramming his football-player-sized frame in alongside him. "What happened?" he asked quietly. "Did you catch him?"

Chase met Luther's serious, navy blue gaze. "Yes, sir," he said, smothering a burp. "He's out of the picture." With his superlative hearing, Teddy's sigh of relief did not escape him.

"Why didn't you tell us?" the black man asked. "I been searchin' alleyways for your body," he added under his breath.

"Sorry," said Chase. "Just needed a moment."

He didn't miss the significant look that passed between the two.

"Are you okay, Chief?" Luther finally asked him.

Chase considered the question. "Nope," he said.

Silence descended weightily upon the table. His two companions glanced at his half-empty beer. He knew what they were wondering—just how much had he drunk?

"What's wrong?" Luther prompted.

"I've hit a wall," Chase said. "Can't do this anymore." Hearing himself talk was like listening to someone else. At the same time, the words couldn't be more true.

"Happens to all snipers," Luther comforted. "You've lasted longer than most."

Chase snatched up his beer and saluted them. "Thirty-eight kills," he said, with a twist of his mouth and a burning in his belly.

"So we'll rotate you out of sniper duty and put you somewhere else on the team," the lieutenant suggested.

"Right." Chase took another swig.

"What do you really want?" Luther asked him.

"Maybe I could get a bad psych eval and be discharged," Chase suggested, half-seriously.

"Oh, come on," Teddy protested. "You ain't crazy, Chief."

"I think he's crazy in love," Luther suggested.

Chase scowled at him. "You've been talking to Hannah," he accused.

"She is my wife. Do you deny it?"

"Hell, no," said Chase. And since he was being honest with himself he added, "I told her not to wait for me. What the hell was I thinkin'?"

"I don't know," said Luther. "What were you thinking?"

"You sound like my shrink when you talk that way."

"Sorry, but from Hannah's description of her, Sara sounds pretty amazing."

Amazing. Chase felt his eyes sting. Shit, maybe he was drunk. "I don't how it happened," he admitted, hoarsely. It wasn't like he'd been hit with a bolt of lightning. She'd crept into him so subtly, it was more like she'd been there all along.

Teddy offered a sympathetic wag of his head.

"We still have an objective to complete," Luther reminded them.

Chase filled his lungs, trying to clear his head. "Yeah," he agreed. "I'm with you," he ground out.

"In a couple of weeks, we'll be home," Luther added. "I'll talk to the XO. He and Commander Montgomery are pretty tight. Maybe they can find you something cushy that'll get you to retirement."

"Right." Chase nodded. He wasn't going to count on it. The only thing that would get him through the next four years was if Sara said yes to the question he wanted to ask her, in person.

With her arms folded against the December chill, Sara watched bemusedly as Dean Cannard backed his cruiser toward her porch steps. It was obvious he was delivering the live Christmas tree that stuck out of the half-closed truck. This wasn't his first attempt to win her with unexpected gifts.

She really ought to tell him he was wasting his time, but he killed the engine and popped out of the driver's seat with such an eager smile that the gentle rebuke never made it past her lips.

On Christmas Eve, she and Kendal planned to join her mother, who was still recuperating from a fractured hip and two broken ribs. Sara'd bought an artificial tree to take to Dallas with them. It was stowed in its box in the bed of the truck.

"You can't have Christmas without a proper tree," Dean enthused, tugging at the rope that kept his trunk half-closed. Dainty snowflakes settled on his police jacket and glinted in his black hair as he threw the trunk open and put his arms around the strapped boughs.

He hefted the tree out and propped it up against the porch rail, going back to his trunk. "Figured you didn't own a tree stand, so I bought that, too." He hefted a bright red metal stand and showed it to her.

"Thank you," Sara said, dredging up a smile for him. "Why don't you bring it in?" she offered.

"Wish I could." He shot her a regretful look. "But I gotta run to the office. There's a grand larceny case that needs my attention right now." He left the stand on the porch and reached into his pocket. "I'll come back this evening and set her up for you," he promised. "Meanwhile, I've got just enough time for this."

With a twinkle in his eyes, he produced a sprig of mistletoe. "You can thank me now," he invited.

Sara hesitated. With a constricting heart, she remembered Chase's intoxicating kisses. Nothing would ever compare, and yet Chase had told her not to wait for him. Dean, on the other hand, was determined to woo her. And it wasn't as if she was betraying Chase, who'd never hinted at a future for them.

In two months, she'd heard nothing from him. Was she really so foolish as to hold out hope that that would change?

Dangling the mistletoe over his head, Dean waited, eager for a glimpse of passion. Sara hid her eyes to keep from disappointing him. Putting her hands lightly on his shoulders, she tipped her chin up and kissed him, half-hoping for a spark.

It'd be so much easier to love a man like Dean.

His lips felt cool and firm, but the kiss didn't move her. It was merely a comfort to touch another human being, to feel less adrift. With a sigh, she dropped to her heels and opened her eyes, masking her disappointment.

"I have to go," he said with regret.

"Yes." She stepped away. "Thank you for the tree."

"You're welcome. I'll be back this evening. Oh, I almost forgot." He fished inside the inner pocket of his jacket. "I brought your mail up."

"Thank you." She'd been looking forward to a walk to the end of the driveway to fetch the mail, but okay.

"Well, see you tonight." With a wave of his hand, he jumped into his cruiser and roared away.

Sara flipped idly through the stack, which was mostly junk mail. A letter-sized envelope caught her eye, and she pulled it out, recognizing the name of the sender with a gasp. Hannah Lindstrom! Why would Hannah be writing her unless something had happened to Chase!

With her heart in her throat, Sara tore open the seal.

She shook open the letter inside and two paper tickets floated out. Airplane tickets, she realized, as she leaned over to snatch them off the snow-dusted grass: one ticket each, for her and Kendal, to fly from Tulsa to Norfolk.

Sara turned to the letter for an explanation.

I have it on the best authority that Chase loves you!
Come and welcome him home. I'll pick you up at
the airport. Yours truly, Hannah.

Sara stood there, unmoving for nearly twenty minutes. Chase loved her? How could Hannah be so certain? Yet, apparently, she was, enough to spend gobs of money on airfare.

Tears of hope and fear and relief rushed from Sara's eyes to sting her cheeks. Was she going to do it? Could she bear the risk of rejection for a second time if Chase didn't really want her?

Turning in a semicircle, her gaze settled over the headstones of his family members, a visible reminder that life was short. Rachel would be the first to insist that she give love another chance.

With a shriek of excitement, Sara made up her mind and raced inside to tell Kendal of their plans.

Poor Dean would find only a note tonight when he came by to assemble her tree.

Chapter Nineteen

"The CO wants to talk to you," Luther informed Chase, putting away his cell phone. The four-man SEAL squad and their pilot had just exited a C-17 Globemaster transport plane and were crossing the tarmac at Oceana's airfield. They'd just touched down from a sixteen-hour flight, routed through Bonham Air Force Base in Germany, when Luther's cell phone rang. It was quarter to midnight, and Chase was running on fumes.

"Now, sir?" Chase asked, savoring the bite of cold air after two weeks in the tropics.

"Yes. I'm coming with you."

Peering up at the taller man's profile, Chase tried to guess whether an impromptu meeting with the powers that be was a good thing or whether he was going to get his ass chewed for the poorly executed Nigerian job. Couldn't this wait until after Christmas?

"Isn't it Christmas Eve?" he asked, consulting his mental calendar.

"It will be in, like, fifteen minutes," Luther confirmed. "You're still on Pacific time."

Oh. Well, that sort of explained why the CO was still at the office at this time of night. The man worked obsessive hours, perhaps to mitigate rumors of his Playboy lifestyle— a lifestyle that had ended abruptly in a disfiguring accident.

"You want a ride?" Luther asked Chase, heading toward his Ford F150 pickup truck.

"I got my motorcycle," Chase replied.

"You're going to freeze," Luther warned him. "It's supposed to snow tonight."

"It'll wake me up," Chase assured him. From his evaluation of Commander Montgomery, he had better be incredibly coherent, or the man would show him no respect.

By the time Chase swept through the gates of Dam Neck Naval Annex on his Harley, his face felt frostbitten, his ears ached, but his brain was wide-awake. Shucking his biker's gloves, he strode toward the halogen light that glared over the entrance to Spec Ops. Luther, who was waiting on the other side of the door, pushed it open for him.

His face, which had stared off the cover of *Sports Illustrated* more than once when he played professional football, betrayed not a hint of what Chase was walking into: a dressing down or a rally for moral support.

"They're waiting," Luther said.

They? Who was they, exactly? With butterflies in his stomach, Chase followed Luther down the hallway into the CO's office.

Both the CO and the XO were in the room. Commander Montgomery sat behind his desk. The lamplight cast an unkind light on the scarred portion of his face. Chase didn't know him well enough to read his stone-faced expression, but his hazel eyes struck Chase as guarded.

Hadn't he been the driver in that accident that had killed two much younger women? Obviously, he hadn't been to blame or he wouldn't be in command of Team Twelve today.

Lieutenant Renault, aka Jaguar, was standing behind the CO looking like the cat that ate the canary. Chase knew the man like a brother, and seeing contentment in the man's gold-green eyes, he heaved a silent sigh of relief. "Sirs," Chase greeted them, snapping both men a smart salute.

"At ease, Chief, Lieutenant." The CO waved them both into armchairs. "You must be crusty as hell after all that travel."

Chase was way past crusty. Right now, the only thing that kept him going was the hope of getting to the ranch in time for Christmas.

Lieutenant Renault crossed to the window to draw the blinds against the night sky, and Chase's curiosity went through the roof. This had all the earmarks of an under-the-table job.

Drumming big-knuckled fingers on the surface of his desk, Montgomery frowned at the paperwork before him. From where Chase sat, he couldn't make out what the man was looking at. Was that his personnel file?

"You've been a sniper for what, fifteen years?" the CO queried. Greenish brown eyes assessed Chase impassively.

"Sixteen, sir," Chase confirmed.

"You've had thirty-eight kills as opposed to a career average of nineteen." Was that a flicker of respect in the man's murky eyes? "One shot, one kill. What happened with Faisal Fashanu?" he inquired.

The fucking Nigerian. The man had opened his eyes

and looked at him, that's what'd happened. "I hit a wall, sir." It had taken three shots to make him close his eyes forever.

Montgomery grunted. "I see you reenlisted in August, but now you want to be rotated out of sniper detail?" He sent Chase a vaguely disappointed look.

"Yes, sir," Chase confirmed.

"We'll have to scrounge to come up with a replacement," the commander groused. "It's not easy to find a man with your experience, not to mention your language skills." He flipped through the pages of Chase's personnel files, noting the many commendation letters. "Are you sure you want to give up what you do best, Chief?" the man inquired.

Chase didn't hesitate. "I am absolutely sure, sir."

Montgomery studied him, his eyes as hard marbles. Chase stared back. He would make no excuses for the way he felt. "You tell him," Montgomery said to Lieutenant Renault.

"Ever heard of Camp Gruber, Oklahoma, Chief?" Jaguar asked, his eyes far warmer than the commander's.

Startled to hear the name of his home state, Chase sat straighter. They couldn't have . . . "Of course, sir." Camp Gruber was an hour's drive southeast of Broken Arrow. "It's a training base, if I'm not mistaken."

"You're not," Jaguar confirmed. "It trains National Guardsmen and law enforcement personnel, primarily. They're looking for an active duty, field artillery expert to instruct the trainees. You'd fit that billet, wouldn't you, Chief? It's a four-year assignment, which would put you at twenty years, eligible for retirement."

Chase could scarcely hear him through the humming

in his ears. The room seemed to fill with sparkling dust as he regarded his colleagues in stunned silence.

"Merry Christmas, Chase," said Luther softly.

His buddies had gone to bat for him, Chase realized, feeling his heart expand. They hadn't just rotated him away from sniper duty, they'd eased the pain of long-distance love by securing orders for him at a base, commuting distance from Broken Arrow. Hot damn! "I'd sure as hell fit that billet, sir," Chase replied with feeling.

"Good," said the CO, slapping the folder shut. "You'll PCS to Oklahoma over the holidays and start work there the first of the year. You've given the teams a good sixteen years," he added, with unexpected fairness. "There's no shame in that."

Chase leapt to his feet, his opinion of Montgomery soaring. "Thank you, sir!"

"Don't thank me," the commander retorted, heading for his coat. "Your superiors, here, have badgered me nonstop for two weeks. They wore me down," he confessed.

"Yes, sir. Good night, sir."

Montgomery punched his arms through a Navy-issue trench coat and headed for the door. "Turn out the lights when you leave," he said, considerate enough to give them all a moment alone.

"God damn," Chase said, eyeing his teammates. "I don't know what to say. I fucking love you guys."

Lieutenant Renault chuckled. "Well, that pretty much sums it up, and we fucking love you, too, don't we, Luther?"

"Absolutely," Luther replied. "We'll toast to your new job at my place tomorrow, starting at 1600. Hannah's been planning this party for a while."

"Oh, damn," swore Jaguar, glancing at his watch. "I

told Helen I'd stop by the store and pick up confectioner's sugar on my way home."

"Food Lion's open twenty-four hours," Chase divulged. "Ya'll go ahead. You've got women waitin' for you. I'll get the lights." He didn't have the heart to turn down Luther's invitation. Tomorrow at 1600, he'd be in Oklahoma.

The thought warmed him as much as it terrified him.

"Say hey to Hannah for me," Chase called, as the two men left the room before him.

"You may have more than that to say to her," he thought he heard Luther mutter.

Chase stuck his head out of the door. "What's that, sir?"

"Oh, nothing." Luther shot him his best Boy Scout smile.

Then he and the XO disappeared down the hall murmuring confidences under their breath. Chase narrowed his eyes as he locked the door. He sensed a conspiracy, but he was too tired to guess what it could be.

Sixteen minutes later, he dismounted his Harley before his small, white, bungalow-style house and unstrapped his duffel bag to carry it inside. The scent of woodsmoke hung in the air. Christmas lights twinkled on the facades of every house on the street but his. It wasn't the first time he'd come home to a house plunged in darkness, colder than a witch's tit.

With his senses dulled, he inserted a key into his front door before noticing the amber glow behind his drawn curtains. By habit he reached uselessly for the SIG that was stowed in his duffel bag. *Who the hell is in my house?*

At the sound of a key jiggling in the lock, Sara jerked awake. She was slouched at the foot of Chase's utilitarian couch, while Kendal lay along the length of it, fast asleep. At last, following hours of agonizing uncertainty, Chase was back.

She'd paced the floors of his modest, one-and-a-half story home, reviewing Hannah's reassurances and wondering, but what if the woman was wrong? What if Chase took one look at her, and said, "What the fuck are you doing here?"

She was about to find out. Her heart trembled with mixed anticipation and dread.

The door swung open, there stood Chase, looking stupefied, clutching a sea bag to his chest. "Sara!" he breathed.

Oh, God, he looked gorgeous, with his sun-streaked goatee and glinting earrings.

His bag hit the floor. "What are you doing here?" he asked. A low murmur from Kendal drew his gaze. "You're both here!"

"Is that okay?" Sara wanted to stand up, but there was no way her legs would bear her up right now. "It was Hannah's suggestion. She mailed us airline tickets and met us at the airport. We can leave if you—"

Before she could finish her sentence, he'd crossed the room and pulled her to her feet. The rest of her words were cut short as he crushed her to him, so that every inch of their bodies touched. "Stay," he said in her ear. And in the next instant, he was kissing her, with such fervor that any misgivings Sara still harbored evaporated.

At last, he lifted his head. "You came for nothing," he rasped.

"What?" Her misgivings returned.

"I was gonna fly to Oklahoma tomorrow," he explained, with laughter in his blue eyes.

"You were?" she asked. "Why?"

"Why? Because I wanted to say, 'I think I love you, Sara.'"

Her breath caught at the confession.

"No, in fact, I *know* I love you. And I wanted to ask you if you'd wait for me. But now I don't have to."

"What do you mean?" The contradictions pouring out of him confused her.

"I just got reassigned."

"You did?"

"Yes, to Fort Gruber. It's right down the road from the ranch—a bit of a commute, but it beats the hell out of goin' overseas."

"How's that possible?" she asked, her head reeling.

"Luther and Lieutenant Renault," he answered with a grin. "They went to bat for me."

"I can't believe it," she whispered.

"Think you can stand to have me around?" he asked. "Bet you got used to bein' there alone, just the two of you."

"I don't think I would ever have gotten used to it," she answered honestly.

"Me neither. Don't know how you did it, Sara, but you got to me like no one ever has." His eyes turned suspiciously bright. "I could never go back to bein' who I was before."

"Oh, Chase." This was all happening so fast. She was dizzy with euphoria.

He drew her hand from his shoulder to the center of his

chest. "Feel this?" His heart beat with a steady *thump-thump*. "This is for you," he added.

Her eyes welled with tears of joy. "I can't believe this. Wait till Kendal hears. He's going to be thrilled!" If any-one adored Chase as much as she did, it was her son.

They turned their heads to look at the boy. He slept so peacefully, one hand tucked beneath his chin. "Should we tell him?"

"Yep," said Chase, "but not yet. I've been dreamin' 'bout you for two months. Just give me half an hour with you alone," he begged.

Like teenagers, they slipped into the darkened kitchen and up the crooked stairs, giggling. Under the eaves of Chase's sloping roof, on a bed that creaked outrageously, they made love.

"You know what makes me happiest?" Sara said after-ward, stroking the soft whorls of his tawny chest hair.

"What's that?" he asked on a sleepy note.

"Knowing you'll never be alone again."

He rolled up on one elbow to gaze down at her, his eyes lit with an inner glow. "You promise?" he asked her. "'Cause I tried that, and I didn't like it."

"I promise," she whispered, pulling his head down for a long, dreamy kiss.

At this rate, telling Kendal was going to have to wait till morning.

Epilogue

Four months later

Spring was a time when animals got restless, shaking off the lethargy of a long, cold winter. That was obviously the case on the ranch. Cinnamon, Kendal's golden retriever, adopted from the local shelter, bounded across the field in pursuit of a hare. The pair of swallows nesting under the porch eaves darted in and out to fetch larvae for their young. And Sara, who watched Chase tinker under the hood of the truck as she washed their morning dishes, wondered if he'd ever get around to asking her to marry him.

By all indications, he was about to set out on his Saturday morning atonement. He'd made a habit of visiting the victims of the skinheads because he felt, on some level, responsible for what had happened at the country club. With a *clang,* he closed the hood of the truck and headed for the house.

He entered into the kitchen, catching and holding Sara's thoughtful gaze as he approached the sink to wash the grease from his hands. "You want to come with me this mornin'?" he asked, with a speculative look.

"Um," she said, handing him a towel to dry with. He had more courage than she did, visiting victims of violence, some of whom were scarred for life. "Okay."

"Great," he said, turning toward the rear of the house. "Let me just fetch somethin'."

He never said what he'd fetched as he joined her in the cab of the truck.

They zipped past pastures, verdant with spring grass. Past the Goodner's cattle, who swished their bovine tails at the early mayflies. Past the overpass to Highway 51 and the convenience store on the corner. At last, Chase pulled into a driveway, much shorter than theirs. They stopped before a brick rancher, an older home that looked a bit neglected.

"Who lives here?" Sara asked him.

"Melody," said Chase.

The little girl who'd lost both parents and now lived with her grandmother. Sara swallowed hard. She wished she were as strong as Chase when it came to life's harsher aspects.

He led her to the front door. "Bell's broken," he explained, lifting a hand to knock.

A moment later there came the shuffle of footsteps, then a little old lady opened the door and blinked at them. "You brought Sara!" she exclaimed in delight.

"Yes, ma'am," Chase admitted.

"I hope that means what I think it means," the woman added, with a gleam in her eyes.

Sara cut Chase a questioning look.

"We'll see," he equivocated.

"I'm Doris," the woman said, extending a welcoming hand. "Melody's been looking forward to this day." She turned and let them into a house that was cluttered and worn.

Sara reached for Chase. Melody's shoulder, she recalled, had been so badly broken that she'd had reconstructive surgery and still required therapy to regain use of it. He squeezed her hand reassuringly.

"Melody," Doris sang out ahead of them. "Chase brought Sara to meet you!"

They turned the corner, into a room filled with sunshine and stuffed animals. Sara met the girl's bright blue gaze and faltered. She was struck by a sense of recognition.

Chase pulled her toward the bed. "I brought you a surprise," he said, bending to kiss her cheek.

Melody leaned into him as if she'd known him all her life, but she kept her eyes on Sara. She couldn't have been more than six years old, yet she struck Sara as an old soul, wise beyond her years.

"Hello," said Sara, glancing at Melody's left hand, which lay unmoving on her lap.

"You're very pretty," said the little girl.

"Thank you. So are you." From her flaxen head to her bare toes, she was ethereal, summoning the instinct to shield her from future horrors.

The girl gestured for Chase to lower his head again, and when he did, she whispered in his ear.

"Yes," he said. "In a little while. How's your therapy goin'?"

"I can wiggle my fingers," she said, showing him.

"Atta girl," said Chase.

Sara watched with her heart in her throat.

Doris slipped shoes on the little girl's feet.

"How's she sleepin'?" Chase asked the woman.

"Oh, 'bout the same," Doris answered, wearily.

Sara could only guess that Melody suffered nightmares. Chase turned his attention to the patient. "All set?"

Melody nodded. Sara'd always guessed that Chase had a soft spot for children. But seeing him with a little girl in his arms, one who looked so much like their own child might, made her melt.

He gestured for Sara to follow as Doris led them back down the hall and out the rear door. "Have fun," the old woman called. She lingered at the doorway, watching with a bittersweet smile as they ventured into the over-grown yard together.

Chase put Melody on her feet, and the girl ambled toward the tire swing to sit on it expectantly.

Sara couldn't take her eyes off her.

"What do you think?" Chase asked her.

"I'm speechless," Sara replied. She'd had no idea that Chase was such a ministering angel, that he'd developed a special bond with this small child.

"Go ahead and give her a push," he invited, "but not too high."

Sara spent the next half hour playing with Melody, first on the swing, then at the wrought-iron table, where they enjoyed imaginary tea with Chase. It was deeply gratifying.

"My mommy used to play tea with me, too," Melody remembered with a sorrowful glance.

"She did?" said Sara gently.

"Yes. She looked a lot like you."

The observation made Sara's heart clutch.

"Would you like to be my mama?" Melody added very seriously.

Startled, Sara glanced at Chase, expecting him gently to tone down Melody's expectations.

Instead, he smiled a little smile, his blue eyes watchful.

"He has a ring for you," the little girl divulged. "You want to see it?"

The blood drained from Sara's face.

"Show her," Melody urged, with a smile replacing her sorrow.

Chase reached into the pocket of his jeans and withdrew a velvet pouch.

Sara nearly fell off the wrought-iron chair as he produced the loveliest diamond-and-sapphire ring she'd ever seen. "Figured you couldn't say no if she asked you," he admitted with a crooked smile.

As if she'd ever say no.

"You went through a lot with Garret," he added, sobering. "I hope that didn't put you off marriage."

"You have to be married if you're going to take me home," Melody explained.

Sara reeled, and yet it seemed only natural that, having been adopted herself, they should adopt this little girl.

"Her grandmother needs some help," Chase explained. "You think you can handle all this?"

Sara wanted to pinch herself. Never in her wildest dreams had she expected Chase to propose like this, certainly not with this added bonus. She shook her head, overwhelmed.

"I already brought Kendal over," he added, looking more and more worried by her continued silence. "He played with Melody last week. They got along great."

Knowing Kendal, he'd taken to the little girl instantly.

Sara's eyes grew wet. "Oh, Chase," she said, last. "You don't even need to ask. I've been yours since you rescued me. You've given me a whole new life," she added, her voice quavering. Her gaze shifted to Melody, who looked delighted by her answer. "The least we can do is give Melody a new life, too."

"I love you, Sara," Chase said, his own voice gruff with emotion. He held out the ring for her to put on.

With a smile for Melody, whose face reflected hope for the future, Sara slid her ring finger into the circle of gold. It fit her perfectly, just the way Chase fit her. Just the way their little family was going to fit.

About the Author

Daughter of a US foreign officer, Marliss Melton enjoyed a unique childhood growing up overseas. As one of five children, she was encouraged to think creatively and wrote her first book at age thirteen. Following college, Marliss pursued her dream of publishing while teaching high school English and Spanish. A Golden Heart and RITA finalist, she writes both medieval romance and romantic suspense. Her husband, a warfare technology specialist, is her real-life hero. She juggles her writing career with the challenge of raising five children—hers, his, and theirs.

Dear Readers,

As the creators of potent military heroes, we authors would like to know if our warriors, both medieval and modern, surrendered to love in a similar fashion. Dante Risande from *Lord of Temptation* and Chase McCaffrey from *Time to Run,* both Warner Forever books published in February 2006, have bravely answered these very personal questions.

Paula Quinn: Dante and Chase, what happened after you met Sara and Gianelle, our irresistible heroines?

Dante: I went to Devonshire to investigate a Saxon noble suspected of treason. I left, taking with me a beautiful servant accused of murder, spilling insults and planning her escape the moment I closed my eyes. Gianelle wanted no part of me after spending years as a slave, she wanted naught but her freedom. I wanted to protect her. And to do that, I had to buy her—to possess her, body and soul. But winning her heart was another matter.

Chase: Sara asked me to help her run away from her husband. Of course I said, no. After sixteen years in the service, the last thing I needed to do was to screw up my career. But there was somethin' about the way she looked at me that made it impossible to just walk away. That's when all the trouble started.

Marliss Melton: Gentlemen, how would you say that your lives have been changed by Gianelle and Sara?

Dante: Gianelle smiles at me like an angel and then she snubs me, rebuking every attempt I make to please her. I was a devilish rake, never considering the hearts I had broken. For the first time in my life, I care about what will become of a woman after I take her to my bed. *Merde,* it scares the hell out of me.

Chase: Emotions used to run off me like water off an oiled tarp. Now I can't get away from the way things make me feel. Shit, the first time I made love to Sara, I cried like a baby. I've tried goin' back to what I used to be, a sniper without empathy, without remorse. But it's too late now. Somewhere along the way, Sara crept inside of me. She's made me a different man. Funny thing is, I don't much mind.

There you have it, readers. Even the toughest warriors, regardless of the era in which they live, are helpless when it comes to love. In fact, it's apparent to us authors that the bigger they are, the harder they fall.

Sincerely,

Paula Quinn
LORD OF TEMPTATION
www.paulaquinn.com

Marliss Melton
TIME TO RUN
www.marlissmelton.com

If you liked this book—
and like Romantic Suspense. . . .
You'll LOVE these authors!!!

Karen Rose

"Utterly compelling . . . high wire suspense that keeps you
riveted to the edge of your seat."
—Lisa Gardner, *New York Times* bestselling author

Don't Tell
(0-446-61280-4)

Have You Seen Her?
(0-446-61281-2)

I'm Watching You
(0-446-61447-5)

Nothing To Fear
(0-446-61448-3)

Annie Solomon

"A powerful new voice in romantic suspense."
—*Romantic Times*

Blind Curve
(0-446-61358-4)

Like a Knife
(0-446-61230-8)

Dead Ringer
(0-446-61229-4)

Tell Me No Lies
(0-446-61357-6)